MOUNT
MISERY

D0814854

MOUNT MISERY

A Novel

Angelo Peluso

TALOS PRESS

Copyright © 2014 by Angelo Peluso

Skyhorse Publishing books may be purchased in bulk at special discounts for sales promotion, corporate gifts, fund-raising, or educational purposes. Special editions can also be created to specifications. For details, contact the Special Sales Department, Skyhorse Publishing, 307 West 36th Street, 11th Floor, New York, NY 10018 or info@skyhorsepublishing.com.

Skyhorse® and Skyhorse Publishing® are registered trademarks of Skyhorse Publishing, Inc.®, a Delaware corporation.

Visit our website at www.skyhorsepublishing.com.

10 9 8 7 6 5 4 3 2 1

Library of Congress Control Number: 2014947755

Cover design by Erin Seaward-Hiatt
Cover photos: Thinkstock

Print ISBN: 978-1-940456-13-3
Ebook ISBN: 978-1-940456-18-8

Printed in the United States of America

For Mother Ocean and all her creatures . . .
known and unknown

CHAPTER 1

Alessandra stood naked in waist-deep water, her body framed as a silhouette against the moonlight, as Jorge took off his clothes and walked from the beach to join her. She spread her arms playfully and invited him to move closer. The lovers embraced and kissed, slowly at first but then more passionately. Jorge nibbled at Alessandra's neck and she closed her eyes. The inner warmth of arousal blended in striking contrast with the cool water of the Long Island Sound. It was a nice feeling. Alessandra turned her head and for a moment opened her eyes. As she looked west down the beach, she saw what appeared to be many small yellow orbs moving erratically in the water, all headed in her direction. She thought that odd, but nighttime has a way of playing tricks with the eyes and the mind, and Alessandra had a vivid imagination. She closed her eyes, re-opened them, and the yellow orbs were gone.

Alessandra then let herself succumb to Jorge's touch and again closed her eyes. As the two moved in the water, the yellow orbs homed in on the vibrations caused by their love making. The orbs moved closer until they were just a few yards from the couple. An eerie illumination surrounded Jorge and Alessandra. She was the first to feel the presence of something unusual: a welling up of water that pushed her off balance. Jorge felt it too. It was like a wave. Alessandra opened her eyes. Her shriek startled Jorge. And then he saw the ghostly luminescence within which they appeared trapped. Instinctively, he knew they had to exit the water. He took

Alessandra's hand and walked toward the beach. But there was no escape route.

The attack was astonishingly swift and merciless. The killers tore and ripped flesh from their bodies. Jorge died first. His feet were severed just above the ankle bones and both hands were bitten cleanly off. He bled out in seconds. Alessandra tried screaming for help but a fatal bite to her neck had severed her vocal chords. She was dying and being eaten alive. Her body went into shock. The final blurred memories of her short life were all that comforted her. As the last drops of her blood emptied into the Sound, her killers continued to feed.

When the attack ended, the only evidence of their existence was clothing strewn about the beach and a small, tattered knapsack. Alessandra and Jorge weren't missed until the following day when they failed to report for work at the local vineyard. A lifeguard found the clothing and old backpack and put them aside in the lost-and-found locker.

CHAPTER 2

Two days later . . .

A dory drifted quietly along an outer edge of Mount Misery Ledge in the central Long Island Sound. Two fishermen sat inside the rented dory patiently awaiting the next fish to bite. It was just before noon on a calm and sweltering dog day of late August. A slight wind wafted out of the southwest and the tide ran strong west to east, energized by the extra pull of a growing full moon. Building clouds were a sure sign of an impending late afternoon thunderstorm.

The 17-foot boat was seaworthy, a hull design that had endured for centuries. A 9.9 horsepower Mercury outboard engine sat securely on the dory's transom. It was more than adequate to move the two anglers efficiently from spot to spot until they found fish. Under average sea conditions, the rig could be trusted to get fishermen to the fishing grounds and then safely back to port. The boat and motor could well handle much of what the Long Island Sound was capable of dishing out and almost anything but the most unusual circumstances.

Tomas and Salvador rented the dory from The Fishing Shack, located off the main launch ramp in downtown Port Roosevelt. The Shack has been a local institution since 1911. Its fleet of rental boats provided many casual and weekend anglers with the opportunity to get out on the Long Island Sound and enjoy a day of fishing. With the rental arrangement, the proprietors of The Shack did all the work and the renter had all the fun. Some regulars often drove out from

New York City to escape the metropolis mayhem and oppressive summer heat to cash in on the bounty of fish species roaming the waters of the central Sound.

So it was with Tomas and Salvador. They made the trip east from Queens during predawn hours and were first in line when The Shack opened for business at 6:30 a.m. sharp. Once they arrived, others slowly followed; many more than there were dories. Some were in line for bait, some to buy ice or other various fishing essentials like hooks and sinkers. Several small groups were there to rent boats.

Theo and Cindy, the husband and wife team who owned The Shack, were punctual. The door to the building always opened precisely on time. They had been in the fishing business for all their married years and they loved it. The two especially enjoyed meeting new people. The Shack was, above all else, a democratic place, a true melting pot where fishermen of many ethnic origins would visit and congregate, simply to share in their passion for fishing and tell a few lies about the big ones that couldn't be conquered. As Theo prepped the dories, Cindy held court as she sold bait and ice to customers. She always dispensed timely and friendly information about where the best fish bite was happening. She told Tomas and Salvador that if they wanted porgies to anchor up on one of the rock piles just outside the harbor. "But if you want big striped bass, head for the northeast corner of Mount Misery Ledge."

The two fishermen were thankful for the advice. Cindy never steered them wrong. They paid the dory rental fee, stocked up on bait and ice, and made way to the fishing grounds. After exiting Port Roosevelt Harbor, they cast anchor at a submerged rock pile slightly west of the harbor entrance, paying out rope until the anchor caught and the dory came to rest. Fish of all varieties and sizes like bottom structure, especially rock formations, and porgy are no exception. A large school sat directly above and around the submerged boulders. Porgies are pan-sized fish, prized for flesh that delights the taste buds of both fisherman and large predatory fish. Using small pieces of clam as bait, the fishermen caught one porgy after another until their arms ached. They enjoyed a good day of fishing, one of the best all summer. Such was their success that they couldn't close the lid on their cooler for all the fish piled inside. The two fishermen would later use some of the porgies as bait, hoping to entice a large bass.

Tomas sat in the stern of the boat and pulled on the motor's starter rope; the small engine immediately came to life. He aimed the bow of the dory toward the shoal and twisted the handle throttle full speed ahead. Once upon the shoal, he cut the engine and the dory drifted with the current. The duo talked, joked, and ate cold pork sandwiches. They drank a couple cold beers. Cold beer, stored on ice along with the dead porgies, was just what they needed to crack a nagging thirst from the heat and to wash down the leftover pork. They didn't mind in the least the taste of fish that rimmed the necks of the beer bottles. Hardcore fishermen get used to the constant scent and taste of aquatic creatures.

Like many weekend fishermen, Tomas and Salvador didn't understand the hydrodynamics of the shoal they drifted over, and they really didn't care to. All that mattered was they were told it held big bass. But others who fished the area regularly and studied it knew exactly why it was a productive fishing hole. Baitfish of all types would congregate on the shallow portions of the shoal only to be swept off as currents accelerated during tidal changes. At times during the season, sand eels, menhaden, butterfish, Atlantic silversides, and anchovies would congregate in mass on Mount Misery Ledge. Larger, more predatory fish, like striped bass and bluefish, recognized this pattern and had become conditioned to wait along the deeper edges of the shoal to intercept and attack the hapless baitfish as they swept into deep water and turbulent rip currents. With the tide now being pulled east in the Sound, bait would flow with the current and get deposited off the northeast edge in ninety feet of water. This was a perpetual process, one repeated for as long as life inhabited the Long Island Sound. On this day, big fish would indeed be waiting.

The fishermen drifted repeatedly over this precise location and waited for a coveted striped bass to strike their baited hooks. The dory would flow off the shallow part of the shoal until it moved well into deep water. Since the pair didn't have an electronic depth recorder, they could only guess at the water's deepness. Cindy told them to drift for about one hundred and fifty to two hundred yards once they passed navigation buoy number eleven. They followed her instructions. She was right on the mark with the porgy fishing advice so catching bass would hopefully follow.

The dory would be taken with the tide and with the flow of bait-fish, a drift repeated for as long as it took to get a bite. As each drift approached the terminal point, Tomas would start the outboard motor and reposition the boat well up onto the shallow part of the shoal. The outgoing tide was running fast, moving the dory rapidly through the fish zone. They made frequent moves.

Putting fresh-cut pieces of porgy on their hooks and tossing the chum bucket overboard, the hopeful anglers endeavored to excite the feeding senses of any cruising stripers. A keeper bass would make their day. Two big keepers would be a Godsend. They had made more than a dozen drifts without so much as a touch. But their luck was about to change. Approaching the dropoff point between shallow water and the ninety-foot ledge, both fishermen felt something take their baits. They were patient as line slowly moved off from their reels. "Count to ten," Salvador said, "and then set the hook." First one and then the other had strikes from powerful fish. They both hooted and hollered and proclaimed victory over their hooked adversaries. Steadily, they reeled in line and brought the bass closer to the boat. And then it happened. Both rods slammed down violently and with alarming force onto the gunnels of the dory. "What is this?" Salvador said.

"I have one too, mi amigo! A big one."

Both were indeed large fish. The fishing rods were doubled over, bent close to the breaking point—straining in wide parabolic arches as both fishermen pulled back against the weight of two seemingly immovable objects. Big, wide smiles set upon their faces until both realized something odd had happened. The big fish swam toward each other and began pulling away in unison, like two Clydesdales. Neither fisherman had ever felt such strength. The fish pulled as if their entire existence depended on it; the fishermen held on not realizing it was their lives that were in peril. Reeling lines in against the pull of the fish's weight was futile. It was as if the quarry had caught their pursuers. The combined strength and speed of what was now attached to the ends of the super strong braided lines was enough to overcome the weight of the dory, the motor, and the anglers.

The fishermen were certain two monster bass had taken their baits, even though they had no idea what large bass felt like. Were these the trophies they had anticipated? No, they had to be much more. The fish fought ferociously for their freedom as dogged and powerful headshakes transmitted power up the line, through the fishing rods, and into the hands of the fishermen. Tomas and Salvador didn't realize they were completely overpowered and overmatched by what had taken their baits. In ignorant bliss, they cheered and howled as the fish gained dangerous advantage. But their expressions of joy quickly turned into grimaces of concern. The fishermen tried, to no avail, to gain control of their catch. These fish were big and meant serious business. The fight was intense and furious, like nothing they had ever before experienced. Neither had ever caught anything larger than a seven-pound tautog, or blackfish by its more common name. These fish were no 'tog. The two perplexed anglers held tightly to their rods but their captors were in total command. The fishermen again tried reeling in the lines against the pull of the fish but that was not to be. The applied force of what was now secured to their hooks was enough to completely overcome the boat's inertia.

The dory began to move. Slowly at first, but then accelerating as if the engine was in gear and the throttle had been pushed forward. The dory left an impressive wake, much to the bewilderment of other boaters, who looked on in astonishment—some foolishly cheered and offered encouragement. None were more bewildered by the events taking place than the two anglers connected to their unknown prizes. Tomas yanked on the motor starter rope while maintaining a death grip on the fishing rod. The motor coughed to life as the fish pulled the small boat up on plane. Putting the engine in reverse did nothing to halt the dory's forward progress. It was as if they were being drawn through the water on a sleigh. Their joy at hooking two huge fish turned to pure terror. As the dory passed Mount Misery Inlet, more than a mile from where the fish were first hooked, it came to an abrupt halt. The sheer power of the beasts snapped the strong lines that bound them.

The fishermen spat Spanish curses at losing their *keepers*, but quietly they were each relieved to be detached from their now-lost trophies. As quickly at the battle had begun, the pulling ceased. The fishermen looked at each other in disbelief and puzzlement.

"What was that?" Salvador said.

"I don't know." Tomas didn't know what had happened either. Both fishermen no longer felt resistance against their rods. They reeled in their lines, which gathered easily onto the spools.

"Shit," they said in unison. "Go to hell you bastards!" But that's exactly from where these fish had come.

The two sat sulking with bowed heads as nervous water moved undetected toward the dory at an alarming rate. Dorsal fins broke through the surface. Salvador was seated in the front of the boat and had begun winding the remainder of slack line when the first fish struck the chum bucket with a force that knocked both men from their seats. The fish ripped the bucket from the cleat that secured it, and then ripped the stainless steel cleat cleanly from its anchor point. The creature rolled, an enormous forked tail emerging from the water. The fishermen did not see it since both were lying flat on their backs. They tried regaining balance and composure by gripping the gunnels and pushing themselves upright—only to be knocked down yet again by a second torpedo-like blast that hit the dory off the port-side bow. Salvador stood fore of the dory's mid-line when the jolt caused him to fall forward violently. As he stumbled and fell, his head hit the front seat, his right arm snapped as it lodged between the seat and the cooler. The weight of his body was just too much for the aged, brittle ulna and radius bones. The sound was like a rifle shot. The scream was blood curdling. Tomas righted himself and tried starting the motor. In haste, he over-choked the carburetor and the engine coughed as the starter rope was pulled. He tried another pull but froze in disbelief as the largest fish he had ever seen clamped its huge maw on the engine's entire lower unit, propeller and shaft. It shook its head ferociously as if trying to rip the motor from the dory's transom.

The entire boat shuddered, on the brink of being torn apart. The fish's long and muscular body quivered in violent spasms. The fisherman gasped. If this wasn't bad enough, many other large fish now circled the dory. He had no idea what they were. His body trembled uncontrollably. Salvador pleaded in agony to the heavenly Father as he became aware of the compound fracture to his arm, bone protruding through flesh, blood pouring from the wound. "Please God, help me."

His appeal was answered almost instantly. The attack ceased as quickly as it had begun.

CHAPTER 3

Just before dusk that same day, Mimi Vandersleet walked with her standard poodle, Pisces, along a beach that lead from Boulder Point to Plover Dunes, two towns located east of Port Roosevelt. It's a nice stretch of coarse sand and pebbles and, in late summer and early fall, it is usually devoid of large crowds typical of most other Long Island beaches during the high season. North shore beaches are not as popular as south shore areas like Jones Beach, Robert Moses, and the Hamptons. Those beaches are more suitable for comfortable sun bathing, having finer sand and larger waves; beach goers who preferred lying on soft sand always headed south. North shore beaches that face the open Sound are strewn with pebbles, rocks, and even small boulders, remnants of the terminal Hither Hills glacial moraine. That geological formation was the result of the Wisconsin Glacier coming to an abrupt halt more than twenty thousand thousand years ago. The movement of the ice sheet carved out the land that is Long Island and gave the north shore its harbors and beaches, lumpy and bumpy as they are.

But Pisces had no such bias against rocks. He loved running that beach with his owner and taking an occasional swim. Standard poodles are known for their love of water since their roots extend back as gundogs for German water fowlers. Pisces was no exception. He was a big dog, about seventy pounds, and he loved playing in the surf. Pisces was especially partial to swim and retrieve games. Mimi always carried a rubber training dummy with her on their walks, tossing it out into the Sound and delighting in Pisces's willingness and ability to retrieve. She'd toss out the dummy as far as she could, signal Pisces to fetch, watch him swim out to retrieve the object and then return it to land. This game went on for a mile as the tide ebbed, receding to toward low water.

One well-placed throw landed the dummy between a set of large boulders close to shore. A small rip current had formed at the center of this configuration. As was his duty, Pisces eagerly leapt into the water and swam toward his toy. He grabbed the dummy and turned to complete the retrieve. As the big poodle swam back toward the beach, Mimi heard Pisces let out with a terrifying yelp. She saw three huge forms with enormous forked tails emerge from the water and slash viciously at the poodle. Mimi panicked. She screamed! "Come, Pisces! Come!" But her faithful companion was incapable of responding. The dog's legs had been bitten off. Mimi jumped into the surf and started to swim toward her dog, but as she did, Pisces let out one final death yelp and disappeared. The rubber retrieving dummy was all that remained on the surface of the water, ringed by blood. Mimi returned to the safety of shore to call police.

Not more than twenty minutes later and farther down the same beach, Mickey Rosen's Chihuahua named Killer, succumbed to a fate similar to that of Pisces, but with much less drama. The little hound enjoyed water as much as his larger poodle cousin but he wasn't inclined to venture too far from the safety of land. The tiny pooch preferred to relax in a little ring-tube raft its owner had made so his little dog could float effortlessly on the small waves. Mickey would often tie a long length of light rope to the raft and walk along in the water, Killer in tow. That was the day's drill, but at one point while Mickey waded along, he heard a humongous splash behind him and felt a strong tug on the line. When he turned back around to investigate the source of the disruption, he felt instant terror. Much to his astonishment, Killer was gone. When asked later by police about the incident, Mickey thought he remembered seeing a very large forked tail where his beloved Killer had been moments before. County police were at a loss to explain the disappearance of either dog. The official incident reports chalked the episodes up to unusual and coincidental drowning.

CHAPTER 4

Jimmy McVee clocked out from his job as a line repairman for Island Power and Light as usual at 3 p.m. This had been a good day—his primary work order had him close to home, repairing power lines in downtown Port Roosevelt. A turbulent summer storm the day before had knocked out electricity to the Town Hall and adjoining businesses. This had become a priority repair. Jimmy lived in Port and this day's commute was a snap: out of the house, into his car, and down the hill straight to Dunkin Donuts for some hot coffee and a bagel. While in town, he could also check out the fishing activity at the local boat launch ramp. Jimmy always had fishing on his mind and he liked keeping tabs on the action. When he worked locally, he'd usually make pit stops at the ramp to drink coffee before work and then again during his lunch break. At this time of year, there'd always be someone either dropping a boat in the water or taking one out. He spotted a captain he knew well and watched as the twenty-foot, center console Aquasport rolled off the trailer. Jimmy waited until the boat was tied off to a dock cleat before approaching.

"Hey Billy, how's the fishing?"

"Not bad. Got a bunch of bass and blues and a few little tunny and bonito yesterday. Released them all. Lots of fish out there. Tons of baitfish too. More than has been around in years. Hoping for the same luck again today."

"All four?" Billy nodded, smiling.

"That's a nice Long Island Grand Slam. What did you catch 'em on?"

"Flies and artificial lures,"Billy said.

Jimmy especially liked fishing with classic old wooden plugs, carved forms that replicated fleeing baitfish when retrieved.

"That's great. Any big fish?" Jimmy asked.

"I saw some very large fish bust the surface out near the Middle Grounds yesterday, over toward Stratford Shoal. I mean really big. Couldn't make out what they were. They were so fast I thought they might be some wayward tuna, but they were behaving very odd."

"Haven't seen tuna around here in a long time. That would have made for some nice sashimi."

"Yeah, it would." Billy said. "Last year, some guys fishing with chunks of menhaden saw small bluefin out near the Stratford Shoal Light house. Been some bottlenose dolphin in the Sound too. Great to see them coming back. Lots of sea life out there."

"Thanks for the update and good luck out there today. I think I'll be out on the beach tonight."

Jimmy knew about those small bluefin tuna. One of his friends was fishing menhaden chunks as bait for bass out in the middle when he spotted what he thought to be bluefin. Jimmy's friend then made a few call-outs on his VHF to other captains to see if they had spotted similar activity. Only one other captain, Jack Connors, had seen them. He too was out in the center of the Sound on a charter, chunking bait for bass and big bluefish, and he too thought they were tuna. Jimmy didn't doubt his buddy for a moment. When he was into boat fishing, he would often encounter unusual species in the less traveled reaches of the Sound, species like oceanic sunfish and bottlenose dolphins, an occasional shark and other non-indigenous fish. The dolphins used to be commonplace, but only recently returned after a decades-long hiatus. Rising ocean temperatures resulting from global warming and a Gulf Stream that moved ever so close to Long Island enabled many varieties of southern species of fish to move northward and near shore. There were even thriving populations of tropical fish inhabiting inshore areas during summer months such as jack and tarpon, so tuna would be no surprise.

What interested Jimmy most was the fact that so many species of fish were in the area simultaneously. With so much bait around, he'd have great fishing later that night.

Many of Jimmy's closest fishing friends preferred night beach fishing during periods of the new moon, but Jimmy preferred the full moon. He knew the current lunar phase would make for some exceptional nighttime striped bass fishing. Stripers preferred feeding during the darkest of hours and, even though the illumination of the full moon would prevent pitch-black darkness, some of his best fishing happened on full moon phases. That predilection had a lot to do with the fact that baitfish frequented the shallows along beaches. The full moon brought with it stronger tides and heavier currents.

Big bass love turbulent water, and the combination of moon-enhanced tidal flows and tons of local bait was a formula that couldn't fail. That was precisely what Jimmy had counted on. After eating dinner and getting a few hours shut-eye, he'd go fishing. His girlfriend knew not to call him when the moon was full, especially during the fishing season, so Jimmy felt no pressure to do anything other than eat, sleep, and hit the beach. He especially loved the August moon, known as the Sturgeon Moon. Early Native American fishing tribes believed the August full moon was the optimal time to catch the largest fish. He checked the tides in his favorite weekly fishing magazine, *The Island Angler*, a publication that kept local fishermen in touch with the most recent on the water happenings. He knew the editor, Ferdie G, very well. They belonged to the same surf-fishing club. Ferdie was plugged in better than anyone around Long Island and was the source for the most reliable fishing information. He was also one of the best surf anglers to ever set foot in the wash. When Jimmy wanted the straight scoop on what was happening in the world of fish, Ferdie was his man. Jimmy would often say that if a fish farted at fifteen fathoms off Montauk Point, Ferdie knew about it.

Jimmy flipped the magazine to the tide page and took the reading for Bridgeport, Connecticut. From that, he deducted five minutes for his location and calculated high tide at 2:07 a.m. It was perfect. He would get down to the beach at midnight, make the walk to his favorite spot, and be in the action as the tide started its outward flow. Jimmy had a plan he liked and he expected to catch fish.

CHAPTER 5

In the world of sport fishing, a surf rat is a unique breed of angler who prowls the beaches and the near surf for striped bass. Some might label them eccentric since nothing is out of bounds in their quest for a trophy fish. They enjoy solitude and freedom and prefer the light of a new or full moon to the rays of the sun. Like all hardcore surf rats, Jimmy loved pursuing fish at night. Jimmy would often say the only hours of the day worth fishing were those of the vampire shift. When operating under the cover of darkness, his senses heightened to a point of acute awareness. It was as if he became one with the predators he pursued.

Lack of light has a way of raising the most primordial instincts to an intense level, even in someone fishing along the congested North Shore of Long Island. But on this full-moon night, Jimmy was especially attuned to his surroundings. He was fishing alone on an isolated stretch of beach enjoying the simple pleasures of silence and seclusion. Jimmy checked his watch—2:45 a.m. He would have a small window of opportunity once the fish started to feed. The tide was coming off full flood stage as he waded out a few yards from the shoreline and positioned himself on his favorite casting rock. He loved being there in the dark, as the ebbing flow and tidal currents brought renewed life to the shallows along the beach.

Jimmy was casting a large swimming plug when he heard the first familiar and welcomed *slap* interrupt the stillness to his left: *Big bass*.

He readied his plug for a quick cast but he didn't pull the trigger. Something else caught his attention. Many more big fish were directly out in front of the rock, tearing into a school of hapless menhaden, a preferred source of sustenance for big bass. Heavy cloud cover didn't allow for much of the moon's light to illuminate the water. Jimmy relied mostly on his sense of hearing to identify the location of the splashes and slaps. Other fish revealed themselves as ghostly ephemeral forms racing along in thin water. Jimmy's eyes had adjusted earlier in the night, allowing him to faintly see the pods of immature bunker leaping onto the beach to evade their pursuers. Death came to those fish either way they turned. Stay in the water and meet with certain demise or jump onto the temporary safety of the sand and commit preordained mass suicide.

Jimmy heard a set of titanic splashes ten or twenty yards out. He lobbed the artificial swimming lure toward the loud disruption. The instant strike was swift, solid, and heavy. "Thank you, Lord." The fish's substantial bulk and its first sustained run had Jimmy thinking a nice "forty" or maybe even his first ever fifty-pounder. But bass that big were more the exception than the rule on this beach. He knew that all too well—he'd be content with a respectable thirty-pound striper. The big fish took considerable line despite the heavy drag setting on his spinning reel. The striper moved east among the boulders as if it understood how to evade capture. Jimmy was tempted to tighten down on the drag but he knew from past experiences that would be a big mistake. He also knew he had to follow the fish or risk losing it as it would quickly gain an advantage and break free. Jumping from the rock and wading back onto the sand, Jimmy applied pressure with his rod. While holding the rod at a forty-five-degree angle, he pulled hard, attempting to turn the big bass back in his direction, but the fish would have none of that. Jimmy's pace quickened as he attempted to cut the distance between himself and the fish. It had now taken more than half the line from his reel spool. He thought that quite peculiar.

While big bass are true brutes and prefer down-and-dirty, dogged battles, long runs like this were not at all typical.

Maybe I foul-hooked this sucker? Jimmy thought. Or maybe—just maybe—it was the bass of a lifetime. He was pumped; a rush of adrenaline prepared him for the balance of this heavyweight bout. After what seemed like an endless ordeal of give and take, Jimmy felt that first subtle sign of submission. He pulled back yet again on the rod and this time the fish inched slowly toward him. It appeared to be well hooked, and Jimmy knew if he took his time the prize would be his. Slow and deliberate pulls gained line and brought the fish closer. The beast came to the surface and shook its massive head fiercely, trying to separate itself from the grasp of hooks. Even in low light, Jimmy could make out the shape and form of an extraordinary adversary. It was bigger than anything he had ever hooked. One more long pull on the surf rod, several turns of the reel handle, and the big fish would be but two rod lengths away. Jimmy re-entered the water in an effort to grasp the fish by its lower jaw. He was unsure if he could beach it so he took the end game of the fight directly to the enormous fish.

Jimmy was in water up to the top of his thighs when he felt the odd sensation of other fish swimming around him—fish that appeared as large as the one attached to his swimming plug. They moved at frenzied pace, bumping his legs as they swam, apparently not at all fearful of his presence. Jimmy tried backing out of the water, but it was too late. The behemoth at the end of his line stopped fighting and rushed in to attack. The first bite to Jimmy's leg sent an electric jolt through his entire body. He screamed in pain as he instinctively grabbed his left calf. No one heard his cry. The second bite was as ferocious and tore through his waders, ripping his entire calf muscle from the bone. Another fish hit his right thigh, severing the femoral artery. Jimmy stumbled forward, not yet realizing he was a dead man. He felt excruciating pain in his thighs and torso as they slashed and bit mercilessly.

He cried out in agony, but still no one heard him. As Jimmy tried to regain footing, he felt the most vicious of all bites and trembled: his left hand had been bitten off above the wrist. Blood spurted from the stump that only seconds ago had been a hand tightly gripping a surf rod. The blood in the water only fueled the fish's feeding pheromones at peak levels, stimulating them to collectively work to destroy their oversized prey. The last thing Jimmy remembered was the vicious bite to his groin. Jimmy McVee's life ebbed five yards from the beach he so loved to fish.

CHAPTER 6

The remains of Jimmy's body washed up on a beach in Smith's Bay several days later. Authorities hadn't a clue what had happened to him. An elderly gent walking his dog was startled when fido fetched a fibula. He immediately called police. When County PD arrived on scene, they secured the area from curious onlookers. The arriving officers had never seen remains as mangled as the ones they were attempting to preserve as forensic evidence. Most of the flesh had been torn or ripped from what was once Jimmy McVee's strong body. The waders were completely shredded. Visible bone revealed deep and penetrating bites. What flesh remained clung to a skeleton that showed signs of large but odd tooth marks. The County Crime Scene Unit was as much at a loss as anyone for attributing cause of death. The lead investigator thought it might be the result of a rare shark attack. Another member of the team suggested the body had been dead for days and the mutilation was the work of crabs or some other wildlife. When the coroner arrived, he took one look at the uniformity and number of bites that were still recognizable and suggested they get the remains back to the morgue. Jimmy's remains were bagged, tagged, and placed on the gurney for transit.

Jimmy McVee's mutilated body parts were laid onto a cold stainless steel table at the county morgue. Although a specific cause of death would have to wait until all standard forensic testing was completed, the M.E. was eager to understand the origins of the bites. In all the years of practicing his art, he had never seen a bite pattern this unique. His curiosity peaked and he called for a biologist from the State University's Division of Marine Sciences to come have a look. Katie DiNardo was assigned the task. She'd also bring along her sidekick, Nick Tanner, an ichthyologist.

Katie DiNardo and Nick Tanner were two of the best minds in the New York State Marine Sciences Bureau, a division of the Department of Fish and Game. Between them, they had more collective research and field experience than the rest of the fisheries crew combined. When they joined forces to solve a problem, it was a tag-team that couldn't be beat. Their superiors at division knew that and it was one of the reasons they were paired on this unusual death. If this incident had anything to do with marine life, these two were best equipped to solve the case. They had worked together on several other tough cases in the past and put the marine bureau in a very favorable light with the high mucky-mucks in Albany. Their division had imposed a hiring freeze and good staff like Katie and Nick were doing double, sometimes triple duty, working like switch engines.

While the medical examiner scrutinized every piece of what was once a vibrant and strapping young man, Katie and Nick looked on. Their attention was riveted on one very prominent bite mark. "What do you think did that? A shark?" the M.E. said.

"I doubt it. That's not at all typical of a shark bite. It's the wrong alignment of teeth and the bite radius is inconsistent with the shape and size of a shark's jaws." Katie DiNardo hadn't a clue what caused these wounds but she was confident it wasn't a shark.

"Whatever it was applied a remarkable amount of bite pressure per square inch. We have indications of multiple shattered bones, and both hands and a foot have been bitten off. The foot was severed cleanly, right through the wading boot. Other than a shark, what indigenous fish could possible do something like that?" the M.E. asked.

Katie just shrugged her shoulders and eyed a number of the other bites. The sequence of the marks and the manner and pattern of torn flesh reminded her of the attack effects of Amazonian piranha, only much larger.

Nick Tanner remained quiet, intently focused on the shape of one specific bite. It was strangely familiar to him. He asked the M.E. if he could take some measurements and photos of the uniquely intact bite mark. While the competent M.E. had already done so, Nick wanted to take his own set of images so he could examine them in more detail back at his lab.

"Sure, go ahead," the M.E. replied. "I can use all the help I can get on this one. Never seen anything like this before."

Once Nick Tanner completed his task, and Katie fulfilled her official duties with the medical examiner, she and Nick rushed back to their lab at the Marine Sciences Building on the campus of the State University. Nick was especially eager to further study the images and measurements. One digital photograph intrigued Nick above all others. He viewed an enlarged version of the image on his computer monitor. It was a complete bite impression from a large piece of the waders Jimmy McVee wore the night he was killed. It was from a section of his torso.

"These bites may have been the work of a fish pack. No way one fish caused all this damage," Katie said.

Nick was absorbed by the bite. "Maybe it wasn't a fish. Lots of creatures swimming around in the sea."

"Like what?" Katie said.

"I just can't seem to put my finger on where I've seen this bite pattern before: a single row of teeth in each jaw, uniform in size, that appear knife-like and razor sharp."

Katie moved closer for a better look. "From what I can tell, the teeth also appear conical, somewhat stubby. My guess is that, considering the bite force, the teeth are also well-rooted in a very hard and powerful set of jaws, but definitely not sharks."

Nick closely examined the image on the screen. He alternated between the raw photography and the enlarged version, using a magnifying glass to further analyze the bite impressions. He counted each and every mark, first the dentary teeth on the lower jaw—thirty-one impressions. Then he counted the premaxillary upper teeth—thirty-nine impressions. These were fully developed adult teeth that had increased in size with each replacement cycle. Nick looked closely at the exact curvature of the bite and visualized the full jaws and teeth. And then he remembered.

The previous fall, while reeling in a legal-sized striped bass off Sandhill Point, something followed and attacked the hooked bass. Nick never got to see the culprit but he did get to see the result of its savage bite. When Nick reeled in his prize, it was only half a bass. Considering the size of the bite radius, Nick estimated that whatever ate his fish weighed about fifteen or twenty pounds. By comparison, the bite impression on Jimmy McVee's waders indicated fish of between seventy-five and one hundred pounds.

"Any idea at all, Nick?"

"Other than it being exceptionally big, no. Similar bite impressions on the victim but all are not exact. The way these bites align, this does appear to be the work of more than one fish," Nick said.

"Maybe it's just a school of some exotic tropical species like barracuda?"

"Possible, not probable," Nick said. "This is not a friendly environment for fish like that."

"Foreign fish—or whatever—of the size you suggest could wreak havoc on an ecosystem; the entire Long Island Sound for that matter. Like snakeheads," Katie said.

"Let's not jump the gun. I'm not certain. It's just a hunch and there has to be a rational explanation for this. I might be looking at these bite marks all wrong. Although there are some significant differences between these bite patterns and sharks, we can't rule out any large predatory marine species at the moment. It could also be some form of jaw abnormality. And who knows what creatures might have slid up north with the Gulf Stream? We are going to need really solid physical evidence to substantiate that opinion."

"Could it be a mammal?"

"I really don't think we are dealing with psychotic seals or sociopathic sea lions, Katie. My bet would be some kind of fish. And my first opinion is that whatever did this fed on the body postmortem."

Katie had a very logical mind and believed completely in the scientific process. But she had a tendency to worry and sometimes overthink a problem. Although lacking in any scientific basis, Katie pondered the alternative—the remote possibility of large, nonindigenous fish in the Sound. Fish that might attack humans if provoked in some way, or fish that might actually feed on human flesh. She was an expert on predatory fish behavior. She studied all the major northeast species in graduate school and defended her thesis on the predation patterns of bluefish, one of the most common and prolific local species. Katie owed her career to those fish, including her PhD. Plus, she had caught plenty, both for research and for pleasure with her sometimes significant other, Captain Rick McCord, a local fishing guide.

There was much that science didn't know about the oceans and its fish. But Katie knew the potential downside of a pack-aggressive fish roaming the congested water of Long Island. Aside from the environmental effects that could result from an invasive species, even local schools of small bluefish could be trouble if they came too close to bathers.

Katie also knew that if the bite marks were not the result of postmortem feeding that could mean trouble worse than any possible shark-attack scenario, including that of the great white or a bull shark. While sharks in general are somewhat social and communal animals, big rogue sharks often tend to be solitary creatures. But other fish travel in large predatory schools. Katie also knew this was a transition point in the season when both predators and prey would stage for the fall migration south. Great numbers of bait and fish would be on the move and would concentrate at key locations around Long Island. Predatory species especially would congregate around the bait. If the culprits to this killing were indeed a species of schooling fish, they would surely have a ready-made buffet at their disposal, and they would have a compelling reason for remaining in the area. And if Katie's and Nick's hunch was right, these fish could redefine the meaning of *big*. With Labor Day just a week away, the last thing Katie wanted on her plate was an unsolved death that somehow involved marine life. She was hoping this death had nothing to do with marine life.

Katie couldn't help but think about the scene from the movie *Jaws* where every yahoo with a boat figured they could catch the killer shark. It would be no different once the local fishing crowd got wind of some over-sized, exotic fish swimming in the Long Island Sound. It mattered not what kind of fish they were as long as they were trophies. If these were big fish, they would all want to catch them. And to add to that dilemma, the largest bluefish tournament in the country came at the end of the month. All elements combined could prove a perfect recipe for chaos. But until they knew all the facts, Katie hoped her research would ultimately provide a logical explanation.

"Katie, what are you thinking about? You look puzzled."

"I think I'll give Rick a call and see if he's seen or heard about anything out of the ordinary. He's out on the water every day and if these fish are roaming locally, there may be some VHF chatter about them or he may have bumped into them."

Katie had already begun dialing Rick's cell phone number. Nick pressed further. "I don't think you want to let the cat out of the bag just yet. We don't know for certain what species made these bites. Can you still trust Rick to keep his mouth shut?"

Katie let the call connect.

"We need to gather more facts about all this before going public. With the holiday coming up, I'll be hung by my nuts if the wrong shit gets out before we prove it."

"Hey Katie, what a pleasant surprise. I just love hearing your voice. Didn't think I'd be hearing from you for a long while. To what do I owe this honor?"

"Cut the sarcasm, Rick. You bailed on me the other night because the bass were running strong. You just couldn't miss another moon bite, now could you?"

"I meant to call. I was with clients. It's just that we got into some nice fish and you know how it is."

"Yes I do know how it is, more than I care to admit. Maybe if I had gills instead of tits things might be different. But I'm not calling about that. Where are you right now?"

"Out with a charter, fishing bunker chunks at the Middle Grounds for bass. Why?"

"Have you seen or heard about anything odd happening in the Sound lately?"

"Like what, an alien encounter? What do you mean, odd?"

"Anything strange . . . oddball fish or something out of place in local waters. Anything that doesn't fit or seem right?"

"Oh, you mean like a coelacanth or some other previously thought extinct prehistoric species? Hey, I did see a large green fluorescent blob come up from the depths the other night. May be a new species of algae. What think?"

"You know, you gotta always be the funny man. Why don't you go do some stand-up at the Port Rosey Comedy Club? You'd be a big hit."

"Katie, where are you going with these questions? Why in God's name are you asking me this? How about a hint?"

"Look Rick, I'm investigating an unusual death and I'm exploring all leads, even a few that are really far out there. I really could use your help without having to divulge all the details just yet."

"You mean that mutilated body they found in Smith's Bay? Since when does a marine biologist investigate a homicide?"

"Who said anything about a homicide? And how the hell do you know about it?"

"I know one of the cops who was on scene. He and his buddies charter me once in a while. I met him in town at Bailey's Pub and he told me some of the sordid details. Said they couldn't yet determine cause of death but murder hasn't been ruled out."

"So, have you encountered anything odd out there in the past few days?" Katie knew she needed to refocus the discussion. Rick could be tenacious and he wouldn't let go if he got a hook into this matter. He would press her to no end.

"Not me but Jack Connors called me on the VHF two days ago and said he thought he saw some small bluefin tuna flying out of the water off of Navigation Buoy 9 down by Boulder Point."

Katie knew Jack, a friend of her mother's, and usually a very reliable source of fishing information. He took her out on a few of her research expeditions and fished with Rick for big striped bass off Montauk.

Small bluefin tuna in the Sound was a very rare occurrence. They'd be in the Sound more by chance and serendipity than by standard migratory wanderings. Usually, they just made a wrong turn out east at Orient Point, the terminal promontory of the north shore, and moved west until they found bait, never staying for very long.

"Was that it? Just the tuna? Is that all Jack saw?"

"Are you suggesting there is something more at issue here? Actually there was more. But maybe you should show me more of your cards first, Katie dearest."

"Cut the bullshit. What else is there?"

"You owe me for this one. Jack said that the tuna didn't appear to be feeding but were being chased. He saw one attacked and eaten by something large and fast with a huge forked tail. Jack was certain it wasn't a shark but he had no idea what the hell was chasing the tuna. Those damn things are so fast only mako sharks stand a chance at nailing them. Only God knows the last time makos were in the Sound. But Jack said he was going to try to catch one if he saw them again."

"Did he get a good look at the fish? Could he describe them? Trying to catch them may be a bad idea."

"I told you, he said he didn't know what they were, just that they were big and fast. What does all this have to do with that dead guy?"

"I'll fill you in when I can. Gotta get going now."

"That's it? No little lovebird small talk? How about you meet me later at Grumpies for a beer and burger?" Rick said.

"Sorry. Can't today. Do me a favor. Be careful on the water. Gotta go. By the way, maybe one of these days you might treat me like a client? Get my drift, buddy boy? Bye."

Kate turned back to Nick. "One of Rick's buddies saw some small tuna being chased by something big and fast the other day off Boulder Point. "They could be our mystery fish."

CHAPTER 7

Katie knew she could depend on Rick in a pinch but their tumultuous relationship was hard on her. She needed his help now but she didn't want to open old wounds. Katie also needed to protect her emotions. That was easier said than done.

Katie first met Rick when she was studying for her masters degree at the State University of New York. Rick would sometimes substitute as captain of the school's marine research vessel when the regular captain was out sick or on vacation. At first she thought him to be an arrogant smart ass but that was just sexual attraction at work. Katie rebuffed Rick's initial attempts to go out together but she eventually wore down and conceded to a first date. Rick would tell her that he had chased her until she caught him. They dated on an off for a few months and then the relationship turned serious. The one night spent in front of Rick's fireplace fanned the flames of passion and for a period of time they were inseparable.

They were an attractive couple, but mismatched by height. Rick was athletically built, about six-two and in terrific shape. Katie was short and petite, well-toned with curves in all the right places and a face that turned heads. Long light brown hair, tied in a ponytail and run through the back of a baseball cap was just the way Rick liked seeing her. There was nothing fancy about Katie. She personified the meaning of down-to-earth and dressed to fit the part of a field biologist. She had that classic LL Bean look. But her looks were often deceiving to those who took her attractive features for granted. Her intellect was her greatest attribute. Unknowing suitors would often be trimmed down to size in short order by her fast wit and biting tongue, especially if they were overzealous in their attempts to hit on her. Beauty, brains, and a personality that didn't take fools lightly made for a real bundle of dynamite.

Rick was a college baseball jock with a pretty good fastball and slider. For a while he had aspirations of a major league pitching career, having been drafted into the Yankees farm team system. But he also had a hot head and somehow managed to piss off the entire franchise until he was branded persona non grata. Following his release from Triple A, he bounced around with a couple of minor league clubs in the Atlantic League. After hitting one too many opposing batters in the head with a ninety-file mile an hour rocket Rick found himself in a Brazilian jiu-jitsu school. The school was owned by a friend who had convinced him that martial arts would be a great outlet to release his pent up aggression and a good way to stay in shape. It was here that Rick ad been taught restraint. He had also been taught how to maim and kill. Rick took to martial arts as easily as he had taken to baseball. He quickly gained respect-ability and proficiency in jiu-jitsu, judo, karate, and kickboxing. Eventually, Rick decided to compete in matches sanctioned by the Federation of Mixed Martial Arts. He had a 4–1 record when an opponent connected with a powerful leg kick that fractured his eye socket and almost took away his sight in that eye. Rick continued to fight valiantly but his coach stopped the bout. Doctors subsequently advised Rick against continuing competitive fighting or risk blind-ness. Katie wasn't silent either. She threatened to leave him if he continued with the insanity. She hated violence, even if it was con-ducted in the name of sport. Katie made Rick promise to end his fighting career. Grudgingly, Rick obliged and shortly thereafter he was on a plane headed for Alaska. He landed a job at the remote Peninsula Creek Lodge guiding wealthy hedge fund managers and other well-to-do sports.

The lodge owner was originally from Long Island and a big-time baseball fan. He remembered Rick's one-time call up to the Big Show at The Stadium. Rick put on quite a display of pitching skill, striking out six Red Sox batters in a row. That left an impression. He knew Rick had been drummed out of baseball and that he liked to fly fish. It took but one phone call to seal the job offer. Rick accepted without an iota of hesitation. Katie was not at all initially fond of the idea but her love for Rick convinced her that this was the right thing for him to do at this stage of his life. He had one too many conflicting demons floating around in his head and needed to get his life squared away. At one point, Katie thought she might join Rick for the summer if she could sway her superiors to allow her a sabbatical to study the spawning habits of Alaska's migratory Pacific salmon. One of her graduate school friends took a job with the Alaska Department of Natural Resources and was up in the Unalakleet area by Nome, counting silver salmon on the North River. She told Katie she could arrange a summer deal for her to work part time as a consultant. The opportunity never materialized and Rick headed north without her.

Rick loved the job. He started work that May, helping to get the lodge in order for the coming season, and ended his assignment in October when the last of the silver salmon had spawned. Rick was into his second summer. He was good at the guiding game—a natural. The guests liked him and the tips were substantial, especially if the salmon were running hard and his sports had a good week, which was often the case in this remote part of Alaska. He could typically earn five or ten times his weekly salary in tips and that was motivation enough to do a good job even if some of the clients were obnoxious. Rick always preferred guiding women clients since they were easier to instruct than the classic Type A characters they accompanied. And Rick felt his charm might just land him a score. It can get awfully lonely in the Alaskan bush after three or four months of nothing but fishing. Some of these ladies were real lookers. Rick had had a little fling with the lodge chef, but when the relationship became a problem the owner told Rick to knock it off and stick strictly to business.

Rick was always amazed that the hotshots would arrive at the lodge with thousands of dollars worth of the newest fly-fishing gear. Most of them couldn't cast worth a crap if their lives depended on it. Most had no skills whatsoever. Many were lucky not to hook themselves with their wild flailing. But every once in a while, a good caster would show up. Often it would either be a guy from the East Coast who did a lot of saltwater fly fishing and who really understood the dynamics of casting, or a steelhead angler from the West Coast who had mastered the art of the cast and the drift. But most of the yo-yos were totally clueless. Half the time they wouldn't even know if a salmon or trout was on the end of their lines unless Rick told them to set the hook.

The funniest thing to Rick was when they all came marching into the dining lodge one by one each morning for breakfast—they looked as if they were ready to pose for the centerfold of a high-end fishing catalog. They all dressed identically and to the nines with the same fashionable outdoors clothing, brand new stuff, just out of the box. Some still had price tags attached. It was if the gear and the look made them fishermen. It was a hoot, especially since most of Rick's gear was held together with duct tape and silicone. Yeah, he felt contempt but it was a job and he did take some joy in seeing these titans of the financial services industry struggle at fly-fishing, beaten by lowly pea-brained fish. Not one ever asked him for help with casting technique. They knew it all. That's why he preferred fishing with the ladies. They wanted to learn and Rick was a very willing teacher.

One particular mergers and acquisitions guy really got under Rick's skin. He was a guest of Ross Simonetti, founder of the world's most successful hedge fund. Simonetti had reserved the entire lodge for some of his best clients and business associates, a $110,000 tab without tips. He also sprang for the two-grand, first-class airfare for each guest and the bill to outfit all the greenhorns: top of the line Orvis rods, three per guest—one for salmon, one for trout, and a spare—reels, line flies, waders, wading jackets, polar fleece pants and pullovers, hats, you name it. The only thing his guests had to bring were themselves, toothbrushes and underwear.

Simonetti was a one-time physics professor at SUNY on Long Island with an absolutely brilliant mind. He made a ton of money at the blackjack tables in casinos all around the world. He had a system and formula for success that had him on the watch list of every gambling house from Connecticut to Dubai. While they couldn't prove he counted cards or *cheated* them with his mind, he fell out of favor fast at all the tables. They harassed him constantly, so much so that it became a huge hassle for Ross to gamble any longer. So he took his talents to another gambling venue—the stock market. He had an idea that if he could apply some market performance modeling with Einstein-like regression analysis and remove the emotion from trading by having computers do all the thinking, he just might score big on Wall Street. He was right on the money with that concept. Ross recruited some of the best scientific and mathematical minds he could find—many were very fortunate former academia colleagues—and he lured away some of Microsoft's best programming talent. Money is a great recruiter. This collection of brainpower formed the best hedge fund team in the world. These guys were so good at what they did that when the global economy collapsed in 2008, their DaVinci Premier Anatomy Fund earned billions. They had the highest returns in the business. Even the Senate Committee on Finance and Banking Reform was impressed. Ross was called to testify before that august but dazed and oblivious group as the bottom fell out of the global banking system. He was cool, calm, and collected and left his audience drooling over what he had accomplished while the rest of the financial world was being flushed down the crapper.

Even though Ross Simonetti was a powerhouse titan in the world of high finance, he was still a humble and down-to-earth guy. That came from his roots, growing up in an Italian-Irish family from the Bronx, which taught him the values of family, friendship, and loyalty. He was one of the wealthiest guys in the world but one of the nicest guys you would ever meet. That was more than could be said for some of his weasel-like business associates and clients who thought their crap didn't stink. This mergers and acquisitions asshole was one of those.

As is customary at Alaska wilderness fishing lodges, the after-dinner hours are reserved for socializing, a few nightcaps, and for arranging the next day's fishing itinerary. This is when the guides are paired up with their anglers. Lodges like to rotate guides so each guest gets different fishing experiences and is given an opportunity to sample some of the hottest fishing of the week. At Peninsula Creek Lodge, all the fishing was phenomenal but the best fishing was a heli-copter ride away to remote tidal creeks off the Pacific Ocean side of the Alaska Peninsula. As a top-end fly-out lodge, they maintained a small fleet of aircraft used to shuttle clients to and from various rivers. The lodge also operated two Enstron F28F helicopters for access to very remote and fish-filled locations, inaccessible to their Cessnas or DeHaviland float planes.

But the Enstrons only had two passenger seats. With sixteen guests and weather-related flying restrictions, the lodge manager rotated clients between aircraft and locations throughout the week. The fee for running the whirlybirds came on top of the weekly rate at six hundred an hour—a drop in the bucket for Simonetti. Although the fishing was exceptional, one or two clients always felt they were getting screwed if they didn't get to ride in the choppers every day. The M&A blowhard was one of them. If Rick had his way, the slime ball would never get to fly in the chopper. He had been a royal pain in the ass all week long for the other guides he fished with, incessantly complaining about one thing or another. Now Rick drew him for the following day. The guy's name was Lenny Kramer. He couldn't cast, he couldn't fish, and he couldn't hold his liquor. He was a rather large man and liked throwing his weight around. He still thought he was playing right tackle for Ohio State. A big dude like this and booze spelled trouble.

It was about 9 p.m. All the other guests had left the dining lodge for their cabins. The morning coffee delivery to the guest cabins came early and the day's fishing was exhausting. Rick, Lenny Kramer, and Peggy, the lodge's assistant chef, were the only ones who still remained in the dining lodge. Peggy was cleaning up the last of the kitchen mess. Rick was in the tackle room, tying flies for the next day. He had a lot of luck this season with a purple, pink, and orange marabou fly. The silver salmon couldn't resist it. Since he knew Lenny and his equally obnoxious buddy would lose a ton of flies due to their incompetence, he decided to tie an abundant supply. Lenny, as usual, had one too many beers and was breaking Rick's balls about getting on the helicopter flight in the morning.

"Come on Rick, there's a couple of hundred extra in tips if you get me on the bird tomorrow."

"No can do, Mr. Kramer. We have the seats already assigned and the anticipated heavy fog in the morning might delay the flight. Don't worry; we'll get our share of fish where we're going. There's a solid run of big silvers just a short hop away in the Cessna."

Lenny pressed Rick with more money because now it was just a matter of personal pride and influence. "A grand. Get me on the bird and there's a thousand-dollar tip in it for you." Rick didn't budge an inch. It was a matter of pride for him as well.

It finally became apparent to Lenny that he wasn't about to get his way. Rick really could use the extra money but he despised the attempt at being bribed by some drunken, rich scumbag.

"This place sucks. I should buy the fucking joint and that fucking helicopter. And then you'll do whatever I want or I'll fire your ass." Lenny mumbled obscenities as he staggered from the tackle room and into the main dining area.

Rick was totally focused on his fly tying until he heard Peggy's voice. "Please, Mr. Kramer stop that. Please take your hands off me." Rick got up and moved into the dining room. The kitchen was off to the left, obscured from his line of sight by a wall filled with fish mounts.

"Please Mr. Kramer. Stop that! Please!" Hearing that second, more urgent plea, Rick sprinted the remaining distance of the long dining room in a flash. He still had his pro ball speed. When he got to the kitchen, he witnessed Lenny groping at Peggy. One hand was on one of her breasts, the other paw mashed up against her crotch, and he had her pinned against the sink. He was massive and the small woman didn't stand a chance escaping his weight and grasp. Rick placed a hand on Kramer's shoulder and squeezed hard on his trapezoid muscle. The big man felt the sting and whirled around. He took a half-hearted swipe at Rick. Lenny had had a lot to drink but he still could be a formidable adversary. "You fucker," Lenny said. "Who do you think you are touching me?"

Rick tried diplomacy. "Mr. Kramer, the young lady does not appreciate your advances. I think you've had too much to drink. How about I walk you back to your cabin?"

"Fuck off! I'll do whatever I want."

"I don't think so Mr. Kramer. Please, let's stop before this turns ugly."

Kramer was so distracted by Rick that Peggy used the opportunity to escape from his oppressive weight and alcoholic stench. She ran from the kitchen and out the front door of the dining room.

"I will break you in two," Kramer said. "I'm the top of the food chain, you worthless prick. I can buy you and everyone else at this dump." He threw a heavy but sluggish overhand right that totally missed Rick. As he did, he stumbled forward. Rick caught Kramer and prevented him from falling flat on his face.

"It doesn't have to be like this. Let's just end it here."

"I'll tell you what, buddy boy. I'm going to get down in a four-point stance, come off the line like a tiger, and tackle your sorry ass right through the front door. How you gonna like that, you chicken shit?"

Although the drunk appeared out of shape as evidenced by his beer gut, Kramer was a powerfully built man and he could inflict some serious damage if he gained advantage over Rick.

"Lenny. May I call you Lenny? Let's have a beer and talk about fishing tomorrow. Come on, let's end this."

"Red 32, Red 32, hut, hut. . . ."

Rick knew Lenny was coming full force on the next *hut*, so he remained on his toes to maintain leverage and avoid a direct impact. Lenny was still quick and covered the distance fast. As Kramer charged off the imaginary line, he sneered, a crazed look in his eyes. In his drunken stupor, he probably thought Rick was a rival Penn State tackle. He came right for Rick's midsection with his shoulder low, head outside the line of impact—perfect tackling form. But Rick deftly sidestepped his attacker and used the big man's momentum to his advantage, driving Kramer headfirst into the sidewall of the dining room. Unable to resist the moment, he yelled "Olay!" as Kramer's bulk crashed to the floor.

Kramer was pissed. Oh, was he pissed. Even as drunk as he was, Kramer wasn't about to be embarrassed by some punk fishing guide.

"You cock sucker, I'll kill you." Kramer was up off the floor and on Rick in a split second. Rick tried to avoid the second charge but the oversized dining room table made an escape move impossible. The big man had a few tricks of his own and, as Rick tried to block the attack, Kramer put a classic lineman's swim move on him and deflected Rick's arms before he could deliver a strike. Kramer grabbed Rick in a bear hug and it was face-to-face, hand-to-hand. He wanted to inflict pain that would be remembered for a long time to come.

Rick knew he was in trouble but he also knew what he had to do to extricate his body from this mess. With all the force he could muster,

Rick pounded both of his hands, palms open, against Kramer's ears, delivering a painful and disorienting ear slap. Kramer yelped like a puppy and for an instant released his grip on Rick. But he recovered amazingly fast. He shook off the slap and hugged Rick even tighter, driving him back into the kitchen and up against the refrigerator. It was just like sacking a quarterback. Kramer's breathing was heavy and, with labored effort, he whispered to Rick that he was about to bust all his ribs. Rick tried to break the hold but Kramer was too strong. Rick had no choice but to go for Kramer's most exposed point of vulnerability. Placing the leading edge of his right hand against Kramer's throat, Rick used his left hand as a sledgehammer and focused a direct blow to the windpipe. Rick held back on the power of the blow; too much force would be lethal. Kramer didn't deserve to die. He just needed to feel pain and remorse. As the power of the strike took effect, Kramer emitted a gurgling gasp and reached for his throat, the pain evident and the fear obvious in his eyes.

Rick moved aside. Kramer fell to his knees but somehow managed to gather another burst of energy. He swung around with cat-like speed and reflexes and tackled Rick's legs, taking him to the ground.

Rick's greatest fighting strength was his ability to grapple, but Kramer had some skills of his own. It was obvious to Rick that Kramer had had some formal training, perhaps as a collegiate wrestler. His moves were a bit rusty, but he knew what to do when he had an opponent on the ground. Kramer tried getting a scissor hold on Rick by positioning one of his thighs on the front of the Rick's neck and the other leg on Rick's back, while locking angles and squeezing to apply a choke hold. Kramer also attempted a simultaneous fish hook move on Rick by trying to insert his finger tips into Rick's nose and mouth and pull until flesh ripped. Rick reacted as someone who had trained all his life for this precise moment; he put a reverse escape move on Kramer and got behind him. Kramer breathed heavily and drooled, every once in a while releasing a ghoulish, gurgling gasp from his pounded windpipe. Rick encircled the big man's head and right arm with his legs and squeezed them together to form a tri-angle. Rick simultaneously pulled Kramer's head down, effectively cutting off blood flow to the carotid artery. Kramer was seconds away from passing out from oxygen deprivation to the brain when the door to the dining lodge sprung open. Ross Simonetti was the first to rush in, followed by Joe, the lodge owner. Rick released his death grip, got up off the floor, and walked out. The following morning, he was on his way back to Long Island.

CHAPTER 8

Nick watched Katie as she rifled through some folders in her filing cabinet. "I'm finding it hard to believe these things might actually be fish. It seems too far-fetched," he said.

"Didn't we get a police report at the beginning of the summer about some surfers out in the Hamptons being attacked by a large school of small fish?"

"Those were small bluefish biting at shiny jewelry and dangling toes. Minor bites and lacerations, but nothing that would compare with this."

"But weren't there also reports of some bigger fish in the mix? Some witnesses said they were sharks. Maybe they weren't sharks?"

"Are you thinking our mystery fish may have traveled up here with those smaller bluefish?" Nick said.

"Perhaps. Bluefish can create quite a scene when they migrate and feed, and the ensuing commotion may have attracted other large predators."

Katie was somewhat on the right track. The movements of predatory fish will often track closely to the migration patterns of prey species. Striped bass, for example, will be found hot on the heels of transient schools of Atlantic menhaden. The school of creatures Katie was trying to identify had entered the waters of the Long Island Sound after oceanic wanderings had taken them far from the place of their birth. They met up with the large school of small bluefish off the Jersey shore where they wreaked havoc with the smaller fish.

This mayhem continued as the creatures moved north. Once off the south shore of Long Island, the school of small blues dispersed. The creatures lost interest in that game and zeroed in on bigger prey.

After spending time off Montauk Point, The Race, and Orient Point feeding undetected on whatever crossed their paths, the creatures entered the Long Island Sound, not far from the harbors that nurtured them as juveniles. These enormous beasts would settle into a late summer and fall feeding pattern, ranging between Wading Neck to the east, the Squeteague River to the west, and out to the Middle Grounds and Stratford Shoal. Those geographic points formed a triangular killing zone. As long as the creatures found food, they would remain. These monsters would attack and eat anything that intersected their path, regardless of size. But they preferred to hunt their prey— nothing was too large for their heinous killing methods. Abnormal growth rates resulted in these animals reaching gargantuan sizes. An attacking pack of these fish could swiftly annihilate anything they encountered in the Sound, humans included. They were the largest and the most deadly species to be found anywhere in the world. They not only grew to phenomenal size but also had become more aggressive than notoriously ill-tempered bull sharks. Their savagery was unprecedented in the natural world. They would often tear into unfortunate prey, slashing, slicing and dicing, leaving body parts in their wake. And when they became satiated, they would regurgitate their meals and do it all over again. They were ruthless in a way that was unique in the animal kingdom. Other animals mostly just kill what they need for survival. But these superior organisms killed wantonly and nonstop.

Katie found the folder she was looking for and she read a loud for Nick's benefit: "Bluefish are one of the most popular game fish found along the East coast of the United States. They range from Florida to Nova Scotia. They are migratory, found worldwide in tropical and temperate oceans, inshore and offshore. They are prized both for their prowess as relentless fighters when hooked and the quality and flavor of their flesh, especially the smaller fish."

"Where are you going with this?"

"This is prime time in our area for bluefish. And what if those other sightings off New Jersey were of large predators traveling with them? They could be our mystery fish. There are bound to be more encounters."

"You know that big money bluefish tournament is coming up soon. Labor Day weekend."

"Great! That is just what we need. All that chum and bait in the water will get every bluefish in the Sound in a frenzied feeding mood, and who knows what that might attract."

Katie then pressed on with her ichthyology diatribe in the hope she might reveal some additional clues to the killing. "Bluefish are often located in shallow bays and inshore waters. When migrating, schools the size of a football field can be been found. Some of these large schools of bluefish number in the thousands. In 1901, a school was spotted in Narragansett Bay, Rhode Island, that was almost six miles long! Can you imagine falling into that mess? Bluefish roam the entire water column, top to bottom, swimming continuously day and night."

"So?"

"If something big is killing bluefish, then they must be even more efficient and ferocious. Perfect killing machines with the Long Island Sound as their hunting grounds. And that sounds like mako sharks to me, despite what the bite impressions suggest."

"We need to focus on the possibility of this being the work of one school of fish. And I'm pretty sure those bite marks are not from makos."

Katie wouldn't let go. "The animals we are dealing with might only be stragglers, cut from a larger group. If they are fish, that would mean a large school. Fish tend to travel both in small packs and entire schools of equally sized fish. And given the time of night this incident most likely occurred, it's possible it was the result of a small pack that had broken away from the main school. And how do you know it's just one school?"

"Because predators like our possible culprits often prefer the interaction of large groupings of peers during the day, but they also break off into smaller packs or pods during the late evening and night. Odds are that if it was marine life that killed the guy, it was a small group of marauding creatures that were part of at least one larger population."

"Yeah. And then all their buddies broke up into equally deadly pods of super-sized killers. School's out," Katie said.

"This is . . . baffling. Science fiction not science fact."

"Why don't you think it can happen, Nick? There are all sorts of recorded discoveries of gigantism in marine species. Look at the giant squid. Those things are monstrous. And it wasn't until the last decade that scientists actually had a chance to study them. Is it so hard to believe that some beast could grow to these outsized proportions? Look, you were the one who said that whatever did this was most likely about a hundred pounds."

"*Most likely* is the issue, Katie. We need more facts. You know me, always second-guessing my conclusions. But one-hundred-pound killers swimming in the Sound? That is simply astonishing, if true. We'd be breaking new ground here."

"Yep. But it is possible and the evidence tells me these things are very real, very dangerous, and very much fish. You are very good at what you do and you can't precisely identify those bite marks, even with all your tools and technology."

CHAPTER 9

About three hundred million years ago, dinosaurs roamed the primordial landmass that would eventually be transformed into Long Island, but it was the receding movements of the massive Wisconsin glacier just twenty thousand years ago that began to carve the land into the shape it is today. By most accounts, the specific geological events that would shape the future of Long Island occurred a mere eleven thousand years ago, a speck in time when compared to the age of planet Earth. Two terminal moraines, the Ronkonkoma Moraine and the Harbor Hills Moraine formed the structural spines of Long Island. The Ronkonkoma ridge is the older and more southerly of the two and formed topography of low rolling hills along the south side of the Long Island Expressway. The higher Harbor Hills Moraine is more recent—about eighteen thousand years; it gave the north shore its characteristic hills, cliffs, and massive boulders. Kettle lakes and rivers were shaped, as was the Long Island Sound, its bays and harbors.

Volcanic upheaval and glacial movements created the fish-shaped island that is now one of the most densely populated suburban areas in the United States. In that relatively recent epoch, water surrounded the Island landmass, framing the beginnings of the elongated, fish-shaped formation we now know as Long Island. It is said that the indigenous Native Americans called the land Paumanok in recognition of its likeness to a fish profile. The distinguished American poet, Walt Whitman, reaffirmed the name in his poetry.

Long Island is a 1,723 square mile piece of real estate nestled between the Long Island Sound to the north and the Atlantic Ocean to the south. It is approximately 120 miles long with a width that ranges between 12 and 20 miles. The Island is the fourth largest land mass surrounded entirely by water in the United States and the largest outside of Alaska and Hawaii. Both the Long Island Sound and the Atlantic Ocean each define Long Island's north and south shores respectively. To the west is New York City. The boroughs of Brooklyn and Queens are geologically linked to Long Island but true Islanders are defined as residents of only Nassau and Suffolk Counties.

One hundred twenty miles to the east of the city is one of the most fabled fishing holes of all, Montauk. It is a place of hardy men and great fish, a formula from which legends were born. It was there the legendary Captain Frank Mundus plied his trade and skill for catching great white sharks. His reputation was as great as the fish he chased, so much so that he was believed the most likely inspiration for the crusty Captain Quint of *Jaws* fame. While it is beyond comprehension for most anglers, Captain Mundus and Donnie Braddick, in 1986, caught the largest fish ever on rod and reel—a 3,427-pound great white. Although that was a remarkable catch, it was far from eclipsing the 4,500-pound behemoth Mundus harpooned previously off Montauk in 1964. Those two fish showed the world that monsters do indeed swim in the waters off Long Island.

Slightly to the north of Montauk are Orient Point and the legendary Race, places in their own right filled with much angling lore and seafaring adventure. Bracketing the Island are both the north shore and south shore coastlines. The fertile waters of the Long Island Sound—approximately 122 miles long—and the expansive and seemingly endless Atlantic Ocean define the character and scope of the Island's marine environment. Remaining true to its original contours, the eastern end of the Island, beginning at about the town of Riverhead, begins the fishtail-like transformation that creates two fluke-shaped peninsulas known locally as the north and south forks.

The Long Island Sound is a large body of water situated between the north shore of Long Island, a portion of the Queens County shoreline, and the Connecticut coastline. It was formed approximately thirteen million years ago, another by-product of the Wisconsin glacier scraping and then receding across the landscape. The Sound is actually an estuary, a body of saltwater nourished by freshwater flows from rivers and streams. Approximately 90 percent of the freshwater that enters the Sound does so primarily from three Connecticut Rivers and one from Long Island: the Connecticut, Housatonic, Thames, and the Nissequogue. This freshwater mixes with saltwater that enters the Sound from the Atlantic Ocean. The Sound has an east-to-west orientation and is approximately 110 miles long and 21 miles across at its widest point. Its surface area encompasses 1,320 square miles and the watershed's drainage extends an astounding 16,820 square miles and well into the Canadian provinces.

Long Island Sound is an extremely productive ecosystem inhabited by significant numbers of fish and other wildlife. Its estuary characteristics enable portions of the Sound to function as highly active feeding, breeding, and nursery areas. The watershed, wetlands, and the Sound itself are a natural wonderland. Almost 175 birds and waterfowl maintain some residence in the area, as do about 170 species of fish and 1,200 invertebrates. Dozens of tropical species of fish annually visit the waters of the Sound as do several coveted pelagic game fish species. Approximately fifty species of fish actually spawn in its waters.

Nearly twenty million people live within fifty miles of the Sound. It is a vibrant, multiple-use natural resource that attracts power-boaters, sail boaters, fishermen, water fowlers, birders, kayakers, divers, swimmers, hikers, and a whole host of other outdoor enthusiasts. In 1987, it was classified as a National Estuary. Unfortunately, a consequence of its suburban profile results in more than one hundred sewage treatment plants discharging about one million gallons of treated effluent into the Sound each day. The extensive range of the watershed resulted in numerous and varied pollutants entering the Sound. At one time, the lobster fishery of the Sound was rated in the top three of such fisheries in the United States, that is until pollution caused a massive die-off of young lobster. The most probable culprits were the meticulously manicured and fertilized lawns of the north shore. While the root cause of the die-off has not been definitively identified, the lobsters have died, and along with them a once thriving industry.

The primary recreational fish in the Sound of interest to fishermen are striped bass, bluefish, fluke, tautog, porgy, sea bass, bonito, and false albacore. The Sound is a magnet for many forms of bait throughout the entire season since its waters stay relatively cool and its backwater harbors and rivers act as natural nurseries. The principle food sources of predatory fish in Long Island Sound are sand eels, silversides or spearing, bay anchovies, adult menhaden, peanut bunker, shad, squid, herring, mackerel, cinder worms, crabs, shrimp, and the American eel. Since most recreational fish are very opportunistic feeders, they will also actively feed on juvenile fish of many species. Large bass, weakfish, and bluefish will key in on larger prey, especially the bunker. The longer bunker remained in the Sound, the longer those large predatory fish would also hang around.

The spring migration of fish into the Sound typically moves from west to east, with the most active early spring fishing occurring in the western-most reaches of the Sound. Much of that movement has to do with striped bass migrating out of the Hudson River, into the East River, and then following time-honored routes into the Sound. During the middle of April, those fish take up residence in the western Sound. As the waters warm, bait and fish become more active in areas of the central Sound, and then along the East End of the North Fork. Some areas of the Sound have greater proclivity toward attracting and holding bigger fish throughout the season, while some areas tend to appeal to smaller fish. But each area will see peak times when big fish move through. Yet, fish are not always predictable and their patterns of travel can change from one year to the next.

The season of the killer creatures had seen abundant bait and strong runs of fluke, big bass, and very large numbers of bluefish. The masses of bluefish ranged in all sizes, from small snappers to tailor and harbor blues, to fish of twenty pounds. For a while, blue-fish, bass, and even fluke had come on hard times from over-fishing but reduced harvest limits and the natural cyclical turnaround of their stocks resulted in a large, revived biomass of those species. For larger predators, there was an abundance of food. But now, the most superior and deadly of all oceanic creatures had found their way into the normally tranquil waters of the Long Island Sound and were on the prowl. They came here to feed.

CHAPTER 10

The needle was buried in the red on the radiation detection device. At first the safety engineer making his daily rounds of the cooling pools thought the instrument might have malfunctioned, since the warning siren had not sounded. But when he obtained a second device, the results were the same. Blood drained from his face and nausea took hold for he knew the potential consequences. His body trembled. After gathering his composure, he rushed to inform his boss.

It had taken almost ten years to build the new East Coast power plant. The facility was completed in 1989 but the 820 Megawatt nuclear reactor was shut down without ever delivering the electricity that was to have been one answer to growing power demands along the East Coast of the United States. Overwhelming public outcry against the plant's safe operation and ineffective evacuation plans were too much to overcome. But before the plant was decommissioned, an incident involving the nuclear reactor had taken place with very unexpected consequences.

At the time of initial plant construction, Ned Mack was named head of the plant's mechanical engineering department. Ned's primary responsibility was to oversee the construction and subsequent online operations of the steam-driven turbine generators. He was considered the best of the mid-level operations managers. Ned had a special passion for power generation and was good at his job. His superiors recognized his talents and ambition and eventually tapped him for this position at the nuclear plant. With all the political furor and sensitivities surrounding construction of the plant, and the nonstop public revolt against the plant, they needed their best management team in place. They'd have only one shot at getting the construction done right and acquiring the approvals to put the plant online. The main project team had botched their most important emergency evacuation drill and the local politicians were up in arms over the failure. There were daily protests by throngs of residents and organizations to cease and desist from further plant construction and operation. Their resistance worked. The combination of a failed evacuation drill, the 1979 Three Mile Island accident, and the 1986 Chernobyl tragedy put the final nails in the new power plant's coffin. Twenty-five years later, the gray hulk of the main reactor building sat idle as an omnipresent reminder of a multi billion dollar fiasco.

Although no commercial power was ever generated at the plant, low-level testing of the reactor was authorized by the Nuclear Regulatory Commission. Ned was part of the quality control team during those tests. He was a disciplined and no-nonsense guy. While he managed with a heavy hand, his employees considered him fair. Ned believed to his core that when working with nuclear power, there was no tolerance for error. His motto was "Zero defects, zero mistakes, zero failures," and he hung signs with those words around the entire workplace. He drilled that discipline into his team every day. That approach worked for most of his tenure at the plant. Ned had no incidents of failure among any of his workers; that was, until one leak of radioactive waste.

Nuclear power plants operate on the principle of nuclear fission, a process by which atomic particles split. As the atoms split at light speed, they generate enormous amounts of heat, turning water into pressurized steam, which in turn drives turbine engines to produce electricity. Uranium, especially "U-235," is an ideal natural element to use for nuclear power generation, since it is one of a select few natural elements that allow for induced fission to occur in nuclear reactors. That capability is essential for the controlled generation of nuclear power. The process is so efficient that a pound of highly enriched uranium equates to about one million gallons of gasoline. The heart and soul of any nuclear power plant is the reactor, the most common of which is known as a Pressurized Water Reactor. Uranium enriched fuel rods are contained within the reactor and sheathed in zircaloy, an alloy used as protective cladding of the fuel rods. A nuclear reactor also contains significant quantities of water maintained at high-pressure levels to prevent boiling. Add to that control rods that assist in managing the amount of nuclear chain reaction that takes place in the reactor, and the plant is good to go. The U-235 nuclei split, releasing heat that is transferred to the water. From there on, the process is simply a heat transfer to the water that turns to steam, which powers the turbines. Ultimately, electricity comes out the other end to power the needs of energy customers. Despite their effectiveness and efficiency as a source of power generation, nuclear reactors generate significant amounts of high-level radioactive waste in the form of spent fuel rods.

There are potentially cataclysmic consequences if those rods are mishandled or disposed of in a careless way, the most catastrophic of which is a total core meltdown and explosion, somewhat like the Chernobyl fire and the catastrophe in Japan. Spent fuel rods are stored in basins of water referred to as spent fuel pools. The water provides a cooling bath for the still-decaying fission products that can take hundreds or even thousands of years to fully decay. Spent reactor fuel is maintained in these water-filled storage pools. The pools are typically forty feet deep, with the bottom fourth of the pool equipped with racks designed for short-term storage of the fissionable materials. Re-circulating water cools the fuel and provides a protective shield from radiation. This nuclear power plant had just such a configuration. Even though this was a limited power test, the spent fuel rods still generated an enormous amount of heat and radiation. The amount of power output generated by the reactor is managed by controlling the fuel rods, and over time the fuel rods decay to a point where they are spent beyond useful life. At that point, they have to be disposed of and placed in the interim cooling pools. This is where the disposal team dropped the ball.

The spent fuel rods were removed from the reactor by a team of highly trained technicians. The logistics involved with the removal to the fuel pools required the use of an automated fuel rod handling system. The transport team had been through numerous simulations of the process and could perform the drill blindfolded. Ned Mack's quality control team was tasked with monitoring the fuel rod removal process. The spent fuel rods were successfully transported from the reactor and placed into the cooling pools. All went well with that phase of operation.

The critical value of fuel pools is that recirculating cold water works to remove the heat generated by the spent fuel assemblies, and the water also acts as protective barrier against the escape of harmful radiation. As long as the water remained a cooling influence on the rods, and as long as it was of an adequate volume to cover the rods, all was well. All nuclear power plants have contingency back-up supplies of water. In the case of this plant, one such source was the water of a large bay set off the Atlantic Ocean. Without adequate cooling, pool water can heat to the boiling point. If that happens, the spent fuel assemblies will eventually overheat and possibly melt or catch fire. The worst possible nuclear power plant accident will occur if either complete draining of the pools occurs or if the heat-exchanging cooling system fails. This can result in the most dreaded of all events: The Meltdown. Under those scenarios, deadly quantities of radioactive materials could be released into the atmosphere or surrounding environment. But a complete meltdown does not have to occur for damaging levels of radioactivity to be released.

Once the spent fuel cells from the plant's reactor were safely stored beneath thirty-plus feet of water, Ned Mack's quality control team triple-checked the various protocols. Although all procedures were followed, one major defect in the cooling system went undetected.

A control valve at the bottom of the pool that allowed an external water source to replenish water lost through evaporation malfunctioned and reversed the water flow. Rather than adding water to the pool, the valves released it back into the bay. Compounding the control valve problem was a failure of the low water alarm system.

The contractor who installed the alarm mechanism cut corners. Despite rigid NRC standards and contract materials commitments, the contractor did just enough to meet the minimum acceptable standards but used sub-par valves. As the water level in the pool dropped to within a few meters of the tops of the fuel rod assemblies, elevated radiation levels contaminated the water being accidentally released into the bay via the defective valve. While the safety inspection of the pool identified the problem, enough damage had been done to warrant an evacuation of the plant. But that never happened. The accident was kept hush for many years and only a few workers and their superiors were aware of the event.

Plant officials attempted to pay off all those involved with large sums of money to keep their mouths shut, starting with Ned Mack. He was offered a substantial lump sum payment in addition to a lucrative pension annuity arrangement to forget what he had seen. He refused. Others didn't. Ned was a principled man and was not about to be bullied or bribed into doing something that went against his grain. After several repeated refusals of their offer, Ned's superiors realized he had become a threat. Sadly, Ned didn't fully understand the magnitude of what he was up against. Ned mysteriously disappeared one day while out fishing. He was officially classified by police as a "missing person," and his disappearance remained an open cold case. Ned's family was never satisfied with the investigation and, although they received a ton of money to make them forget, they never could.

The crisis at the plant following the accident eventually stabilized. As interest in nuclear power generation gained new traction, the possible longer-term effects of the accident were swept under the rug. Since many who had been involved in the leak had died from various forms of cancers, the accident's audit trail from eyewitnesses was weak at best. Aside from the cancers, when humans and other animals come into contact with the harmful levels of radioactive substances, the interaction is known to mutate DNA and genetic composition, potentially causing chromosomal aberrations. That is precisely what happened when radioactive water came into contact with a species of migratory fish that had been in the area at the time of the accident. Some of those fish floated to the surface with mouths agape and clouded eyes, but many resisted death.

CHAPTER 11

Rick's morning aboard *Maya* had been far from ideal. His charter arrived promptly at first light. The lead dog of the charter, Sidney Metzinger, was a Type A orthopedic surgeon who headed a local practice. He chartered Rick for himself, his wife and son, and for a shot at catching a striper, a bluefish, a little tunny, and a bonito: the Long Island Grand Slam. This was the best time of year to attempt that feat. Sidney fancied himself a fly fisherman and was determined to bag his slam on the fly, but as the morning unfolded, Sidney's inexperienced wife proved to be the best angler of the four. She stuck with easier-to-use spinning tackle and caught one fish after another, which did not sit well with the good doctor.

The day started out just fine inside the Port Roosevelt Harbor where Sid immediately hooked a six-pound bluefish from among a small school feeding on peanut bunker by the ferry dock. His wife and son did the same; it was a good start for Rick. The skunk was out of the boat, some of the guide pressure was off Rick, and for the moment he had three happy clients just minutes from the launch ramp. Sid was congratulating himself on the fly-rod catch but it was one of those situations with bluefish that no matter what was thrown their way, they were determined to eat it. Fish actually raced each other to get at the fly first. All in all, it looked like it might shape up into a good morning of fishing.

After playing with the bluefish for half an hour, Rick decided to move on and try for a striped bass that would give Sid number two of the four species needed for his "slam." Rick hit all his productive harbor spots to no avail and moved out into the open Sound, heading east along the beach. Sid's wife caught a nice keeper-size bass at the first spot, and his son followed with two small undersized fish. As his wife released her bass back into the Sound, Sid hooked up with another bluefish that bit through his fluorocarbon leader. Rick retied the leader and added a new fly. He then worked down the shoreline to East End Beach, and then stopped at the inlet jetty off Mount Misery Harbor. It was there that Sid hooked a small striped bass that was eaten by another fish while being retrieved. Rick saw a large swirl behind the bass just before it was stolen from the line. He assumed it was a large bluefish. Sid was pissed. Rick moved the boat to the other side of the inlet where he knew some small school bass stayed throughout the summer. Sid hooked up again but the line immediately went slack. The bass was gone and so was Sid's Deceiver fly. Again Rick saw a large swirl. *That's odd*, Rick thought.

Rick tied on another fly and the doctor was into another bass. He landed this one. While not a keeper, it was a bass on the fly and it qualified as part of the slam. The easy part was now out of the way. While Sid's wife and son were having a blast with a school of harbor blues, Rick noticed the telltale surface-busting of the elusive Atlantic bonito. Their behavior was erratic and out of the ordinary. They seemed especially spooked. Rick knew Sid would have difficulty.

Sid was an abominable caster. The speed and selectivity of the bonito totally frustrated him. His casts were consistently off the mark and pitifully short, and at times wild flailing of the fly rod posed a danger to all those on board. At one point, Doctor Sid hooked his hat and then Rick's shirt. It could have been a lot worse. But that didn't stop his wife and son from catching their share. The frustrated doctor belted out orders for Rick to get closer to the fish so he would have a fair shot at reaching them, and he instructed his wife and son to cease casting. That didn't help either. Rick thought that for this guy to catch one of these speedsters, it would have to commit suicide by hooking itself. Rick checked his watch and was glad to see his six-hour charter come to an end. Sid wanted to hire him for the rest of the day but Rick had had enough and Sid's wife and son had caught plenty of fish.

Rick headed back to the launch ramp at full throttle, only slowing down when he hit the no-wake zone just outside the harbor. At the ramp, Sid paid his bill, adding a decent tip, and said he would call again. Rick had no clients scheduled for the afternoon so he would head back out into the Sound for an afternoon of personal fishing and some exploring. He had Katie on his mind and was still thinking about her call. He'd grab some lunch, fill up with gas, and then make the rounds of all his productive spots to see if he might locate anything unusual. He dialed Katie's number on his cell phone.

"Hi Rick. What are you up to?"

"Just about to grab some lunch and then head out for a solo afternoon of fishing. Care to join me?"

"Can't Rick. Working hard on this case and still need to gather some more facts."

"Well, we might just bump something out there that could help you solve this. There were a ton of small bluefish and bass out there this morning. Aside from some seemingly spooked bonito, I didn't see anything out of the ordinary but we could make the run out east and then back west. We could cover a lot of ground."

"I'll take a rain check for later in the week. What do you mean *spooked bonito*?"

"They were just acting a bit odd and being tougher than usual to catch."

"Huh. That's interesting. Wonder what had them nervous? Let me know if you see anything else. Okay?"

"How about dinner?"

"Rick, you know I'm busy."

"Come on, Katie, we really need to talk and maybe I can help you with this case of yours. And it has been a while since we got together.

I think you've made me suffer long enough. I've done my time in purgatory. Don't make me beg on this one."

"Seven-thirty at Grumpies. Okay?" Katie's reply surprised Rick.

"You just made my day. I'll be there 7:30 sharp. Love ya."

Rick made certain the boat was secured to its mooring and then headed over to Mickey D's. Once back on board *Maya,* Rick hailed his buddy Jack on the VHF.

Rick took a bite of his sandwich and tried again. "Captain Jack, Captain Jack, this is Captain Rick, do you read me, over?"

The VHF crackled, "Got you, Rick. What's cookin'?"

"Hey Jack, just eating some lunch and getting set to head out to the middle. I'll be idling out in a minute. Anything going on?"

"Things got quiet during the slack tide but when she was running hard on the outgoing, there were fish busting all over. Got some nice blues and stripers and played a bit with the albies. How about you?"

"We did okay this morning. Had a challenging sport on board but we managed some fish. The guys wife nailed a slam."

"Nice going, Rick. Ton of fish around right now. Hope the bait stays put. Where you headed this afternoon?"

"Figured I would do some scouting and see if I might help Katie out with her case. She's still going on about something strange out there but won't spill the beans. Got dinner with her tonight so maybe she'll open up a bit."

"Bet you're hoping in more ways than one."

"This is just a friendly dinner, Jack. See if we might get things back on track."

"Man, you two are like oil and water. You will be the death of each other one of these days."

"Hey Jack, anything strange going on out there. I mean any more of those unexplained big fish sightings?"

"Last evening I bumped a large school of little tunny just flying out of the water in all directions. Not like they were feeding, just as if they were running from something. Strange behavior."

"Did you see anything harassing them? Something would have to be big and fast to catch them."

"Nah, nothing. At first I thought it might be bottlenose dolphin. About two hundred were spotted west of here the other day, over by Stork Neck, but I never saw anything break the surface. There would be no mistaking dolphin."

"Got you, Jack. I'm just breaking free of the harbor and getting ready to mash the throttle. Heading east a bit and working my way back. Gimme a shout if you see anything suspicious."

"Count on it Rick. Over and out."

CHAPTER 12

The novice diver had recently finished his certification training at the Long Island Dive Center and quickly outfitted himself with the latest and best diving gear. He bought everything one could possibly need for dives with a National Geographic film team. But the gear he was most eager to try out was his new spear gun, so much so that he was prepared to violate the cardinal rule of diving: always dive with a buddy. Anticipation had gotten the best of him and he loaded his gear into his small fifteen-foot Boston Whaler skiff. He figured the dive would be a quick one; a small rock reef about four hundred yards off the beach, not far from his parents' waterfront home. He'd be down and up in no time with a nice bass skewered on his spear.

Once he exited from Mount Misery Inlet, the young diver motored east to a tight formation of large visible boulders. Like icebergs, what is revealed above the water represents but a small indication of the structure that lies beneath. The diver's handheld GPS guided him to the exact submerged rock cluster he was looking to find. He dropped anchor and suited up, dutifully checking his gear to make certain all was in working order. Satisfied he had done his pre-dive due diligence, he entered the water back first off the portside gunwale. The water was about thirty feet to the bottom. He had fished this area from his boat in the past and knew it held plenty of porgies, blackfish, striped bass, and bluefish. But this was the first time he would fish the rock reef as a diver, alone. If he was really lucky, he might be able to pick up a nice lobster or two hiding in the crevices for dinner with his family. While winter diving in the Long Island Sound offers some of the cleanest water and highest visibility, late summer divers are hampered by algae growth and can expect about four feet of visibility. Since it was late afternoon, the sun's rays angled low, limiting optimal light penetration to brief windows of visibility as he dove to the bottom.

As the diver approached the floor, he spotted a school of porgies suspended above the rocks. He chose not to give his new spear gun a try on the small fish; he had bigger game on his mind. The diver found a trio of rocks that formed a bottom blind he could conceal himself within. Rather than swim about looking for fish to shoot, he opted to stay put on the sand and gravel bottom and have the fish come to him. Most predatory game fish are drawn to rocks and boulders since all the nooks and crannies attract potential food like small baitfish, crabs, and lobsters. The diver knew this from his fishing experience and also knew the probabilities were high that some desirable fish species would eventually swim by within his cone of vision. He had about thirty minutes to spear dinner before the aqualung emptied.

The diver sat patiently, comforted by the soothing release of air bubbles as he breathed. He had always wanted to be a Navy Seal but he didn't have the right stuff. His doctor dad had other designs on the career he should pursue. Remaining motionless, the young man imagined being part of an expeditionary team preparing for an extraction of a covert operative held captive by the bad guys: an undetected swim to the beach, a silent approach to the cottage where the mark was being held captive. Stealth personified as muffled shots from silenced Sig Sauer 9mm handguns hit their target. Mission accomplished.

He saw the fish swim by, moving quickly from the murkiness to within his cone of vision. It was a big striped bass, but while daydreaming, he missed the opportunity to shoot. He readied his spear gun and aimed it through an opening in the rocks, figuring on having another chance. The bass was at least twenty pounds so the odds were good there were other fish of that size swimming with it. Again he saw the snout of another bass fill the opening of his rock blind; the pace of his breathing accelerated as the excitement built. He held off firing the gun until the mass of the fish's mid-body filled his field of vision, and then he pulled the trigger. The elastic band released; *swoosh* . . . as the spear traveled the short distance and struck true in the target. There was no way he could miss at four feet, even in dingy water. It was a big bass, larger than the one he first saw.

The fish reacted quickly to the mortal sting of the spear. With a burst of speed and power, the bass pulled line from the spool attached to the spear gun. The bass was a vigorous fighter and had much stamina. Coming out from his lair, the diver swam after the fish and its blood trail while continuing to retrieve and release line from the reel as needed. Although he could no longer see the bass, the diver was able to stay on track with the angle of the line attached to the spear. After a few minutes of give and take, a tug-of-war of sorts, the diver felt the first signs of submission. The pulling stopped and he detected only minor headshakes and slow, lumbering movements. He glanced at his watch—he had eight minutes of air left, plenty of time to get his prize to the surface.

An even larger fish swam by him with a force that moved water and pushed him off track. *Holy shit! What the hell was that?*

The diver watched in awe as another equally humungous creature passed through his field of vision, then another, and another— perhaps a dozen or more in all. Even though he could no longer see what they were, he could feel their presence. He felt uneasy, like being in a dark room sensing some unnatural force. The young man figured they were a school of really big bass, but he had already taken his dinner and his airtime was running out. He reeled quickly to retrieve the solid mass attached to his spear that no longer fought back. His prize was obviously dead. Based on the amount of line that was put back on the reel, he estimated his fish was about ten or twelve feet away.

The diver was startled as he felt a bump at the end of his spear. It was either another fish or his prize was in the final throes of dying and making one last bid for freedom. He quickly gathered more line and brought the bass to within six feet of his position. He could only see out about three or four feet so the bass was not yet visible to him. His senses were focused, and adrenaline flowed through his veins. The presence of other creatures while one is in the water is unnerving. Not seeing is downright frightening. The diver heard odd sounds in the water. It was a clicking sound accompanied by thumping and grinding noises. As he tried to determine the source of the sounds, his spear gun jolted violently from his hand, saved from total loss by the securing wristband he wore that attached him to the gun. Line flew off the reel as if his dead prize was brought back to life. He had five minutes of air left and he could not afford a renewed or pro-longed battle. *This damn bass must be bigger than I thought.*

The pulling suddenly stopped. The diver re-grasped the reel and wound on more line, the fish all the while coming toward him easily. Yet again, the big fish was very close. A few more feet of line taken in and he was able to make out the snout of the bass. By the size of its head, it was indeed bigger than he first thought. *Oh my God,* the diver thought when he realized only half a bass was still attached to his spear. Something had bitten a fifteen-pound chunk of bass clean off, from the tail to the midsection.

The diver panicked: *shark.* He swiftly kick-started his ascent to the surface, while still clinging to his spear gun and half of what just moments ago was a thirty-pound striped bass. The diver wanted to scream. His eyes widened as panic took hold. One of the demons charged upward from beneath the diver and bit off his left flipper and foot. The diver's mouth and face contorted within his mask as another creature severed his right foot from his leg. He tried again to scream but the sound he made was a high-pitched gurgle. The diver clung to the bass even tighter in his final moments. It gave him comfort. The diver was still kicking his legs as if to swim but he went nowhere as blood trailed from the stumps that moments before were his feet. He could see the surface, his boat just out of reach. But as the diver tried to swim upward, each leg kick only resulted in his body descending further back toward the bottom. The blood scent excited the big fish to feed even more violently—unlike sharks, they liked the taste of humans. Two-dozen killers circled their prey, taking big bites of neoprene and flesh wherever they struck. The bass was taken from him along with his arm. He maintained consciousness long enough to watch as the razor-lined mouth of a one-hundred-pound creature ripped off his face in one swift bite.

The neoprene sleeve from the dive suit floated to the surface, the diver's right arm still encased within. The sleeve was recovered two days later by a lobsterman tending to his pots. The coast guard responded to the grisly find and eventually found the Boston Whaler still anchored above the rock reef. They compared notes with police and identified the victim, whose parents reported him missing the night of the killing.

CHAPTER 13

Rick arrived at Grumpies at precisely 7:30 p.m., but Katie was nowhere to be seen. Rick figured she had been detained by the investigation. If she intended to bag dinner, he knew she would call. The place was mobbed as usual for a Friday night. He called over the hostess and reserved a table for two. The hostess knew Rick. They dated once.

"That will be about half an hour wait, Rick. Is that okay?"

"Sure thing, Becky. I'm waiting for someone so I'll just grab a beer until she gets here."

"Who's the lucky lady tonight, Rick?"

"Just someone I'm lucky to have join me for dinner." Rick smiled but the hostess didn't.

Rick knew many of the people in the bar. The place was a popular hangout for many Port Rosey locals. The restaurant had changed hands many times over the years, but the current combination of sports bar, quality food, and reasonable prices seemed a formula that worked. Rick loved their burgers. He ambled over to the bar and ordered up a summer ale. There is nothing quite like the refreshing taste of cold beer on a hot summer's night. As he raised his glass for a second swig, he noticed Jack sitting at the opposite end of the bar.

"How goes it, Jack?"

"Hi, Rick. Been doing okay. The fishing has been hot. Had some weird shit happen to me after we spoke."

"Like what?"

"I gotta tell ya, I hooked into something that just kicked the crap out of me. When I say big, I mean *gigantic*. I had twenty pounds of bass on the line and then this thing hit."

"You think it was a shark? Maybe a small mako?"

"It could have been a shark but I doubt it. I had the thing hooked and there was no jump. Makos like going airborne. But there were other equally large fish swimming with the one I hooked. When it came near the surface, I saw the backs of other big fish. Couldn't make out what they were. Busted my eighty-pound braid like it was sewing thread."

"That's two odd deals you got into out there in the past week. First those albies flying out of the water being chased by something big, and now these things? I wonder if this has anything to do with what Katie has been up to?" Rick glanced at this watch—eight o'clock and no Katie. "Now she is officially late."

"So what are you thinking those fish were, if you had to guess?"

"There aren't many local fish that can pull that way, Rick. And nothing that eats twenty-pound bass for lunch. Maybe shark or a bottlenose, but I'm not convinced it was either. Dolphins are way too smart to be accidentally fooled by a baited hook. These were some kind of schooling fish. With all the weird weather changes going on and the Gulf Stream moving closer, maybe some odd fish came up from down south."

"I'm with you, Jack, but what are we talking about? Maybe a school of big wahoo or some big king mackerel, or maybe barracuda?"

"Your date just arrived."

Rick turned around to spot Katie talking with Becky over by the front door. They were both smiling. Rick was hoping his one-night stand wouldn't interfere with tonight's plans. He needed to intervene fast.

"Think I'd better go rescue her before my reputation is tarnished even more than it already is. Nothing like the wrath of a cocktail hostess scorned. Just ask that pro golf guy."

Katie saw Rick approach and gave him a quick wave and smile.

"Hey, you okay? Was wondering what happened. You're never late."

"Tough day at the office," Katie said. She gave Rick a light kiss on his lips. "I could use a nice tall one when we sit down."

"Your table is ready. Follow me," Becky said, winking. Rick wanted to give her the finger but he thought better of it.

"Nice table, Rick. In the corner, in the back, in the dark. Perfect for how I feel right now."

"What happened?"

"Another body was found off Boulder Point today. Correction— another body *part* was found. It was the arm of what was once a young scuba diver. Poor kid. Tragic things are happening in the Sound, Rick, and I need to figure out what before it's too late."

"Do you have any clues?"

"We do, Rick, but the one hypothesis we've come to is so hard to believe that we need substantial proof before I even float the idea to my boss or the police."

"What do you think it is?"

Before Katie could answer, their server arrived. Katie cringed.

"Hey hey, how's my brainy and hot Italian princess doin'?"

"Ricco cut the crap."

"Eh, eh, this ain't no act, princess. I'm the real thing. One hundred percent original Italian Stallion and I got the black two-door parked out back to prove it."

"Hundred percent asshole is more like it."

"Not nice, not nice at all sweetie. What can I get for you?"

"I'll just have a pint of whatever you have on tap."

"And you, my friend."

"I'll have another BP summer ale."

"Got it, get it . . . good . . . BRB my nubile Neapolitan nymph."

"I think I need to slap that guy."

"Rick, he's harmless. An asshole, yes, but totally harmless. We go back to high school. Ignore him. I really need your support right now."

"We got some heavy stuff going down and I'm at the center of trying to figure it all out. In the last week, we had a shredded body wash up in Smith's Bay, two dogs mysteriously disappear off Boulder Point, a kid diver disappears and only his arm surfaces, and all signs seem to point to some marine animal as the perpetrator."

"I was talking with Jack before. Earlier today he hooked something very big and very unusual. It ate a twenty-pound striper. But it spooled him and he never got a good look at it."

"When? Where did that happen, Rick?"

"Lady and gent, your drinks are served. Ready to order?"

"Give us a few minutes," Rick said.

"Yes sir, Captain Ahab."

"He said he didn't think it was a shark and that there were other similar fish swimming with it. He is really at a loss for an explanation. I think it happened late afternoon in deep water near buoy 9."

"Do you think it could have been a large school of large fish?"

"Katie, I don't know. Do you think the fish Jack hooked is linked to the deaths? And how fucking big are you talking about? It would take one mother of a fish to eat a twenty-pound bass, let alone kill someone."

"Rick, I'm not talking about one fish. I'm talking about the possibility of an entire school of big creatures"

Ricco was back. Without even looking up, Rick ordered a bacon cheeseburger with fries and cole slaw and another beer.

"I'll have the same," Katie said.

Katie continued, "Rick, there is some evidence that the bite marks on the guy they found match the profile of some kind of fish that could be enormous."

"So what? The guy could have been dead in the water and a bunch of fish, maybe big bluefish, decided to feed on the corpse just like great white sharks feed on whale carcasses."

"Not likely. If we computer model one of the bite marks found on the victim against normal-sized indigenous fish the results indicate a fish that's between seventy-five and one hundred pounds."

Rick's jaw dropped. "There's no fucking way. Are you shitting me? That can't be possible. There's nothing around here that big. Those computer models are all screwed up."

"And if we extrapolate from scientifically sound growth rate charts, a fish of that weight would be at least six feet long."

Rick put down his burger and stared at her. "I think you're overworked Katie. Six feet long? One hundred pounds? Not a shark? That ain't science, Katie, that's science fiction."

"Listen, it's possible. There are aberrant specimens throughout the entire animal kingdoms, individuals that have undergone genetic alteration either through evolution or environmental factors. This is all possible. And what scares me is that we don't know if this is just one small pod or an entire school. I have been having nightmares about all this."

"Here you go my sweetness. Medium rare, just like you like your meat. How can anything so smart look so good? And here is your well done burger Captain. Just like you like your meat. May I get anything else for you?"

"Not now, thank you." Rick was on his best behavior.

"Katie, the biggest fish I have ever seen in these waters was a sixty-pound striped bass caught on my boat by my friend, Chuck. The biggest bluefish I have ever seen caught was twenty-two pounds. You are suggesting a fish five times that size. I'm having a tough time wrapping my head around that. A school of hundred-pound killer creatures with an attitude would just about annihilate anything they came into contact with."

"Exactly. That's what I'm worried about."

Katie expanded on her fear by using bluefish as an example of predatory fish behavior. "Given their cannibalistic nature, bluefish tend to travel in packs or schools of equally sized fish. That is a built-in protection mechanism. The larger fish feed on the smaller ones and on fish of their own kind. Again, if our computer models are correct and the killer creatures are in fact that big, then there are likely sizeable numbers of them around. Jack probably hooked one and saw its traveling mates come to the surface. That would be worse than some wayward shark."

"Katie, eat your dinner and drink your beer. Give yourself a little break from all this. I hear you. I believe you even if it doesn't make sense. Can I tell you that I've really missed you?"

"Being with you is like being on a treadmill: a lot of work to get nowhere. You have this knack for just dropping out without notice or cause and then coming back like nothing ever happened. Like when you went off to Alaska for four and a half months. It was simply, *gotta go, see ya kiddo*. And then you stroll back into my life like some Grizzly Adams expecting me to welcome you with open arms and open legs. It doesn't work that way, Rick."

"This is a lot more than just missing you. I want to make this right and have all this work out. I know you still care. And you have to believe me when I say I do, probably much more than you might realize."

Ricco interrupted at the wrong time and finally pushed his luck with Rick too far. "How was your dinner my sweetness? Some dessert? I'm sweet too."

Rick motioned for Ricco to come closer. "Yes we would like dessert. As a matter of fact what I would like you to do is to get on the next fucking train out of Port Roosevelt and head to the city. Little Italy to be precise. We would like two fresh cannoli from Ferrara's on Grand Street, between Mott and Mulberry, and two espresso, each with a lemon wedge and a splash of anisette. And don't come back to this damn table until you have that. That is what the princess wants. Got it?"

Katie had to laugh at that one. Ricco was as pale as his white shirt and she could tell he was taking Rick seriously. But then again, she knew Rick well enough to know that he just might be serious. Ricco walked away, tail between his legs.

Down deep, Katie wanted things to work out with Rick but he could be such a wild card that his persona could change from one day to the next. Yet, she was willing to give him another chance. It seemed like she was always willing to give him one more chance.

"Look," he said. "I feel like I'm half a person when we are not together. That is just the way it is. I got a lot of shit out of my system over the past few years. I stopped all the cage fighting and put baseball behind me for now. I'd like to really build my charter business up here and in Florida and I have a few ideas for some new fishing products that I think could make me some money. And I want to go back to school to finish my degree and teach and coach baseball at the high school level. I want to settle down, Katie. With you. Sounds like a plan, right?"

"Yes it does, Rick. But we have talked about plans before and each time I got the short end of the stick in those deals."

"I know I've said it before and I know I've misled you but this time is really different." Rick reached for Katie's hand and took it in his. "All I ask is that you give me one more chance. Just one last chance and I will make this right. You don't owe me this but I'm just asking as someone who was once your best friend and lover."

Katie's eyes locked tight to Rick's and she saw something in him that she had never seen before. His eyes revealed a truth, a depth of sincerity that moved her to her core. She believed deeply that the eyes always tell the truth, that the eyes are the only real window onto someone's true being. When they first met and locked eyes like this, the sensations she felt aroused her. At this moment, the sensations went first to her heart. She had a fleeting thought that tonight she might just not go home, or at least not alone.

A half hour had elapsed since Ricco was given his dessert instructions. He came back to the table with two espressos in hand and two slices of cheesecake. "Coffee and dessert is on the house, I couldn't find any cannoli."

Katie and Rick ate the cheesecake, drank the espresso, and laughed about old times. Rick paid the bill and, as they left Grumpies, Becky said simply, "Have fun."

Katie answered, "You can bet on it."

CHAPTER 14

It had been about a year since Katie was last in Rick's home. They had picked up three bottles of wine and some sushi takeout and made love all night in front of the fireplace. There were no inhibitions, and nothing was off limits. Pure passion and lust filled their time together: throughout high school and college, she pretty much stuck to the books and wandered off her conservative path on just a few occasions. While she certainly was no angel, having had a couple of quick graduate school flings in the sack, nothing compared to the time she spent with Rick. That lovemaking was off the charts for Katie and she'd usually enjoy a love hangover for days. She often longed for him but suppressed those emotions, especially when he was off on another of his meaning-of-life expeditions. The relationship had been on shaky ground for a long time and the last thing she needed now was more frustration.

Rick's home was an old captain's house, originally built in the mid-1800s. His grandfather had owned it and passed it down to Rick's father. Rick was the eighth owner of the house, which was set upon a small hill overlooking Port Roosevelt Harbor. Rick put a lot of time and money into restoring it and now he had his home just about where he wanted it. Much of the decor was of a nautical design or had an outdoorsman's touch. And while Katie would have probably done things a bit differently if it were her place, she liked the house and its cozy character. Rick was a bit of a pack rat so the house was filled with all sorts of oddball collectibles and memorabilia. He had some old duck decoys, antique fishing equipment, baseball collectibles, old sporting art and plenty of books, many inherited from his grandfather. Rick was a voracious reader and he loved old books, something he had in common with Katie. Reading also kept Rick's mind off vodka, which had been on his mind every day since being drummed out of baseball.

Katie especially liked the den, even more than the bedroom. The full-wall stone fireplace was part of some very special moments in her love life, not the least of which were some soul-searching conversations with Rick during difficult periods in their relationship. But the flames from the fireplace also fanned some of the most romantic and sensual experiences Katie had ever had. Considering that it was now late August and the nighttime temperature was still in the eighties, ecstasy by the fireplace was not in the cards for this visit. The house was still hot from the heat it had absorbed throughout the day.

"Katie, I'm going to turn up the A/C just a bit and cool down this house."

"That's fine, Rick. Hey, where did you get this collection of old Hemingway books?"

"Found them in a little bookstore in Lambertville, New Jersey. Remember when I worked down in that area for a few months? One day I walked into the Book Nook on Union Street and there they were. Bought all six right on the spot. Great price too. That's a first edition of *The Old Man and the Sea* and a first of *A Farewell to Arms.*"

"Cool. I love reading Papa. Perfection and genius in simplicity."

"You got that right. The man knew how to use words sparingly, not like some of these windbags today. I still take rides down to that shop. You should come with me some time. You'd enjoy it. Beats the pricey books shops in the Hamptons. The trip to New Jersey is always worth the gas and the time."

"I would enjoy that. Maybe I could even find some old marine biology books. You know how I love to collect those. I really like this old French map of Alaska. Very neat. Did you get that down there too?"

"That map was a gift from the chef at the lodge in Alaska where I guided. She got it from one of her Eskimo friends."

"She must have really liked you to give you something like that?"

"Yes she did, but that is all past tense now."

"Where's Jenny?"

"She's out in the back. I keep her in the run this time of year. It's a nice spot with shade and plenty of room to exercise. She's probably sound asleep in her house right now. I'll bring her in later so you two can reconnect."

"Do you still hunt with her?"

"We still hunt some pheasants and ducks but she really loves woodcock. She's the best at that of all the labs I've had. She's getting old—slowing down a bit. But She'll be all over you when she sees you again. All seventy-five pounds of her still loves you."

"And I still love her."

"Would you like a little wine or some port?"

"Port would be delightful. Ruby, tawny, or vintage?"

"Who have you been hanging around with lately?"

"My dad's cellar was full of port. He's got a special bottle of Wares 1977 Vintage that he says he'll open on the night of my wedding. And he has another, a Taylor '77 that he's saving for my sister. He said he'd need them when it comes time to pay the wedding bills."

"He's probably right about that. But I do I like his approach."

"We've had good father-daughter talks sipping all that stuff. I learned all about wine from him. Actually, one of my favorite ports is a premium colheita tawny. Nice and velvety and it doesn't put quite the dent in your bank account as a vintage port does."

"Well, sweet pea, vintage port is too rich for my wallet. Basic ruby good enough?"

"It's all about the company, right?"

"Right. And maybe some day I just might get to taste some of that special Wares port too." Rick smiled. The reference wasn't at all lost on Katie; she winked at him and then quickly changed the subject.

"So . . . Rick . . . what do you think about my killer creature theory?"

Rick handed Katie her glass. "I could see thirty-pound, maybe even forty-pound fish if we really pushed the laws of nature, but seventy-five to a hundred pounds. You'd have to show me some hard evidence for that."

"You don't think the bite marks are enough?"

"Like I said, there are other ways for that to have happened and I wouldn't trust your computer models if my life depended on them."

"Do you think you could take me out on the boat. We might see if we could chum some up. Would that be evidence enough?"

"If they are big, aggressive fish, and if they are in the area, we just might get them to come into some chum and eat a piece of cut bait. And if we do, we just might catch one. If they are something else, who knows?"

"I have another couple days' work back at the lab with Nick to try and decipher the balance of evidence we have but maybe at the end of the week we could make a run and try to tempt one of these fish to take the bait. This ruby port is pretty good. Nice selection."

"Thank you. You know, I'd love nothing more than to have you with me out on the boat if that is really what you really want. I can call some of my guide buddies and see if we might set up a little trap for your mysterious and elusive killers."

"What kind of trap, Rick? If I'm right, these will be some dangerous fish."

"Tell me what you know so far about the incidents."

"I've told you what I know, Rick. There's nothing else."

"There must be something else. I mean, are there any common threads tying the events together? Maybe some less obvious clues to all this?"

"We know for sure that the two incidents with the dogs happened just before dusk and took place close to the beach. Those happened on the outgoing tide. My guess is that the first death also happened close to the beach, mostly likely at night. That was on the full moon with outgoing water as well. And based upon what the parents of the missing diver have said, he took his dive in the late afternoon, same relative tide. And one other thing, the events seem to be taking place within a triangle formed by Smith's Bay, Plover Dunes, and the Middle Grounds."

"Jack said he saw those big fish at late afternoon with moving water. He was out off the Stratford Shoal lighthouse, right in the heart of the Middle Grounds. There's definitely something up with the timing and locations of these incidents. Pretty fishy if you ask me," Rick added.

"Rick, don't make light of this. We could have a very serious problem on our hands here. You know as well as I do that predatory fish become active late in the day and like to feed at dusk and throughout the night. Most of the fish species we have around here are predisposed to those feeding behaviors. Do you agree?"

"Bass, bluefish, weakfish, sharks. We can rule out weakfish, and the bites are definitely not from sharks so that leaves bass and blues. But even huge striped bass don't have teeth. If by some bizarre sequence of events a big bass did attack a human, the only traces it that would leave would be marks like someone got scraped by a belt sander. Here look at my thumb. See what I mean? Their mouths are like sandpaper. By process of elimination that leaves bluefish. Bluefish might be nasty, but the size you're talking about? Totally impossible."

Kate reflected on this. "I'll have some more port please."

"Here you go, kiddo."

Katie was finally starting to feel at ease. The more she listened to Rick's voice, the more she felt amorous tingles build inside her.

"Come over here and give me a hug. I need one."

When Katie made up her mind to do something she did it. And now she had that look in her eyes. She welcomed Rick with a tight embrace and a wanting sigh. She could recognize him with her eyes closed; the soft scent of his cologne was like a mild aphrodisiac.

"When I'm with you, Rick, I can breathe again. I've missed you terribly and I've missed . . . this."

Rick held her close and rested his head against hers. "I've missed you too. It has been way too long. I'm sorry for that."

Katie turned her head, sliding her cheek against Rick's until the corner of her mouth met his. She moved her lips over his and kissed him. She let out a seductive moan. Her lips parted and Rick responded. His mouth covered hers; they kissed deeply and passionately. Rick pulled Katie closer and held her tight, as if he never wanted to let her go. Her hand moved up to caress his face. Rick put his fingers through Katie's hair and held her head with both hands as they kissed. Katie's heart was pounding so hard she was sure Rick could hear it. He released his hand from her face and traced his fingers along her neck all the while looking into her green eyes. She took his hand and placed it on her right breast. Katie's nipple was hard and erect.

They both let their hands wander, touching and caressing as they kissed. Katie rotated her hips and pushed herself as close as she could possibly get. She moaned as her source of pleasure pressed against the ridge forming in Rick's pants.

"This is the most fun I have had in long time," Katie whispered. "Fully clothed."

"We can change that in a heartbeat."

CHAPTER 15

"What are you smiling about? You've got that glow about you, Katie. Were you doing naughty-naughty last night? Did you see Rick?"

"Back off, Nick. It's none of your damn business why I smile or why I don't. We've got a lot of work to do today and no time to get it done. Anything new develop?"

"Well, you're not going to like this but we have a meeting three-thirty today with the head of regional Fish and Game, town officials, and a few members of Suffolk's finest. It seems like one of Senator Howie Charles's senior staff got wind of what has been going on and now they are snooping around for information. Everyone else wants to make sure their ducks are in a row so they can pass the problem to the next guy."

"Why in hell is a US senator interested in a few mysterious Long Island deaths?"

"Got me, but our fearless leaders are shitting their underwear worrying about what Senator Howie is up to. You know him. He's relentless when he sinks his teeth into something. Or maybe he's just looking for more free television time."

"Maybe his handlers know something we don't. Do we have a contact there?"

"Yes we do. I know one of his Long Island aides very well. We've had dinner a few times. And on top of that, the media are starting to put two and two together: the first death, the diver, and the two dogs. They're beginning to connect the dots. Each of the local weeklies

has assigned one of their crime beat reporters to investigate connections between the incidents, and Channel 21 is hot on the trail
as well. It's only a matter of time before the major newspapers pick
up on this. And if Howie gets personally involved, this goes viral.
We don't have much time to figure this out. But it doesn't end there.
The local politicians are all over this, too. Seems a couple vineyard
workers may have gone missing out by Plover Dunes. They can't
prove it is related to the investigation but there was an odd collection
of clothing strewn about the beach. At first they thought nothing of
it, but with subsequent events, they started asking questions. This
could get ugly fast."

"Let's lay out everything we have and go through this one more
time. Rick is going to take me out on the water to see if we might find
something. He is working out a plan with his captain friends."

"And when, pray tell, did you see Rick?"

"None of your concern, Dr. Tanner. Just get all the files we have.
We need to decide on a party line before the meeting and buy some
time until we can get hard evidence."

Nick Tanner had worked with Katie for about four years. He
moved downstate after spending the early part of his career up in the
Lake Ontario area studying the breeding and the migratory behaviors of chinook and coho salmon, known locally as kings and silvers. With the collapse of the west coast salmon fishery, and with
the exception of Alaska's runs of Pacific salmon, some of the best
remaining salmon fishing in the lower forty-eight occurred annually
in the Salmon River and its tributaries in the Oswego New York area.
Nick was the lead ichthyologist and headed a team that had done
a considerable amount of work to document the spawning process.
Nick got his master's at Cornell and at the time was pursuing his
PhD at State University. He was competent, if a bit quirky. It seemed
Nick paid a little too much attention to a male subordinate who then
lodged a sexual harassment complaint against him. While Tanner was
fully exonerated, it seemed best for all involved to transfer Nick to

the Long Island office. He'd been working with Katie and other team members without incident. Katie felt Nick was straight as an arrow.

Rick was on cloud nine after his night with Katie. He had her back and he meant to make it work. The first thing he was going to do to seal the deal was get her out on the Sound with him and fulfill her request. Even if it proved nothing more than a wild goose chase he'd pull out all the stops and give her the best shot at proving or disproving her big creature theory. Rick spent the morning thinking through his idea and a strategy to put the plan in place. He needed to get five or six of his best guide friends to assist him. An armada of fishermen would be on the water during the bluefish tournament, and the extra chatter on the VHF channels could be valuable if anything unusual happened on the water. Many of the weekend warriors really got obnoxious when they got into fish and were very willing to broadcast their successes. The best fishermen Rick knew were secretive about their success and always kept their mouths shut. The rookies posted their catches on some social media site the moment the fish were landed, and Rick would count on it for leads.

Rick placed a call to each of his friends and scheduled a meeting at Grumpies in one of the quieter back rooms to tell them Katie needed their help with a marine sciences project. After they'd agreed to meet at the end of the day following their fishing charters, he called Katie to tell her the news.

"Hey Katie, how you doing today?"

"Just peachy. I have a three-thirty powwow with a whole cast of characters who've found out bits and pieces of what's going on. They want answers to questions they don't even know to ask. Even Senator Howie is in the mix."

"Sounds like you are up to your eyeballs in political alligators."

"If I'm right, the shit's gonna hit the fan. With the last big weekend of the summer right around the corner, nobody is going to want to hear about killer fish roaming Long Island beaches. I really need your help with this."

"That's why I'm calling, Katie. I have a meeting with the guides at Grumpies later this evening to tell them about the plan. I was hoping you might join us to help fill in some of the gaps. The guys will need some time to clean their boats so I figure we should all meet up by six-thirty. How long do you think your meeting will last?"

"I'm hoping it is over by five, the latest. I'll come over as soon as it's done and bring Nick along with me."

"Fine. He's smart when it comes to fish."

"Care to share any details of your plan?"

"About a half dozen captains chumming at key points in the triangle of incidents throughout the entire tide cycle. We'll attract lots of normal bluefish and bass to the slicks and with a little luck they will be a calling card for your creatures. The goal is to get a positive ID, a video or, even better—catch one. Sound good?"

"I really appreciate all you are doing to help."

"What do I get for it?"

"I already paid you in advance last night. Don't push your luck. See you later. I have to go rehearse my script with Nick. We need to buy some time at the meeting. Love ya."

"Love you too. Good luck."

CHAPTER 16

Katie and Nick were the first to the meeting, followed by their manager, Marine Division Head Ted Gunther. Katie liked Ted. In all her dealings with him, he'd proven himself to be an excellent manager: decisive, fair, and smart. He ran interference for her on more than one occasion when Albany questioned some local positions on fisheries management and conservation issues. Ted was educated as a marine biologist and had spent time in the enforcement division. He was the right guy for the job.

"Hi Katie, Nick. I hear we got some strange happenings going on in our neighborhood. Think any of it has to do with marine life?"

"Unfortunately, Ted, that is where all indicators are pointing."

"Sharks?"

"No. But believe it or not, it could be worse. I don't plan on divulging any of that at this meeting since we don't yet have any hard evidence."

"What could be worse than sharks in the Sound that have taken a liking to humans?"

"How about schools of large killing machines?"

"Come on, Katie. This is no joke. How about you Nick, what do you think?"

"Perhaps some species of migratory fish is the main suspect but we need more proof."

"Do you two expect me to believe . . ."

Ted Gunther stopped in mid-sentence as the door to the conference room opened and two county detectives walked in, introducing
themselves as Detectives Dennis Haney and Sam Spinello.

"So have you guys figured out this mess?" Detective Spinello said.

"We were going to ask you the same question. This one's a real
puzzler," Katie replied.

"There are some rumblings out there that these incidents have all
to do with real weird creatures swimming in the Long Island Sound.
There any truth to that?" Detective Haney said.

This time Nick grabbed the ball. "While there are certainly a
number of fish species and marine creatures that have the ability to
take out a human being, there is nothing indigenous to the marine
environment of the Long Island Sound that would be either capable
or inclined to do so."

"Not even sharks?" Haney shot back.

"We should probably hold off on this discussion until the rest of
the attendees get here. No need going through all this more than
once," Ted Gunther said.

Three local county politicians arrived and introduced themselves.

"Hello, I'm Roberta Lowery, councilwoman from Plover Dunes."

"And I'm Jim Delaney, from councilman Steve Leed's office in
Smithville.

"And last but not least, I'm assemblyman Joe Zalette from Port
Roosevelt. Do we now have a quorum to start this meeting?"

"We do but let's give it a few more minutes. Senator Charles's
office called and said one of the senior staff might stop by. Not sure
why but we'll give it five more."

"Hey, maybe whatever is going on with these cases has something to do with national security," Assemblyman Zalette said. His
sarcasm did not go unnoticed.

The conference room phone rang and Ted Gunther answered. It
was the senator's office.

"Okay, thanks for letting us know. I will keep your office posted of developments."

Ted addressed the group. "We can begin. That was the senator's office. They aren't able to attend. Last minute press conference."

"You know what they say about the good senator,"Assemblyman Zalette interjected. "The most dangerous place to be on Long Island is between Senator Howie and a television camera. Must have been a better photo op someplace else."

Everyone in the room laughed a nervous laugh except Katie, who turned to Nick and whispered,"Thank God."

"This shouldn't take more than an hour. I thought perhaps the PDs could bring us all up to speed on the status of the investigations and if there are any other leads that you are following."

Detective Haney from Smithville spoke first. "You guys probably know a hell of a lot more about this than we do. All we have are body parts and shredded waders from a Port Roosevelt resident named Jimmy McVee. He was reported missing by his family and girlfriend and one of the hands we recovered had a good enough print to pull. We got a positive ID but no clues as to what killed him. The M.E. reports odd and unidentifiable teeth marks on the body but apparently not enough evidence to identify cause of death."

Spinello followed."We know he liked to fish. A guy we spoke to at the Port Roosevelt ramp was one of the last to see him and said he was going fishing that night. We followed up that lead and other fishing buddies told us he liked to fish Old Stoney Beach. We think he was on that beach the night he was killed. There's a lot of scuttlebutt that some fish or other creature is the culprit. I'm thinking the most probable perp has two legs and walks upright. What do you marine biology gurus think?"

"Well,"Katie said, "there is unquestionable evidence of bite marks on the first victim found in Smith's Bay. I'm also not aware if the medical examiner has finally assigned a cause of death. I do know that he is unsure if the death is a result of the bites."

Roberta Lowery chimed in. "Can you tell from the bites what did this?"

The choreography continued. It was Nick's turn to answer. "All we know at this point is that the bite radius is wide, the bite incisions deep, and that whatever did this has powerful jaws."

"It has to be a shark. What else could it be?" Lowery said.

Nick continued "We don't think so. We've ruled out sharks. And as Katie indicated, the bites could have been inflicted postmortem. We really need more evidence."

"Listen," Lowery interrupted. "If you mean more evidence as in more deaths, that is totally unacceptable. I have some concerned constituents who are demanding answers. The local newspapers are following this and people are starting to connect the incidents, fueling all sorts of speculation. The owners of those two dogs are causing a panic. I even had one resident who lives here part of the year and the other in Florida tell me that she heard from one of her garden club friends that there are people who bring up baby alligators from Florida and when they get too big they release them in the Sound. Is that possible? Could this be the result of some alligator attack? Those things are always eating dogs in Florida, right in people's backyards."

"While alligators will sometimes frequent saltwater, they are basically freshwater reptiles. They also prefer the warmer climates of the southeast and Gulf Coast states. Louisiana and Florida have the two largest populations of alligators in the United States. The northeast is just not a hospitable climate for alligators. They would have an extremely difficult time surviving in our latitudes. Alligators are cold-blooded and often use the warmth of the sun to regulate their body temperatures. That being the case, it might be tough not noticing a thirteen-foot long, eight-hundred-pound reptilian taking in the rays on a local beach. And there would be foot and tail drag marks all across the sand. I highly doubt this is an alligator."

Ted Gunther rolled his eyes and Lowery pressed on undeterred, totally missing the sarcasm. "There is evidence to suggest that two vineyard workers might have also gone missing on one of our beaches. At first we thought the debris found on the beach to be the result of some litterbugs, but a recent review of that junk indicates that some unfortunate souls may have been dragged away and killed. That's where the idea of an alligator or crocodile came from. One of the guys in our office said he believed a Komodo Dragon is also capable of tearing apart and eating humans. Is that possible?"

Nick knew that before this got ugly, he needed to field question. He was also glad that this dope had steered the discussion in the direction of a reptile and not a fish. "Ms. Lowery, the Komodo Dragon is indigenous to Indonesia. There really is no way that reptile could have done this."

"But there are always stories of people keeping strange pets and of them escaping, even from zoos and wildlife parks. That might be an angle to consider."

The wall clock read quarter to five and Ted Gunther needed to get the meeting back on track so he jumped into the mix. "Roberta, you are correct. Those things do in fact happen but I believe I can accurately say that we are not dealing with an alligator, a crocodile, a Komodo dragon, or any other large reptile. Even with the limited evidence available in this case, we can rule those things out. And I would think the two detectives would agree."

"I guess my gut is leading me down the path of either a human killer or a shark," Detective Haney said. "They seem to be the most likely perps. All this crap about bizarre creatures is a bit much to swallow."

"We agree with you, Detective," Katie responded, "except your opinion about the sharks. This is definitely not a shark attack."

Assemblyman Zalette then asked the question both Katie and Nick dreaded.

"Considering that we now have two, maybe four, fatalities linked to odd activity on our beaches and in the water, is it not the prudent thing to make this all public and perhaps even provide warnings about going in the water? Don't we have an obligation to advise the public and warn them of a potential danger?"

Katie had mixed feelings about full disclosure at this point since she didn't yet have the positive proof she needed, and she knew a premature public release could cause unnecessary hysteria. Before she could reply, Delaney joined the discussion.

"You all know that the first mangled body washed ashore in my district. The fifth precinct has been on top of this as Detective Spinello can attest. Other local officials and I have received inform-ation from the medical examiner's office that the body was at some point assaulted by some form of marine life, perhaps as either a killer or a post-death scavenger. No one seems to really know. One such incident based on those facts is certainly extremely troublesome but may not warrant such drastic action as public notification or closure of beaches. And I do think we need to consider the possibility of these deaths being homicides. I'd prefer not to cause any unnecessary fear without having hard evidence."

"I agree," Detective Spinello said. "But if we have one more related incident, I think we had all better consider some form of public noti-fication. My bet is that the daily and weekly news rags are close to breaking this story. I'm surprised we haven't seen more coverage and I'm even more surprised we weren't invaded by the press today. I guess someone's good at keeping a secret."

"That may be true," Zalette said, "but if our esteemed US senator gets involved, this will all be prime time news in a heartbeat . . . fact, fiction, and everything between."

Katie looked at her watch. Five p.m. She wanted this to be over, so she could get to the captain's dinner with Rick. It was looking like the meeting would begin to wind down when, out of left field, Detective Haney asked an unexpected question. "Ms. DiNardo, I understand that you and your associate, Mr. Tanner, have conducted extensive research on all forms of local marine species. It is part of what you do, right?"

"Yes, that is correct, Mr. Haney."

"And I also understand that you and your associate assisted in processing the evidence at the site of the Smith's Bay incident, called in by the medical examiner for the combined extensive experience that you and Mr. Tanner have with marine life. Is that correct, Dr. DiNardo?"

"This is beginning to sound a bit like cross examination, Mr. Haney. What's your point?" Ted Gunther said, providing some air cover for Katie.

"Well, I further understand that Ms. DiNardo and Mr. Tanner conducted a review of photographs of the bite marks and did some computer analysis. It would seem that with their combined expertise, the resources of the entire Marine Division of Fish and Game at their disposal, and hi-tech computer imagery, they must have some idea what the bite marks are from. This ain't rocket science. Is the bite that of a minnow, a bass, a shark, an orca?"

"Detective Haney, both Katie and Nick are two of the best we have. They've worked as a top team on all the tough assignments that come through my office. They have briefed me on all their efforts thus far on this case and I can assure everyone in this room that it is too premature to make any definitive statements about the nature of the bite profiles. We could be as wrong as we could be right. In all fairness, without further evidence, Katie and Nick can't draw any hasty conclusions."

"In all fairness to the public, Mr. Gunther, we owe them some answers and some protections," Detective Haney protested.

"Well put Mr. Haney. When the time is right and we have all the facts at our disposal, we will disclose the findings."

"That is all well and good, Mr. Gunther," Lowery interjected, "but let's hope the further evidence they need isn't more bodies."

"On that note, if there are no more questions, this meeting is adjourned."

As the politicians and detectives filed out of the room, Ted Gunther motioned for Katie and Nick to stay back.

"We don't have much time to solve this. We are sitting on a powder keg here. If someone scoops us or if there is another unexplained incident, this thing is going to blow sky high."

CHAPTER 17

Katie dialed Rick. "The meeting just broke, I'll be on my way in a few minutes. Nick is coming with me."

"Glad you can make it. Everyone is here. We are having a nice jawboning session and downing a few beers. I haven't gotten into anything yet so we will wait for you to get here. How'd the meeting go?"

"It went well, Rick, but if there is one more incident, I'm going to be up to my eyeballs in pissed off politicians."

"Don't sweat it. I'll see you in a bit. Drive safe. Lots of summer loonies out there tonight."

"Go slow on the brews with your buddies. What I have to say is going to be tough enough to swallow."

Rick had invited some of the best north shore captains and guides to sit in on the meeting with Katie. These folks were on the water every day, usually for two half-day charters. One of them also often guided on beaches at night in addition to his daytime boat charters. As members of the North Island Boat Captain's Association, they all knew each other well and often worked together during tournaments or for overflow bookings. Rick requested a small private room off the main dining area. He knew Katie would want privacy for this meeting.

Captain Jack Connors was the first Rick called. He had been one of Rick's closest friends and a mentor. Despite his sixty-three years, Captain Jack was as spry as any of the other guides half his age. When it came to fishing, he could keep up with the youngest of them and stayed in shape by walking and jogging the local beaches whenever he wasn't out on the water. Jack fought in Vietnam as a Scout Sniper in the Marine Corp's Expeditionary Unit. His mild disposition gave no clues to the thirty-one confirmed kills he made during his tour of duty in Vietnam. He had number thirty-two squarely in the crosshairs but before he could squeeze off the round, his spotter fell dead following the unmistakable sound of a hollow *thwack*. An enemy sniper had fired first. Jack was never the same after that and spent his remaining time in the military as a shooting instructor at the Marine sniper school in Camp Lejeune. Following the military, Jack pursued a career in private security. Now retired from that occupation, he spent all his time fishing, duck hunting, and carving wooden decoys. Jack had uncanny visual acuity. Rick knew Jack would see things on the water that others would otherwise miss.

Captain Joey Marrone was the youngest of the guides. In his late twenties, he was already one of the best and most popular fly-fishing and light-tackle guides on Long Island. What he lacked in experience he more than made up for in enthusiasm. Joey also guided surf anglers during the graveyard shift. When pushed to choose, he would tell you that being a surf rat was his first love. If it were possible, he would fish twenty-four-seven. But as with many guides, another source of income was often needed to help pay the bills, so Captain Marrone worked a number of odd jobs in construction. Those jobs were somewhat tight this summer since the Great Recession had taken its toll on the Long Island construction industry, so Joey was determined to fish nonstop. He was on the water more than any of the other guides that Rick knew and he fished the widest range, west to east, within the Sound.

Captain Valerie Russo was also added to the list. Tough and capable, she was one of the first women on Long Island to break into the traditional man's game of sport fishing charters. Rick had helped her out in the beginning, often sending overflow charter bookings to her. As a single mother of four boys, she was constantly on the go with their school and sports activities but she could still be found on the water every day in season. She always made the most of her guiding opportunities and quickly became a very popular captain. Rick liked her for her tenacity and willingness to keep at it and do whatever it took to find fish for her clients. He knew Valerie would make it her business to seek out what Katie was trying to uncover.

Captain Sandy Bassonet was a communications expert who'd much rather be on the water chasing fish than chasing down problems with fiber optics. Sandy preferred to fish light tackle but most of his charters liked bottom fishing so he'd go wherever the money brought him. Since he was a full-time network engineer for a large cable company and a part-time fishing guide, he used all his vacation and personal days to get on the water. Although not out every day like the other guides, Captain Bassonet had that sixth sense about fishing and could find fish when most others struck out. Rick fished with Sandy often and admired his skills. Sandy was a renowned big bass and bluefish expert; this was the primary reason Rick selected him for this scouting mission. While catching small fish is a relatively easy thing to do, consistently catching large, chopper bluefish and bass over twenty pounds is much easier said than done. Sandy had also won the prestigious annual Long Island Sound Bluefish Tournament three times and held the current New York State bluefish record.

Captain Al Robinetti, was a former high school science teacher. Once the early-out retirement package was offered by his school district, Al signed on the dotted line, bought himself a boat, and grew his fishing passion into a full-time business. He still did some math and biology tutoring for high school students wanting to pass the state proficiency exams, but he put strict limits on that part-time activity so he could maximize time on the water. Al steadily built his guiding business to the point where he was booked solid from May until the end of the fall run in November. Most of Captain Al's fishing was done in the Long Island Sound but he spent much of the fall off Montauk. With two master's degrees in biology and environmental science, Al was sure to be an objective participant in this project who spoke Katie's language.

The last of the captains was John "Sully" Sullivan, a sometimes surfer, sometimes snow boarder, and sometimes commercial fisherman who owned and operated two recreational party boats. He was fond of using the Hawaiian "Shaka" hand expression—a closed fist wagged with thumb and pinky spread apart to convey that all is right with the world. But to put bread on the table, Captain Sullivan fished every day for a living. He kept two sixty-five-foot party boats in Port Roosevelt Harbor: the *Port Rosey Queen* and the *Port Rosey Princess*. During the summer months, Sully packed the rails of each boat with up to seventy fishermen on the hunt for bluefish and striped bass trips. He ran two cycles of trips each day with each boat as well as nighttime trips. With two boats dumping buckets of smelly chum, there was a good chance Sully would run into what they were looking for. Sully also liked to fish the deeper Middle Grounds that the other skippers might miss. Rick was confident that if some oddball fish were swimming in the Sound, this group had the best chance of tracking them down.

CHAPTER 18

The school of killer creatures numbered about three hundred, all between 60 and 120 pounds. The biggest were over 6 feet in length. They represented the apex of their species. Spending most of the daylight hours in the deepest parts of the Long Island Sound, these creatures marauded endlessly in continuous search of food. At dusk, the entire school would slide inshore to the shallow edges of shoals and along troughs parallel to the beaches. It was here they separated into smaller pods of eight, ten, or twelve fish and hunted like wolf packs. Much like the social hierarchy of wolves, each pod of hunters was led by a large alpha male. Their size was not a normal trait among fish-like animals where the females are typically the larger of the sexes. A dominant male ruled over each pack, while the largest and most violent of the males was respected as the leader of the entire school. It was an alpha male that Jimmy McVee had hooked and that led the attack, culminating in his death. That cold-blooded organism and his schoolmates were far from being satisfied.

The gargantuan beasts were a unique phenotype of their species and began life as minute larvae. While they controlled much of their environment, early life was governed by the currents upon which they drifted and by their ability to escape being eaten. The species spawned on the Continental Shelf, in an area off the Carolinas. Even though that was the primary spawning grounds, there were also secondary spawns off the New Jersey coast and off Long Island.

While specific procreation habits and behaviors of this genus are not well understood, the crop of altered killers was given life in the Long Island Sound. Once spawned, the fingerlings moved to safe havens and were nurtured in the protective and fertile backwaters of local harbors like Mount Misery, Port Roosevelt, and State Channel Harbor.

While victims themselves of food-chain predation, the creatures grew more rapidly than normal. By the end of their first season, these oversized juveniles had transformed from the hunted to the hunters, cannibalizing much smaller and normal members of their species, and anything else that was beneath them on the evolutionary ladder. As pack hunters, they were capable of assaulting much larger, smarter, or more highly evolved prey. During the fall of their first season, the yearlings had grown to about a foot in length and made way from the sanctuary of backwaters out through the harbor inlets and into the more perilous waters of the Long Island Sound. This exodus began their migratory journey to wintering grounds in the warmer waters of the southeast United States. Although these immature killers were superior to other fish species, they were, nonetheless, subject to severe predation during their first passage south. They were high on the menu preferences of many inland and oceanic predators like striped bass, fluke, weakfish, tuna, and sharks. Even as young adults, many larger fish and mammals regularly sought out these fish as a food source.

Once fully-grown and part of a hunting pack and a larger school, very little else in the oceans could challenge them. Those members of the year classes that survived the process of natural selection became formidable adversaries and quickly turned the tables on any species that diminished their early numbers. Within a year, they were eating the same fish that ate the smaller and less fortunate members of their unique clan. Revenge was sweet and constant. Human traits are not often assigned to fish behavior, but in the case of these killers, an exception had to be made. They were vicious, vengeful, and vindictive, with a malevolent neon-yellow eye and piercing stare that was intended to cause its victims to make mistakes. That is all it took.

What made this altered species so much more of a potential hazard to humans than sharks was the frequency with which they came into contact with people. While their range was worldwide, they frequently remained in areas from Nova Scotia to Florida and readily mingled with bathers, swimmers, and surfers throughout their entire range. There are numerous annual encounters where fingers, ears, and toes are bitten, sometimes bitten completely off by juvenile fish of two to three pounds. Very often those instances were mistakenly attributed to small bluefish swimming in massive schools near inshore beaches. The sixty-, eighty-, and hundred-pound adult mutants were nothing less than brutal killers when they turned on to feed.

When these killers were young, they would travel in small schools up and down the East Coast. One year when the school reached the popular beaches of the Garden State, it came upon an equally large school of small menhaden or bunker. They fed in a frenzied blitz, tearing, ripping, and shredding the prey. They fed until their stomachs were full and then regurgitated their kill, only to continue the feeding and killing spree. When the predators and their prey reached a popular New Jersey shore community, an unfortunate swimmer found herself in the midst of the frenzy. The fish mistook her silver earrings for the flashes made by fleeing bait. They tore indiscriminately at the earrings and succeeded in biting off the woman's two ears. The carnage continued farther up the Jersey shore. At one point, the school moved in off-beach as panicked bunker leapt out of the water onto the sand to escape the snapping jaws of their pursuers. From within the chaotic fury, the creatures corralled the bunker in an attempt to prevent the prey from escaping. The killers jumped from the water, some landing well beyond the high water mark; jaws snapped, still trying to kill their victims, even as they themselves wriggled back to the safety of the ocean. Kill at all costs, even at the risk of being stranded on a beach and suffocating. Nowhere else in the natural world does that scenario play out in quite the same way.

The massive body of creatures then traveled farther east and settled in for a while off Staten Island. There, they continued to ravage juvenile bunker and each other; these fish have no problem eating their own. The feeding chaos attracted the attention of sharks that moved into the fray. It was always the sharks that received public attention, allowing the mutants to sneak under the radar and remain unmolested by humans.

As is consistent with the hierarchy of the food chain, the bigger fish and mammals eat smaller species. Predatory fish typically swim in schools of similarly sized specimens. This creates a level playing field with respect to feeding tendencies, and works to prevent cannibalism among equals, but some species like these killers will readily cannibalize those of their species lower on the size ladder. That was the situation offshore of the Gateway National Park in Brooklyn, New York. The mutants ravaged their smaller kin. Unlike the predation behavior of other species such as sailfish that employ a planned herding method to feed, an all-out feeding frenzy is pure chaotic madness with fish striking out at anything that moves. These freaks killed and fed upon their lesser relatives. They then regurgitated the fresh meal so they could continue to feed their insatiable appetites. Creatures like these are cursed with a wanton lust for slaughter. They are cannibals and they are merciless. The odds of human encounters are astronomically greater than the potential for meeting a shark. Therefore, the odds of humans being killed by a chance meeting with these mutant fish were also extraordinarily high. Their predatory behavior this summer along the north shore beaches of Long Island had already accounted for more deaths than nationwide shark attacks. These killers were only just getting started.

CHAPTER 19

"This damn place is always packed. Between the regulars and the holiday tourists, we'll be lucky to find a parking spot."

"What do you expect?" Katie said. "They've got great burgers and the Yankees are playing the Red Sox. There probably isn't a gin mill from Jersey to Maine that's not stuffed to the gills right now."

"Look! There's a guy stumbling to his car. Quick, step on it before that old lady in the beemer convertible beats us to the spot."

Katie hit the accelerator pedal and squealed into the parking space.

"Grandma flipped you the bird."

"Boston fan."

"Better hope Grandma isn't packin' a Glock. You know how tough they can be!"

Once inside Grumpies, the hostess ushered Katie and Nick to a small back room where the captain's cabal was deep in discussion about the effects of ethanol on fuel injectors of the newer four-stroke engines. Captain Bassonet was in the middle of explaining that ethanol will eat your gas tank. "Throw up all the shit into the fuel injectors and stop you dead in your tracks. The guys at Sea Haul have been having a banner year towing disabled boats back to port."

Captain Valerie Russo was listening intently since she had just experienced a similar problem, but as she looked away from Bassonet, she spotted Katie. "How ya doin' sista'? Been a long time. You're looking good. Life must be treating you well. Who's your sidekick?"

"Hi. This is my business associate, Nick Tanner. He is the head ichthyologist at the marine fisheries bureau."

"Nice, a fish dude," Valerie said.

The group exchanged pleasantries and once Katie's and Nick's drinks arrived, Rick closed the door to the private room. "The nature of this discussion is not one we want out in public quite yet. Right, Katie?"

"Have you told the group anything yet?"

"Figured I'd wait for you to get here. You know, 007 stuff."

The group laughed a nervous laugh. They had heard all the rumors about the happenings in the Sound but nothing yet concrete or official, and they expected this meeting to enlighten them.

"Thank you all for coming. I guess I should start by saying we have recently been challenged by a number of unusual events that have taken place in and around parts of the central Sound that have warranted investigation by the Marine Fisheries Bureau of Fish and Game and local police authorities. By all accounts, these happenings appear to be separate and distinct anomalies but there are also some very odd coincidences."

Katie knew she wouldn't be able to bullshit this group one bit. They were too water savvy and collectively they knew the local marine species almost as well as she did.

Captain Robinetti, the ex-school teacher, raised his hand. "Does this have anything to do with the recent deaths and disappearances we have been hearing about?"

"It may. There is forensic evidence linking a few of those tragic events to some sort of marine animal species. Nick and I have evaluated whatever evidence has surfaced and there are some common threads and connections but we can't at this point render a final opinion."

Valerie spoke next. "I've been up to my eyeballs in charters lately and have not been keeping up on current events. Maybe I've missed something. I read about the Smith's Bay and Boulder Point deaths, but what else is going on out there?"

"That's probably a good place to start, Val, especially if others are not familiar with the total extent of recent developments. Less than a week ago, some body parts washed up on the beach in Smith's Bay. That made the headlines and I'm sure all of you are aware of that incident. Farther east, we had two migrant workers and a couple dogs mysteriously disappear out by Plover Dunes. During that same period of time, there were a number of odd sightings and incidents taking place on the Sound. All I can tell you at this point is that it appears as if those situations may have involved a large, unknown species of fish or other creature."

"Are you saying that you think fish may have killed those folks, and that fish had something to do with the other disappearances?" Captain Bassonet said.

"That is not an easy question to answer, Sandy. We've found bite marks but we do not know if those wounds were inflicted postmortem."

"This is some heavy shit," Captain Sully interjected. "If you had to venture a guess, Katie, what kind of fish would you say did it?"

"The nature of the wounds and the bite profiles do not at all match those of any shark species. No marine mammal did this either."

Sully pressed. "Well then, what do those bite marks match?"

Jack Connors was seated at the far end of the table directly facing Katie. He sensed a bit of tension brewing and joined the discussion. "Listen folks, I think I may have had a run in with whatever it is we are talking about here. About a week and a half before the first death, I spotted what I thought to be bluefin tuna chasing schools of false albacore out in the middle. To some of you younger captains that may seem a bit far-fetched but small bluefin have been known—on rare occasions—to briefly venture into the Sound. I tried to catch one but didn't have any luck. Earlier this week, I encountered what appeared to be the same school of fish and accidentally hooked one that ate a twenty-pound bass I was reeling in. When all was said and done, I landed only ten pounds of fish. The bass was bitten in half."

"Sounds like sharks to me," young Captain Marrone chimed in.

"As I said," Katie replied, "we are pretty sure it wasn't a shark."

"And as I asked before," Sully repeated, "How do you know that? What do the bite marks match?"

Katie was in a bit of a box. Nick once again took the reins and fielded the question.

"Sully, Katie and I have done extensive work on the limited bite evidence available to us. We've excluded entire classes of fish that would have had the physical attributes and temperament to engage in this type of unusual and violent behavior. All the usual suspects have been eliminated, even some of the tropical species that may have ventured up north on warmer ocean currents. We know that no striped bass is biting a person in two. I have been around fish all my life and have studied them in the world's five oceans and I can tell you what *didn't* do this. Where Katie and I are struggling a bit right now is with what actually *did*. Odds are it is some fish-like creature."

"I have to partner up with Sully here," Captain Robinetti said. "It would seem to me that unless we are looking at a totally new species of fish, the bite marks have to match to something we know. And if you aren't considering some tropical visitor then whatever did this has to be indigenous to the area. Right?"

Katie answered, "Al, you are perfectly correct. We do have an idea. But it is a far-fetched one and not yet provable. That is where we need your help to get further evidence. Based on the computer modeling Nick and I did of the bite marks, the closest species match is to some form of aberrant fish."

"So you are telling us that some weirdo fish may be responsible for two deaths and unknown disappearances?" Captain Robinetti shook his head in disbelief.

"That ain't far-fetched, that's far out," Sully added.

"As I said, we don't know for sure but the configuration of the jaws, teeth, and bite marks all point to a species that we can't identify."

"Not for nothing, Katie, but are we talking about normal-sized fish or some super-sized version?" Sandy Bassonet said.

"This is where things get real sticky, folks, and what I'm about to say may be beyond comprehension but it's what Nick and I have been struggling with. If our calculations of the bite marks are correct and if the killers are indeed some kind of fish, then the fish that attacked the Smith's Bay man ranged in size from sixty to one hundred pounds. But I have to stress, we really don't know what these creature are."

The room went dead silent at Katie's revelation.

"Sweet Jesus!" Sandy proclaimed, "I can't get my head around that one. One-hundred-pound killer fish in the Sound? Holy shit! No need to be greedy, I'll take a sixty. If I can bag one of those puppies that will be my ticket to guiding fame and fortune."

"Not so fast, Sandy," Rick said. "We really need to keep this under wraps for now. This is speculation, not yet fact. If Katie and Nick are right, we could have panic on our hands all around Long Island. Something in the water could be killing people."

The group was too stunned to respond.

Captain Joey Marrone finally spoke. "Listen, I haven't been at this game as long as many of you have but I've caught my share of big fish since I started guiding. I have a ton of double-digit bass and bluefish to my credit and for many of my clients. Biggest bluefish were about twenty pounds. Those fish beat the shit out of us. Granted, I fish light tackle but blues that big can tear up tackle like they're nothing more than play toys. How the hell are we supposed to catch one of these monster things for you to examine?"

"Stand-up tuna gear," Jack answered. "Or you might want to try some shark gear. This ain't about sport, it's about getting one of these things to the boat. And it ain't going to be easy. Based on what I've seen, I may even consider a harpoon."

"Look, I don't want anyone getting hurt in all this," Katie said. "I really just need some extra eyes out there to see if we can ID one of these creatures. If we can get a piece of fin for DNA analysis that would be more than enough. A video would be great. And if one can be safely landed that would be the icing on the cake. I know Rick has a plan of attack that he wants to talk over with you so if there are no further questions, I'll turn this over to him."

Al Robinetti raised his hand again. He wasn't through grilling Katie.

"Yes."

"I realize this isn't an easy situation for you, but the pieces of this puzzle don't fit. If we accept your suspicion that the killer may be a fish, are we talking one rogue fish, a few fish, or an entire school? And how the hell do fish in the Sound get to be as big as your estimates? We all know how ferocious even small bluefish can be. I can't comprehend the thought of a school of some eighty-pound mutant and unknown species marauding its way through the Long Island Sound. They'd wreak more havoc than sharks or barracuda. That's a tough pill to swallow."

"It is for me, too. But remember, our only solid evidence up to this point is a set of bite marks from one victim that appear to match the jaw configuration of a fish. The second victim had an entire arm severed. Were the culprits the same? We don't know. We don't even know if the other incidences and disappearances are even related. But what I can say is that whatever is doing this most likely has fins, and gills and swims."

Jack spoke. "I've seen them, whatever they are. They are big, they are fast, and they are smart. I say 'they' because what I've seen was more than one. I'm not saying a school of thousands of fish like we see with small cocktail blues but there surely were dozens of them. I don't know, maybe even hundreds. There aren't many creatures out there that can run down little tunny. I only know of a few. We've eliminated sharks and big bluefin tuna ain't biting no human in half, so where does that leave us? I think between us we gotta try to get a profile of these things for Katie and Nick. It's that simple."

Jack's comments presented an ideal point for Rick to re-enter the discussion to present his game plan to the group.

"I totally agree with you, Jack. Your collective experiences on the water will prove invaluable with all this. I also want to reinforce what Katie said: We don't want anyone doing anything foolish that could result in an injury or worse. We believe we are dealing with a fish and each of us, me included, feels we can conquer anything that swims. That's just the way fisherman are built. And you all know that is true. We are usually very well prepared for whatever it is we fish for, sharks and big game fish included. But the difference with this situation is that we don't yet know what we are facing off against. We don't know what they are capable of. Just imagine a pack of rogue tarpon with a mouth full of large, razor-sharp teeth and a real bad attitude. So the plan is really to observe and report. You don't need to vary from your normal fishing patterns. I just want you to be aware of what we may be up against and to stay alert to any situations that might warrant further investigation."

"Am I hearing you right, Rick? You don't want us to catch one of these suckers?" Captain Bassonet asked.

"I'm saying I don't want you to put yourself in harm's way to catch one until we know what the hell it is and how it behaves. If you do get one the end of your line, use all good judgment and caution. Jack's already told us he hooked into one of these fish and couldn't land it. That should be a warning to us all. A good photo at this point is as good as the fish itself. And as Katie said, a piece of fin for DNA analysis will tell all of the story we need to know, if it can be obtained safely."

"So what's your plan, Captain?" Robinetti said.

"The plan is simple defensive-zone coverage. Like in football. In your case, you patrol Eagles Neck to Sandhill Point. Don't vary your typical game plan. Just be aware of your surroundings and the fact that the fish we are looking for might be in your zone. Chances are with all the bonito, albies, and small bluefish that are around to the west, these bad boys might pay you a visit.

"That's the drill, Al," Rick continued. "I'll make the rest of this short and sweet. Working from west to east, Joey, you cover the zone from Sandhill Point to Port Rosey Harbor; Valerie, you take it east from there to Plover Dunes; Sandy, you run the mid-range depths to the east and west of Mount Misery Ledge; Jack, you take the Middle Grounds and Stratford Shoal; Sully, your two party boats run their normal routes along the triangle from Can 11 to Can 9 and then out to the middle. Katie and I will be on my boat. Our plan is to play free safety and range throughout all the zones. We will keep in touch on the VHF, channel 68, since a lot of boats will be out this weekend and the chatter might be of value to us. We just might hear something revealing. You all know how much bullshit there is on 68. Guys just can't wait to report a catch or a sighting. We can chat on channel 19, but if we need some privacy, use the cell phone. Just say, *I got a heads up*, and dial it down. Is everybody in? Any questions?"

"Yeah, I have one," blurted Captain Marrone. You all know my boat. Low freeboard, close to the water. If I do hook one of these things, any suggestions on how to handle it? Based on what I'm hearing, do I throw a flying gaff into the damn thing, try to tail rope it, or shoot it? I'll have clients on board and the last thing I want is a three-ring circus with one of these monsters tearing up the place, or worse yet, taking a chunk out of someone."

"Leave that to me," Sandy Bassonet exclaimed. "I'm real good at catching monsters. I'll be out there with my brother-in-law and two other experienced fishermen and I will definitely be trying to catch one of these fish. There's fame and fortune riding on it. I'll bring some tuna and shark gear along and we'll be certain to get one to the boat."

"Let's not get too cocky. None of us is quite sure what we are up against so be careful," Rick said.

"I want to emphasize the *careful* part," Katie added. "If we all work together and just stay alert, this should all work out just fine. See you all out there."

Rick mentioned one final instruction. "I know you all are on the water every day. If you see anything, just report in. I want to make sure we are all on the water the days of the bluefish tournament. Our best chances of an encounter will happen when all those rods are on the water."

With that, the waitress opened the door as a loud roar erupted from the bar.

"Jeter just hit a walk-off homer. Can I get you another?"

CHAPTER 20

On the beach with Rick, Katie felt like she could finally exhale. "That was a good get-together. I just hope we did the right thing, Rick. I'm so fearful that someone else is going to get hurt and I could never live with myself if that happened."

"Look, Katie, they're all very good at what they do. I really don't think any one of them will try something stupid and get hurt for a fish. This is their livelihood and they are professionals. They won't take it too far."

"Sandy concerns me a little bit. I have this feeling he may view this as a game just to see if he can catch one of these things."

"He'll be okay. Talks toughs."

Looking out into the water, Katie tried changing the subject. "This beach is just beautiful tonight. It's been a long time since we took a walk like this."

Rick stopped walking and leaned over to kiss Katie on the forehead. "I really miss this part of it. I know I sometimes act like a prick but when we are apart, it hurts. I'm glad you're back with me. I miss you more than I miss fishing. Well, sometimes, that is."

"You really are such a jerk."

"Hey, how about we strip down and go skinny-dipping like we used to? Just a quick swim. In and out."

"With everything we just talked about?"

"Oh, come on, Katie. What are the odds of something happening right here, right now? The damn Sound is almost 120 miles long.

Those fish could be anywhere, if they are still around at all. And we still don't know for sure what this deal is all about."

"No, Rick."

"Well then, I'm going in." Rick stripped his clothes. "Last chance, sweat pea. Come on. Just like old times."

"Rick, please don't do this. I realize I should be rational about it but I'm very anxious . . . even a bit scared. I've seen what these fish can do."

Rick was not to be deterred. He made up his mind to go in for a nighttime swim and that was what he would do. As Rick swam parallel to the beach, a pod of the mutant killers cruised about a mile offshore. The pack broke away from the main school at dusk and had since been hunting for food. There were dozens of other patrols scattered about the Sound from Smith's Bay to Plover Dunes, all on the prowl. Their hunting forays on this night would result in multiple kills.

A lateral line running along each flank of their bodies detected the slightest vibrations in water that signaled the presence of prey. Through a network of sensory receptors known as *neuromasts,* the lateral lines helped the fish navigate and avoid other marine species and objects. It also helped each member maintain contact with the others.

The alpha male now sensed something in the water: disruptions in the pattern of impulses His instincts told him these vibrations were being made by struggling prey. The rest of the pod sensed this too. None of the pod was yet certain of the source or the nature of the vibrations, but they all instinctively sensed food. The alpha male changed direction and headed straight toward the beach, his charges in hot pursuit.

"The water is so warm, Katie, come on. It's refreshing." Rick was like a kid in a bathtub splashing water everywhere trying to wet Katie. He swam back and forth off the beach at a distance where his spray could reach her. He'd cup his hands and pushed the water toward Katie. His movements and motions further excited the pod of killer fish.

"Rick, stop this childish behavior. Hurry up with your foolishness and get out of there. Please!"

Rick was about five yards from shore. He stood on a shallow ledge beyond which the water dropped off to ten or twelve feet. It was a natural corridor for game fish to cruise in search of prey. Fish would orient to that edge during the period of a receding tide and travel along its course. When baitfish or other prey were encountered on the shallow shelf, they would burst from the deeper water, attack, and then retreat to the sanctuary of the deeper recesses beyond the ledge.

There were no other fish in the Sound that could challenge these evil creatures or threaten them, but imprinting that had taken place when they were young and vulnerable still motivated their behavior in shallow water. All varieties of marine life prowling the shallows at night looked to make meals of them when they were juveniles. These creatures never forgot those experiences. They were cautious killers.

"Get out of the water. I'm tiring of this game."

"One more quick swim down the beach and back and I'm done."

"You're impossible. Hurry up!"

The pod was now less than a half-mile offshore and each fish was fully aware of Rick's presence. Their collective senses worked in overdrive to determine his precise location. Their bodies stiffened as they swam, a sign of agitation, aggression pheromones fueling their every action.

"On second thought, I think I'll swim out to the lobster buoys," Rick said to an already disquieted Katie.

"Cut the shit, Rick, and get the fuck back here. Now! If you swim out to those pots, I'm outta here. For good. Do you understand me?"

"I'm just messin' with you. Chill out! You're wound up. Calm down."

"Get out of the water now! I want to leave." Katie sensed something she didn't like or understand. Something that elicited a primal fear response. She had always depended on her instincts and intuition, especially in bad situations, and now she was feeling those exact emotions.

"Okay, okay. Don't get upset. Give me another minute and I'll come out."

"I have a bad feeling."

The killers were about a quarter mile from the beach, a distance they could travel with lightning speed. Their combined senses confirmed that what they were tracking in the water was indeed food. The signals were not like other prey fish, but they were familiar messages, signals that had recently led to a large creature they attacked and fed upon. Not being certain of what it was he sensed, the alpha male had to be vigilant.

Like all other aquatic predators, these mutants had the ability to sense their world by acquiring life-sustaining information and cues from the watery environment. As apex predators, they evolved with immensely heightened senses of sight, touch, and feel. They were able to hear signals through vibrations absorbed into their body and smell and taste potential prey through chemical receptors within their brains and nervous systems. Through an arrangement of nostrils and an olfactory rosette, the alpha male and his pod mates were able to detect and distinguish chemicals, often in minute quantities. In a much purer *sense,* they actually tasted through taste buds in their mouths and on their lips and tongues. Physiologically, the alpha male and his pack had many of the same senses as humans and other animals; only theirs were sharpened to the finest point by a jolt of radiation their ancestors received decades before. Within a period of only thirty years, these fish had transformed into one of the most vicious and efficient killing machines ever to swim the world's oceans. Now in the Long Island Sound, they were bearing down on yet another unsuspecting victim.

CHAPTER 21

Nick Tanner and Valerie Russo were still seated at the table well after the others had departed from Grumpies. Valerie had intentions of getting to know Nick on a much more personal level so she volunteered to drive him back to his car parked on the State University campus. They realized quickly they shared a couple of interests—desserts and espresso. When the waitress showed them the dessert sample, it was an indulgence that neither cared to dismiss. Nick was a sucker for New York cheesecake and Valerie simply could not resist tiramisu.

"It's a bit like eating the forbidden fruit," she said playfully.

"This is pretty good cheesecake," Nick said between bites. "I'm pleasantly surprised. Didn't expect this at a sports bar. I've eaten lunch here before but never had time to enjoy dessert."

"They don't bake the desserts on premises. They buy them from Port Patisserie in town. One of the best bakeries on Long Island. They were recently featured on one of the cable food channels."

"How's the tiramisu?" Nick said.

"I've had better. At least one of my urges is satisfied."

Nick was absorbed in his cheesecake.

"Did you know that tiramisu is one of the most popular Italian desserts and a relatively new creation? Some claim 1981 as the year of origin, others 1969," Valerie, said.

"No I didn't. Don't think I ever tasted it."

"Are you kidding me? You've never had tiramisu? You just don't know what you are missing!"

Valerie cut a small piece of the dessert with her fork. "Here, give it a try," she said, licking her lips seductively as Nick took the small wedge of dessert into his mouth.

"Wow, that is pretty good."

"It is made of savoiardi that have been dipped in espresso and sometimes rum."

"Savoiardi?"

"Literally, of Savoy, but better known as Ladyfingers. Do you know what they are?"

"Of course I do. I love dunking them in my coffee. My maternal Italian grandfather got me started with that when I was a kid. Funny thing, one of my uncles used to belong to a singing quartet called The Ladyfinger Boys. At his house, the biscuits were always on the table with coffee."

"That's very nice to know. So you're an old pro with fingers? How lovely."

"Yep. Ate my fair share over the years."

"Shall I continue with my description of this lovely dessert? Still interested?"

"By all means, go on. I'm intrigued."

"Okay then. After the fingers are soaked in coffee and rum they are layered with a yummy concoction of sugar, egg yolk, mascarpone cheese, and sabaglione. Do you know what sabaglione is?" Valerie licked the index finger of her right hand.

"Actually I do. It's an Italian custard. Right?"

"I'm impressed, Nick. Very impressed. It is a very light custard usually made with Marsala wine or some other liqueur."

"Valerie, I have to ask, how does a charter boat captain know so much about Italian pastry?"

"The New York Institute of Culinary Arts. Studied there . . . pastry arts and baking. After graduating, I worked at a few of the best restaurants and hotels and I even did a stint at in Atlantic City as a head pastry chef."

"So what happened? How did you get involved with fishing?"

"A significant other I worked with was into fishing the southern New Jersey backcountry and I would tag along. After a while, I got pretty good at it and actually fell in love with the sport. I decided that I wanted to become a professional guide. So I moved back home to Long Island and got my captain's license."

"Why didn't you just stay in New Jersey?"

"The relationship turned bad, really bad, and I needed to put that part of my life in the rear view mirror. And before I forget, the last step preparing tiramisu is to sprinkle some cocoa powder on top and then refrigerate it before serving. Delicioso!"

"Well thank you for that pastry education. You are a woman full of surprises. I like that."

"You have no idea. So tell me, how did you become a marine biologist?"

"It's ichthyologist to be precise."

"Oh yeah, that's right. You are the fish man."

"I guess you can say that. Ever since I was a kid, I was into fish. I raised tropical fish and even sold them to pet stores. Helped pay my way through college."

"Where did you go to school?"

"Here's the *Reader's Digest* version. I was born and raised in New Jersey, Hunterdon County, not far from the Delaware River, where I spent most of my spare time fishing and exploring. Went to a Catholic elementary and middle school in Raritan, and then Hunterdon Central High School. Then I came out to Long Island to attend the State University, where I thought I would pursue pre-med studies but after two years I decided to follow the passion of my heart and study fish. I had good grades and got into Cornell, where I double-majored in marine biology and marine zoology . . . ichthyology for short. Got my master's, came down to Long Island to work with the Marine Division, and worked toward my PhD at State University. Partnered up with Katie D and here I am."

"Impressive credentials there, mister." Valerie had always been turned on by brains.

"Any ladies in your life?"

"Never really had the time. Some close friends but nothing serious."

"Can a friendship between a man and a woman ever be really close without getting serious or sexual?" Valerie winked.

Nick laughed. "That can be a dilemma for sure. Been there, done that, and have the tee-shirt and the scars to prove it."

Captain Russo felt more encouraged.

"So what's your real take on the happenings in the Sound?"

"I think Katie put all the cards on the table," Nick replied.

"Gargantuan fish?"

"Very possible but we don't know for certain," Nick was unsure where this discussion was headed and he was uncomfortable with the questioning. He didn't know Valerie well and wasn't sure how far he could trust her. "We have some ideas, we are following some leads and hopefully after this weekend we will have a better handle on it. Katie put all the issues in full view and with full disclosure of the facts as we know them." Nick couldn't have been more measured in his response.

"How long have you worked with her?"

"Three years. She is very good at her job and we make a good team. This has just been one of the toughest challenges we've faced since working together. But we will figure it out and we'll get through it."

"I have an offer for you," Valerie said.

"What's that?"

"I have a charter both days this weekend but the guy is a real Wall Street dirt bag. I wouldn't mind ditching him. If you'd like, come out on the boat and set up shop. We'll see if we might get some intelligence on the fish you're looking for. Consider it a scientific expedition. I could use a few vacation days."

"How will that sit with your sport? Won't he be pissed?"

"The guy is such a wuss and, if I must say so, he has a thing for me and he likes being bossed around. Strange dude. As soon as I tell him I can't fish him this weekend, he'll be crying like a baby and begging me for another booking. If he really wants to fish and not gawk at me for six hours, I can easily get him on another boat. I've done it before and he always comes crawling back."

"Why do you even bother with someone like that?"

"Because only one letter of the alphabet makes a difference in how we each view the world. I like big tips and he likes big tits."

"You don't mince words, do you?"

"Not in the least. What you see is . . . what you get."

"Well if you have the room and if it is no inconvenience, I'd love to step aboard and fish with you. Mind if I bring some of my scientific electronic gear?"

"Not at all. Sounds sexy! I'll bring a very special dessert."

"That's a deal. Hey, it's getting late and I need my sleep. Can I take you up on that offer to drive me back to my car?"

"How about a nightcap at my condo?"

"I'll take a rain check. Come on, let's go."

CHAPTER 22

Rick waded from the water at a snail's pace and toward a very anxious Katie, who was standing on the beach. "A drink in town, and then maybe some nookie-nookie?"

"Yeah, whatever," Katie replied. "Just get a move on it and get out of the damn water."

Katie's somewhat implied agreement to Rick's request should have been enough to motivate him to sprint from the water, but he was milking this moment for as long as he could. He liked toying with Katie since he knew it would piss her off, and then reconciliation would be sweet.

As Rick procrastinated, the killers cruised about five hundred yards off the beach, rapidly closing the distance to their prey. Rick was thirty feet from the safety of the sand, taking his sweet time exiting the water. He had not a care in the world and thoroughly enjoyed being immersed in the warm water. Finally in disgust, Katie began walking back to the parking lot.

"See you at the truck, Rick. I've had enough of your bullshit."

"Katie, hold on. I'm right behind you." Rick did not want to lose an opportunity to spend the night with Katie.

While Rick contemplated a night of bliss, the fish sensed their next meal escaping and accelerated. Powerful sweeps of their abnormally muscular caudal fins propelled them forward at astonishing speed. The vibrations broadcast by Rick's movements fueled a growing frenzy among the aroused creatures. Their robust and oversized circulatory systems pumped natural chemical stimulants rapidly throughout their bodies . . . fueling a crazed killing high. Their eyes glowed a freakish luminescent yellow and locked in on the direction of the vibrations. Soon they would be able to see their prey. In their agitated state, the killers snapped their large conical teeth, generating eerie, clicking reverberations that echoed throughout the water column. Each assassin could hear the other's sounds, signals acting collectively as additional aggression stimuli. With jaws snapping open and shut at a robotic rate, the fish raced toward the source of food. All other life in their path fled—all except Rick.

Rick was still in water up to his waist as the pod approached to within three hundred yards of his position. Although he was only ten yards from shore, the angle of the bottom was steep and dropped off quickly. Ten yards on land could be sprinted in quick order but the resistance of waist-deep water rendered the task of walking ashore a much more demanding effort.

Rick called out once again for Katie to wait for him. She stopped and turned toward him, but in the darkness Rick could not see her clearly. He could barely make out her partial silhouette framed by moonlight. Rick quickly turned back around to face the open Sound. He sensed something very peculiar. He had always believed he had a throwback survival gene to Neanderthal ancestors and that is what made him a good outdoorsman. Often while hunting, Rick would sense game well before it sensed him. And when fishing unfamiliar water, he always knew where to cast, where the fish would be. He could enter a strange woodlot or be placed in the middle of a large body of water and he would find his way. To Rick, it was as if he was blessed with a primitive sixth sense for survival, and now his instincts sensed very real and immediate danger.

The hunting pack was closing in on him at astounding speed when Katie saw the yellow glow of aberrant eyes. She screamed loud enough to wake the dead as her eyes followed dozens of glowing yellow orbs moving through the water straight toward Rick. He saw them too and turned back toward the beach. With a forceful running motion, Rick plowed through the water. It was five yards to the safety of the sand. Katie ran toward him. The fish could now see their target clearly and zoned in on the large prey. Rick was in thigh high water pushing forward hard with all his strength and endurance.

"Hurry, Rick! Hurry!" Katie screamed. "They're right behind you!"

Rick felt an easing of resistance as he crested the top of the trough and was calf-high in water.

"Rick, jump! Jump!"

With all the strength his legs could muster, and with fear as a propellant, Rick leapt from the water as the massive snapping jaws of the alpha male took dead aim. He felt something brush his leg as he went airborne. Rick landed on the beach just inches from the edge of the surf. The abnormally large head of the creature landed along side of him, snapping mouth agape and full of stiletto teeth. The animal was partially in the water with half its body alongside Rick's. Katie grabbed a piece of baseball-bat sized driftwood and threw it at the fish to distract it. It struck the killer's mouth and was instantly chopped in half by the rapidly opening and closing vise-grip jaws. Rick scurried up the beach as the fish tried to grab hold of his leg. He reached for a large rock to bash its head, but as he did, the monster slid back into the water and disappeared. Katie and Rick watched in horror as glowing yellow eyes streaked back and forth parallel to the beach, a sign of an agitated pack of fish looking for another chance at their meal.

"What the fuck was that?" Rick finally blurted as his composure and heartbeat returned to normal.

"I don't know, Rick. I didn't get a very good look at it but whatever it was it was big and grotesque and it came within inches of grabbing you. It appeared to be some kind of fish. And what was with those eyes?"

"Do you think that was them, the fish you're looking for?"

"Rick, when was the last time a fish from the Long Island Sound tried to eat you? You tell me. Was that them?"

"Holy shit, Katie, that thing had a mouth like a garbage can with chain-saw teeth. It had to be six, seven feet long at least. If that is what we're up against, we have one hell of a big problem. There had to be a dozen of those things swimming together."

"You know, I told you not to go in the fucking water. You asshole!"

"Do you really think they were some monster fish?"

"You are impossible, Rick. Did you see the rest of the pack? I have no idea what kind of fish they were. I've never seen anything like those glowing eyes."

As Katie spoke, Rick turned his attention back to the water and noticed something reflecting faintly in the moonlight. He moved toward the shining object. It was embedded in one half of the driftwood that Katie tossed at the creature.

"Whoa, Katie, look at this. It's a tooth . . . a big mother of a tooth!"

Katie examined the find and all she could think of was DNA.

"DNA could be extracted from the root pulp of a well-preserved tooth. And this tooth is complete and as fresh as they come."

Katie's fear and anger instantly turned to excitement as she realized the significance of what was in her hand.

"Rick, this could be the smoking gun we have been looking for. This tooth gives us the ability to compare the bites to the Smith's Bay body parts against the bite impression in the driftwood. We also can extract DNA from it and find out once and for all what these fish are. I need to call Karen Hammond at Riverstone National Labs. We need to get this tooth analyzed immediately."

"Katie, it's one-thirty in the morning. I don't think Karen would be at her desk just yet."

"We'll deal with the tooth first thing the morning."

"Fine. Let's get out of here. This beach has me creeped."

The killer pack wasn't done. They still needed to eat. Having expended excessive amounts of energy in their unsuccessful attempt to kill Rick, they were agitated and they were in need of food. The one cardinal rule of predatory hunting is to consume more caloric value than the energy burned to capture a meal. The alpha male and his marauding mutants violated that tenet of the wild and now they had to find sustenance. The pod resumed the hunt, staying close to shore. It was during the hours of darkness inshore waters become alive with many feeding fish that feel secure in darkness, roaming the edge between land and sea. The pack would use those feeding behaviors to their advantage.

Large striped bass, weakfish, and other fish venture into the shallows during this period to feed, unmolested by other predators or humans. Large bass of thirty pounds or more have very few natural enemies in the Sound but tonight would be different. A school of big striped bass had locked in on an even larger school of Atlantic menhaden. The bass had the bunker corralled in a u-shaped indentation in the contour of the beach. To put it mildly, what transpired along that stretch of surf was nothing less than a massacre. Bass tore into bunker from every direction. The lucky menhaden were swallowed whole, while others were pounced upon and slapped by the powerful tails of huge bass. Tail swipes dazed the bunker, allowing their pursuers to ingest them at a more leisurely pace.

The feeding attracted the attention of the killers. The scent of death and the vibrations from struggling prey and attacking bass acted like homing signals. The alpha male and his pack were about two miles from Plover Dunes where the bass blitz was taking place; they could already sense the life-and-death struggle. The killers traveled at a sustained speed of thirty-five miles an hour with bursts up to sixty, all the while their senses attuned to the stimulating signals from the bass and bunker confrontation. It didn't take long for the pod to reach the melee. They wasted no time and charged indiscriminately into the mix, jaws snapping wildly as teeth slashed at every living thing in their path. But it was the large bass upon which their sights had been fixed.

The alpha male was the first to tear into a cluster of feeding stripers, biting the lower third tail section of a bass clean off a forty-five-pound fish that had just consumed an equally ill-fated bunker. Other killers did the same. With the tails severed, they couldn't escape; they just struggled and slowly descended in the water column. And with their prey incapacitated, the assassins attacked and consumed their victims without having to chase them down. Within a heartbeat, the bass had endured the same end as their prey. The doomed fish struggled to maintain equilibrium as blood emptied from gaping wounds and entrails flowed like the tentacles of an octopus.

The big alpha male was completely aroused by the slaughter and death that surrounded him and, with lightning speed, he turned to bite yet another bass in half. He swallowed the largest section of fish and then targeted another victim. The entire pack was in a crazed state of feeding fury. By the end of the carnage, the entire school of large bass had been obliterated. The marauders were temporarily satiated but they would feed again as they greeted the false dawn.

CHAPTER 23

Katie awoke early. She had succumbed to conflicting emotions the night before but was so relieved Rick hadn't been killed that she felt compelled to make love to him. After all the exhausting pleasure, she had trouble sleeping, while Rick was sound asleep. All that Katie had on her mind were the origins of the fish tooth. She was eager to call her friend Karen at the lab to get DNA confirmation of what it was that attacked Rick on the beach. Katie was optimistic that a major part of the puzzle would be solved with an analysis of the tooth. But after witnessing what tried to kill Rick, Katie was also more certain than ever that she was facing a problem of monumental proportions.

Katie showered and then put on a pot of coffee. She once again re-examined the piece of wood containing the tooth. Katie looked at the wall clock in the kitchen . . . 6:45 a.m. It was still way too early to call Karen. But it wasn't too early for her phone to ring. *Who the hell is calling me at this time of morning?*

It was Katie's boss, Ted Gunther.

"Katie, you need to get to Plover Dunes, ASAP! The sand is littered with the heads and mutilated bodies of huge striped bass. The entire town is freaking out. Some early morning beach joggers sounded the alarm. Enforcement dispatched a team of officers to see if it might have been the result of poachers but that is not what's been reported back. All the heads appear to have been bitten off, not severed with a knife. I got a bad feeling these bass and your cases are connected."

"Ted, I have a hot lead I'm working on this morning. I really need to follow this up. Can't this wait? Can Nick do it alone?"

"No, Katie. I need another set of eyes and ears. This might be a media event and I need you to help Nick put a lid on it if things get out of control. You need to buy me a little more time."

"Ted, we found a tooth last night that came from a fish that tried to attack Rick west of Plover Dunes. I think this is the best lead we have to solving this whole mess."

"What tried to attack Rick last night? What have you been up to, Katie?"

"I was on the beach when a pack of enormous fish came in while Rick was wading ashore. They tried to kill him. Or at least one did. Ted, it almost got him. We got a look at it and we got a tooth. I think these may be the killer fish and I can prove it with DNA from the tooth."

"Katie, get over to Plover Dunes now. Figure out that scene first, then go deal with the tooth. I'll let county PD know you are on the way. And let me know what you find. I have to brief the director first thing this morning. And keep what you find quiet until we can figure out a PR angle. If the police or other emergency services types ask just deflect the question and say that you need more time to evaluate the situation. Okay?"

"Give me some credit, Ted. I think I can handle the bureaucrats and press well enough. I know what to say."

"Fine. Call me when you assess the situation at the beach. Bye."

"Rick, get up. I gotta go. Where are the keys to your truck?"

"What's the matter, Katie? What are you doing? It's early and I'm not going fishing today. Let me sleep."

"I have to go over to Plover Dunes. There's a pile of striped bass heads and bodies on the beach and people are in a panic about it."

"Striped bass heads? Maybe someone was just cleaning fish? There are a lot of folks who fish that beach at night. Maybe they hit the bite just right. There's been a pile of big bass in the area recently. Maybe even poachers?"

"I don't think so, Rick. Sounds more like a massacre from what Ted just told me. I gotta get there right away."

"Hang on . . . Give me a minute to shower and get a cup of java and I'll drive you."

"Okay. But hurry. The faster we do that, the faster I can call Karen and get this tooth to the lab."

As Rick showered, Katie paced the floor of the den. Her mind raced a mile a minute. *Bass heads*, she thought. If the fish that tried to eat Rick had elevated levels of chemical stimulants in their bodies, the result of their failed attempt to kill Rick, they would have been one pissed off pack . . . agitated, hungry, and aggressive. They obviously had continued their hunt and came upon the feeding bass. For the killer fish, it would be like finding the mother lode. That had to be it. Rick escaped but the bass were slaughtered in his place. It made sense; it was a very natural predator response to the hunger drive.

"Rick, are you almost done? We gotta get going."

"Just a minute. Brushing my teeth. Pour me a cup of coffee, please."

It was just about a twenty-minute drive from Rick's place in Port Roosevelt to the Plover Dunes. They took Rick's Ford F-250 pickup and drove out on Route 28, against the westbound commuter traffic headed to work and toward the city. Rick pointed to a development off to the right-hand side of the road and began to reminisce. "Katie, when I was a kid growing up, those condos were a peach farm. I used to hunt quail and woodcock back in there with my first lab, Santee. She was a great gun dog. Boy, do I ever miss that. Progress, I guess. That's what they call it, right? Build something on every postage stamp-size piece of Long Island. The only escape around these parts now is the Sound. And that is slowly but surely being screwed up too. With all the nice lawns around here, there's more nitrogen running into the Sound than the water can handle."

Rick was on a roll: "Algae blooms, dead lobsters, tainted shellfish. Guess that's progress, too. And some geniuses from Canada want to put up a natural gas platform right in the middle of the Sound off Boulder Point. Could you imagine the sight if that damn thing ever got sabotaged and was blown up! Lights out, Long Island!"

Katie got in a few words as Rick took a breath. "Man, you are on a tear this morning. I figured you'd be a lot milder after last night. What gives?"

"Did you ever think, Katie, that maybe those fish are trying to get even for all humanity has done to them and their environment? Look at what those assholes did to the Gulf of Mexico. They could do it here too. Fucked up an entire way of life. Generations of traditions. The roots of this country's heritage destroyed. And nobody seemed to give a shit while it all was happening. Politicians too worried about their re-election campaigns, an oil company executive watching horse races as one of the most fertile ecosystems in the United States was being wiped out. Whatever is going on here with these fish is another example of things gone haywire in the last decades. I'm beginning to think the Mayans were right. This has been the decade of turmoil and the end, whenever it comes, will not be pleasant."

"Come on, Rick, let's face some facts here, Mayan doomsday predictions aside. And I agree with you about the Gulf accident. That was like the Keystone Cops. But for the most part, the Sound is very healthy. Yeah, there are pockets of hypoxia in the western regions but here in the central Sound and points east, it is a pretty health estuary, with plenty of oxygen. Just take a look at what a phenomenal fishing season this is. Do you think an unhealthy ecosystem would produce the enormous varieties of life we have been seeing the past few years? Tons of sand eels, Atlantic silversides, football field–sized schools of bunker, squid, you name it. And how about all those species of game fish that come into these waters? Striped bass, fluke, bluefish . . . and all the pelagic species like Atlantic bonito and false albacore and Spanish mackerel. The Sound is a very fertile place, Rick. Fertile enough for you to still make a living from fishing."

"Katie, my Katie. Sounds to me like you are buying into all the chamber of commerce bullshit and hype."

"Oh, come on, Rick, you know I'm right."

"Hey, you know I was telling you about years back when I hunted woodcock over at the peach farm. Well one day, I come out of the woods and there is a woman picking peaches. She starts to pet Santee, my black lab, and asks me what I'm hunting for. I tell her woodcock. So she asks me, what's a woodcock? I tell her that is what Pinocchio has"

"Rick, you are really incorrigible and a real idiot, and you always change the subject when I'm right about something. That is pretty funny about the woodcock."

"Holy shit, look at all the cars in the parking lot. Must have been quite a happening down there on the beach."

There were cop cars and vehicles from all emergency services units parked in the lot and a few four-wheel drives were on the beach. And the local news crews were also on scene. As Katie and Rick reached the sand beach, they heard a familiar voice.

"Dr. DiNardo, glad to see you here."

"Well hello, Detective Spinello. The feeling is mutual."

"Seems like our unknown perps have stuck again. You should go examine those carcasses, Dr. DiNardo. They show very interesting bite marks. Might shed some light on your investigation."

"Do you guys have any new leads?"

Spinello shook his head. Who's your friend?"

Rick stuck out his hand and grasped detective Spinello's hand extra firmly, proclaiming, "Captain Rick McCord, *fishing guide.*"

"You are up and about early. Are you involved anyway in this case?"

Rick thought for a moment and wondered, does he mean in ways other than sleeping with the lead marine biologist? He smiled and said simply, "I offer Ms. DiNardo my captain's services whenever there is a need."

"And have you done so yet with this case?"

"Other than drive her here this morning, no."

"Odd that you didn't come with your partner, Nick? He's been here for a while. Been taking measurements and snapping away photos for almost an hour now. Seems to be intrigued by what he found. Did you oversleep this morning? How about you, Captain?"

"I'm here now," she said, cutting him off.

Nick Tanner spotted the trio chatting and rushed to the rescue not a moment too soon. "Morning, Katie. Hi Rick. You need to come check this out."

Katie walked away without so much as a glance at the detective.

"Later," Rick replied as he too left detective Spinello standing alone.

"That detective has been all over me," Nick said in muffled tone. "He is pushing hard to get some answers. Said he's attending a meeting later on today with other cops and town officials along the north shore to decide if they need to post warnings on the beaches for the Labor Day weekend."

"What are you finding, Nick?" Katie said.

"These are our killers. Identical bite patterns just tore through these bass. Adult bunker as well. The bass found the bunker and the killers found the bass.

"I figured as much, Nick, based on what Ted told me and the experience Rick and I had last night."

"We have a tooth, Nick," Rick said with a wide smile on his face.

"Now this ought to be good. How?"

"Last night they tried to eat me while I was in the water."

"Are you shitting me? You know what's swimming around out here and you go in the water at night? Are you two crazy? And you, Katie, where the hell is your head?"

"Not me, just him . . . the idiot," Katie replied. "It all turned out okay and we got a tooth embedded in driftwood. Right after I finish up here, I'm going to call my friend Karen at Riverstone Lab and ask her to do a DNA analysis."

"I don't even want to know how the tooth wound up in drift-wood, but I'm almost certain these fish are a phenotype of some existing species. Let me see the tooth," Nick said.

Katie pulled the large tooth from her pocket and handed it to Nick. It was all too oddly familiar. Perfect match to the bite marks. "You are one lucky dude, Mr. McCord."

Katie felt somewhat relieved being one step closer to solving the problem but Nick's conclusion did not provide an identity to the killers.

"They are some kind of bizarre and brutal fish, Nick. That much I was able to ascertain from last night's encounter."

"Katie, I'm thinking we need to put out a statement just warning folks to be cautious of large schools of aggressive fish. These things are getting more violent."

"I need to call, Ted. Then I need to bring this tooth over to the lab. The DNA mapping is the only way we will know for sure."

"I think that's a waste of time, Katie. It could take a week or more to get the DNA results back. Even if your buddy expedites it, we are looking at three or four days, easy. And the big weekend is only three days away. I think we are on solid ground with our hypothesis that the culprits are fish. We need to declare our findings and have the department issue a public statement and warning. We need to protect our asses and the public."

Katie dialed a number on her cell. Three rings later: "Hello, Ted Gunther, Marine Fisheries . . . Ted, it's Katie. I'm at Plover Dunes."

"What did you find?"

"You are not going to like this, Ted, but what happened here was caused by the killer fish and Nick and I are now almost certain they are some mutated species. We think the department needs to issue a public warning for the holiday weekend."

"Your timing is just peachy, Katie. One of the biggest tourist weekends of the year and you want me to go public about killer fish in the Long Island Sound. I can see the headlines now."

"Ted, we just need to warn folks to be careful and if they spot any suspicious activity to get away from the water."

"Do you have any idea how this is going to fly upstairs? The two of you need to get back here right now and we are all going to call the commissioner."

"Ted, I need a favor. I'm going to call my friend Karen at Riverstone Lab and ask her to expedite a DNA mapping of the tooth we found. If you could make a call to her superior, it might grease the skids and get the results back before the weekend."

"Katie, you are asking me for a small miracle. Holiday weekend, a test that normally takes a week or more to do right, and you want it in two days. I'll see what I can do, but you and your sidekick get your butts back here on the double."

"Okay, but I'm going to drop this tooth off first . . . Rick, you need to drive me to the lab. And Nick, you need to get back to headquarters. I'll meet you there when I'm done. We have to huddle up with Ted about the press release. Give some thought to what we might want to say."

"You mean beyond the fact that beach goers should keep their asses out of water because there are one-hundred-pound fish in the Sound killing people, dogs and anything else that gets in their way. Okay, I'll give some thought to how we might sugarcoat that."

The trio began to walk from the beach, but as they did, Detective Spinello blocked their paths. Katie knew their escape would not be an easy one without some explanation.

"So what have the esteemed marine biologist, ichthyologist, and fishing guide concluded? This certainly was not perpetrated by some small baby bluefish, now was it?"

Katie was suspicious of Spinello's implication and chose her reply carefully: "Detective, we need to take these findings back to our headquarters and conduct further evaluations. We are still not fully certain what is behind all this and any conclusions that might be drawn have to be tested and validated."

"Well, Dr. DiNardo, there is wide gap between suspicion and knowing for certain. By this time, you must have an idea. Scientific process aside, if you had to make a guess right at this very moment, what would it be?"

"I'm a scientist, Detective, not one for outlandish speculation or guesses. As you do, I deal in facts and evidence. Too much is at stake here if we suggest the wrong opinion."

Detective Spinello wasn't about to let go without pressing the issue further. He was a highly decorated police officer whose track record included solving a number of very high profile and challenging crimes. He was instrumental in providing the FBI and CIA with dead-on leads that resulted in the infiltration of a Long Island–based terrorist cell with the arrest of more than a dozen covert operatives. Spinello was a street-smart cop, growing up in the Brooklyn where many of his childhood friends moved on to less than distinguished careers with the mob. Most of them were now away at "college" serving twenty-to-life. He learned the real-life game of cops and robbers at an early age and could have been swayed to the dark side had his family not moved from Brooklyn to Long Island during Spinello's early high school years. His parents enrolled him in Saint Patrick's High School, where he excelled at sports and academics. It was at Saint Pat's where Spinello decided he wanted to pursue a career in law enforcement. He attended John Jay College and was graduated first in his class.

"Forgive me, but I just can't seem to understand how all this talent can't come to a conclusion about what did this and if it is related to the other deaths and events. What's so tough? I've solved murders in less time!"

Nick jumped in. "Look, Detective, there are a lot of variables at play here. On the surface this seems to be the work of some form of marine life. The exact species we can't say for certain just yet. Some of the analysis that needs to be conducted to verify our observations is complex and takes time to finalize. I'm hopeful that before too long we will have an answer or at least some more conclusive evidence. That's he best we can do."

"Before too long? And how many more massacres like this one will we have to endure until then? Maybe next time, it will be a group of school kids out for a swim and not striped bass."

Rick was beginning to get antsy and Katie was reading his body language. He didn't tolerate interrogation and, if this went on much longer, he was certain to say or do something they would all regret. He was not one for authority figures.

Katie spoke. "Detective, we have a lot of work ahead of us. We really need to get moving. You'll be the first to know."

"I'm sure we will talk soon, Dr. DiNardo. Enjoy the rest of your day. You too, Fishing Guide Rick."

"Asshole," Rick mumbled as the trio walked from the beach.

"He's only doing his job, Rick. But something tells me he knows more than he is letting on. I gotta call Karen about this tooth, pronto."

CHAPTER 24

The phone rang twice. A woman answered. "Hello?"

"Karen, it's Katie. How are you?"

"I'm fine. It's been a while. What are you up to?"

"I'm saddled with this complicated and high visibility case and I need some help. Got a favor to ask."

"As long as it doesn't involve a felony, I'm game," Karen said.

"I need you to map some DNA from a fish tooth. And to do it as fast as you possibly can."

"I heard some of the scoop about all this. The scientific community is hearing lot of chatter about some bizarre occurrences in the Sound. And I heard you were in the middle of it. As a matter of fact, your boss called my boss just a little while ago and asked if we might help out. Sounded urgent. Said you'd be calling me with the details. Want to fill me in?"

"Well, now. I'm impressed at Ted's initiative. I'm over by Plover Dunes and can be at the lab in about twenty minutes. I'll give you the details when I see you."

"Okay. I'll call security and get you on the visitor's list. They'll give you a pass and I'll meet you at the entrance to the Visitor's Center."

"Can you make it two passes? Rick is driving me."

"You back with him again? Thought that whole fling was over and done with. Guess he's really gotten inside your head, sweetie. That guy can be trouble. But if that is what you wish, two passes it is. See you in a bit."

The Riverstone Lab was founded in the late 1940s as a multidiscipline, national research facility. Over the course of its existence, the scientists received numerous Nobel Prizes. The facility houses several research labs for a staff of thousands, including scientists, engineers, and support operations. While most of the Lab's charter and mission remained within the realm of energy and physics research, the lab maintained an active biology department that focused on genome and DNA research.

Karen Hammond was employed in the DNA Unit. Her friendship with Katie extended back to their childhood. They attended the same preschool, middle school, and high school. Coincidentally, in high school they finished their senior year as numbers one and two in their class. Katie was valedictorian and Karen salutatorian. They were also both all-county players on the girl's lacrosse team. That closeness and likeminded makeup prompted their schoolmates to refer to them as the "K&K Twins." Karen obtained her PhD in molecular biology from the State University of New York, where she also did her undergraduate work. She'd been employed at the lab since her PhD. Her area of expertise related to cellular responses to environmental influences. Although she has had numerous offers to work in the private sector, Karen's love of pure science and research kept her well anchored at the government facility. For her, it was an ideal environment to pursue admirable career goals defined by her strict research parameters. While the private sector of the US economy would eventually benefit from discoveries and research made at the lab, the profit motive was not Karen's prime mover. For her, it was the journey toward new discoveries that motivated her scientific findings. Results were her reward. While the lab was the recipient of numerous private foundation and corporate research grants, Karen was able to insulate herself from the eventual commercialization effects of her DNA research. At this stage of her career and life, she was a purist, not yet seduced or corrupted by the almighty dollar.

The armed guard at the entrance to the lab asked to see two forms of identification from both occupants of the vehicle, and the vehicle registration. Rick produced his driver's license and a photo ID card from The Wholesale Outlet as well as the DMV vehicle registration. Katie presented her driver's license and her work ID badge from Fish and Game."We are here to see Karen Hammond."

Without so much as an acknowledging glance at either Katie or Rick, the guard took all IDs to the guard shack and entered information into a laptop that sat upon a wedge-shaped bench. He double-checked the registration against the license plates. Seemingly satisfied, he re-entered the guard shack and printed two visitor's badges. Handing Rick and Katie back their respective IDs, he added, "Please peel off the backing and affix the badge to the upper left-hand side of your chest, above the shirt-pocket area. The passes are valid for today only and must be returned upon your departure. Do you need directions?"

"We are meeting Dr. Hammond at the admin building."

"Straight ahead, first left, and then the first right. You'll see a sign for the visitor's parking lot. Please park there. Enjoy your day."

"Thank you." A little more efficient than the typical rent-a-cops you find at places like this, Katie thought.

As they pulled away from the guard shack, Rick couldn't resist a dig. "Katie, I think you need to reposition that badge on a bit higher on your chest. It shouldn't be resting on your boob like that. The middle of your name is kind of pointy." Rick laughed.

"Rick, buzz off. I'm really in no mood for your silly jokes right now. Karen knows who the hell I am. Pay attention to your driving. Make the first left and the first right. There's the building, and there's Karen standing out front. Prompt as usual. Park this thing."

"Prompt? You mean anal . . ."

"Hey there, K1, how goes it? Nice to see you. Nice to see you too, Rick."

Rick nodded.

"Right back at you, Savage. Thanks for getting us in here. Is there a place we can talk?"

"There's a small cafeteria inside. We can sit and talk quietly. I don't think we have any tours today."

Karen had been given the nickname "Savage" in high school, but not for the aggressive nature of her lacrosse play or academic competitiveness. Due to their high school rankings, the K&K Twins were individually referred to as K1 and K2. Since Katie's grade point average was slightly higher than Karen's, she was designated as K1. Both girls were in the same advanced biology class. Their teacher was an avid mountain climber. When he overhead Karen referred to as K2 by one of the other students, he told the class that K2 is the second highest mountain on earth, only surpassed by Everest. The teacher advised that K2 is also known as the Savage Mountain. The Savage part stuck. Katie would always toy with Karen that even with nicknames she was number one. Karen was quick to remind her best friend that although Everest was the higher of the two mountains, K2 was unquestionably the most dangerous and difficult climb. She'd always add with a mischievous smile, "Not many make it on top of K2!"

Rick went to get coffee while Katie and Karen found a table in the cafeteria. Katie removed the large tooth from a plastic bag and handed it to Karen.

"The fish it belonged to and his buddies tried taking a chunk out of Rick's ass last night. Almost got him."

"Too bad. What kind of fish do you think it was? It obviously had bad eyesight."

"From all the evidence I've seen, I'm inclined to say it is some phenotype or mutated form of fish. I need you to help me prove it."

"So there's a school of these things?"

"My guess is that there are numerous hunting pods that belong to a much larger school. They most likely break into packs to hunt and then reassemble into a larger community once they've fed. We have no idea how many fish there are but the ones that tried to eat Rick seemed to number about a dozen. Weird fish, Karen . . . big head and glowing yellow eyes. It appears for the moment the fish are only in the Sound. So far no reports of any similar incidents along the south shore. But that could change in the next hour or with the next tide. My guess is these are pelagic fish and roam wherever the hell they want. We have a little experiment going on this weekend with some of Rick's captain friends to see if we might get a handle on them."

"Now that ought to be good. From what I've been hearing through the grapevine, your incidents are more like mayhem, mutilations, and massacres. Hope you don't add to the death toll with your experiment."

"Gruesome would be the perfect description. I've never seen anything like this before, Karen. Not even with shark attacks."

"That's lovely. How long has this been going on?"

"Started about a week ago. Now that we are coming up on the holiday weekend, we need to be sure of our facts before going public. Based on what I've seen and what my partner and I have concluded, we need hard evidence before breaking this news. All this could sound like a bunch of science mumbo-jumbo, and if we aren't careful, there could be a panic."

"I'll extract samples from the root pulp. That should give us our best results."

"How long will it take?"

"Typically with tissue of this type maybe five days, but we have some new analysis technology under development at the lab that involves direct visualization of DNA using nanotechnology and electron microscopy. If I can get clearance to use it, I might be able to have this done in about two days. Can you live with that?"

"If that's the best, it'll have to do."

Karen would use an extraction process that first breaks down the cell walls of the pulp tissue to gain access the internal genetic material. The pulp sample would go into a piece of equipment known as an Eppendorf tube with a detergent and enzyme proteinase. The solution would break down the tissue sample's cellular structure and nuclear membrane and ultimately release the DNA. A lab tech would add a salt solution containing isopropyl alcohol and place the tube in a centrifuge. The effects of centrifugal force cause the deoxyribonucleic acid, DNA, to separate from solution and clump into strands. The DNA would go through the centrifuge again, forcing the strands to bind together, then removed and allowed to dry. When complete, the DNA extracted from the tooth pulp would be ready for analysis to determine the origins of Katie's fish.

"Karen, I need you to analyze a few things with this DNA. First, I need to know if the tooth came from a known species of fish. If not, what does the DNA most closely match? Second, I want to know if there are any anomalies in the genetic makeup of the tissue. Has anything caused changes or mutations? My gut tells me these are not simply giant guppies."

"I'll also use *FISH* to help me profile the DNA. Stands for Fluorescence In Situ Hybridization. It will allow me to map the genetic material in the DNA, including specific genes or portions of genes. From the standpoint of your needs, it is important since this enables me to analyze any chromosomal abnormalities or other genetic mutations. If your fish are some genetic monsters, I will be able to validate that. I may even be able to tell you how it happened."

"Terrific, Karen. I appreciate all the help. This whole situation is like a ticking time bomb and I'm running out of time."

"Have the K&K Twins completed all their work?" Rick returned from his coffee run. "I brought you each a coffee light with a tad of sugar to add to your already sweet dispositions."

"What a ball buster," Karen responded, "But thank you. Despite what some may say, you do have some socially redeeming qualities."

"Who's the ball buster?" Rick shot back.

Katie intervened. "We're done, Rick. Karen has a lot of work to do and I need to get back to Fish and Game. Let me hear as soon as you find out anything, K2."

"Figure two days. That would be my personal best."

"Okay, we are outta here. Let's get together for dinner after all this is over. We have a lot to catch up on."

"Just leave your buddy at home."

Rick turned back toward Karen and with a smile said, "I love you too, sweetie."

On the way back to the truck, Rick asked, "What's up with Karen? Why the nasty attitude toward me? What did I ever do to her?"

"It's not what you did to her, Rick. It goes back a long way to when you and I broke up and you headed up to Alaska. Karen was my crutch. She was there for me when you weren't. It was a dark time for me and she was my salvation. She helped me through some tough days. In her eyes, you were a real shit. Can't say I blame her."

"You two stick together like syrup on pancakes. That wasn't an easy time for me either. But that was then and this is now so she'll just have to deal with it."

"We'll talk about this some other time, Rick. Now I just need to get back to work and figure out what we are going to tell the director. Waiting for those DNA results for two days is going to seem like an eternity."

CHAPTER 25

The bait shack had been open for business almost two hours when Jack Connors walked slowly up the stairs leading to the front door. While he was in good shape, jogging and mountain biking regularly, sixty-four hard years had begun to take some of the spryness from his legs. His double tours of duty as a US Marine scout sniper in the jungles of Vietnam had had the most impact on his physical and mental aging. He rarely talked of his combat experiences, but when he did, Jack would often respond to inquiries about the Vietnam War with his own altered version of a famous quote by Henry David Thoreau, "The mass of Vietnam vets simply lead lives of quiet desperation." Jack had seen more than his share of the horrors of war, and he had perpetrated many of his own horrors in the name of honor and duty. To this day, he had endured his own personal times of quiet desperation. Jack wasn't ashamed, nor did he ever feel a sense of guilt for what he had done for his country. He did what he knew was right and necessary, but sometimes late at night he would see the faces again as clearly as he had seem them through the scope mounted on his sniper rifle. Faces frozen in time and mind just as they were before he held his breath and squeezed the trigger.

Jack would have preferred to have been on the water at first light but he'd had a late night carving mallard decoys for one of his duck hunting buddies. He specialized in working decoys, those that are actually used for waterfowl hunting rather than purely decorative "birds" whose only functional purpose is to sit on a display shelf and look pretty. His carvings were all about function rather than form. Jack's decoys were in local demand by hunters as well as collectors of American folk art, but these days he only carved for his friends. When the demons of his scout sniper days would relocate to his consciousness, Jack found comfort in carving, the feel of wood and the shape of an evolving duck. The creative process cleared his mind and his soul. His were oversized decoys called magnums, much larger than the real-life ducks he hunted. Jack found that the bigger the "deek," the more easily it caught the eyes of greenheads. He painted his decoys with a unique impressionistic style that worked well to fool waterfowl. It took a lot of concentration and finishing time to transform blocks of basswood into an impression of a live mallard. When asked how he did it, Jack would say that every block of basswood had a decoy locked inside and it was his gift to give it freedom. Jack carved and painted birds throughout the previous night until he was completely exhausted. His head didn't hit the pillow until almost two in the morning and even then, the faces in the scope kept haunting him. This late morning start would have to do.

Jack had called Theo at The Shack the day before and told him to hold out some fresh bunker and two frozen chum blocks. This was to be a bluefish day, hopefully, a big bluefish day. With two days to go before the big money tournament kicked off for the holiday weekend, Jack wanted to take a practice run and fish a few of his favorite spots. Jack had been fishing these waters for more than fifty years and knew the local fishing better than anyone. His morning outing would be a secret honey hole off the northeast edge of the Stratford Shoal in the Middle Grounds, around half the distance between Long Island and Connecticut. Jack would run and gun, shoot and scoot, testing the waters to make sure fish were around.

While others knew the general whereabouts of this location, Jack planned to stay on the move. He didn't want to draw the attention of snooping eyes spying his intended fishing spots; the key to his success was to fish around one specific period of tidal movement. One of Jack's fondest sayings was that there are fishermen who are good at finding fish, and wannabes who are good at finding the fishermen who find fish. Jack also believed there were no longer any secret spots in the Sound, just spots that held their secrets. With fifty grand on the line, Jack didn't want to take any chances, so cloak and dagger was to be the order of the day. He told his wife that if conditions were right, he might stay on the water throughout the night and use the cover of darkness to explore other spots that might produce big fish.

"Top of the morning to you, Theo."

"And the rest of the day to you, Jack, I've got that bunker and chum for you. Been getting some good reports of big blues running the deep edges of the shoals and offshore structure. There's a ton of bait out there too. It's shaping up to be a good tournament. From what I'm hearing, they've gotten a record number of fishermen signed up already."

"Now that's just great. Every weekend warrior from the Bronx to Orient Point is going to be out on the Sound this weekend. Not to mention boats from Connecticut and other transients trailering from around the tri-state area. I hate fishing the thing but there's a ton of cash at stake."

Jack was also thinking that he promised Rick he would help out with the covert operation to gather some G-2 on those killer fish. Damn, this was beginning to feel like one of his long-range reconnaissance patrols behind enemy lines.

"I'll put this stuff on your tab," Theo said, and then added with a big smile, "You can settle up when you win the fifty Gs. What do you think will win it this year?"

"It'll take a bluefish of about eighteen to twenty pounds and I'm going to pin those suckers down right now."

Jack gathered up his bait and chum and walked back to his truck and trailer parked in the adjacent launch ramp lot. He loaded the bunker baits in the cooler that sat securely tethered with bungee cords behind the bench seat of his center console. And then he tossed the chum blocks in the fish box.

Jack's boat was an old style Sea Craft, a hull from the late seventies. He bought the boat with the money he saved while on active duty. There was not much to spend his meager military pay on in the boonies other than booze, hookers, and gambling, and Jack didn't gamble much. Those old hulls were some of the best center consoles ever built. Jack's boat was a Classic 20. He loved that boat more than any other material thing in his life. It was his ticket to freedom. Whenever life started to suck, which was more often than not these days, he filled up the gas tank and headed to the water. Jack learned early on in life that water was for him a therapeutic elixir, a chemical compound with extraordinary medicinal properties. Jack simply loved being around water; he adored being on it. He also hated crowds and that motivated him to find sanctuary away from the typical fleets that congregated on all the known hot spots. That penchant enabled Jack to build a coveted library of GPS coordinates of fishing spots that other fishermen would kill to acquire.

Jack admitted he was, first and foremost, a bait fisherman and big striped bass were his favorite quarry. He had become very proficient at catching big bass on all forms of local baits, dead or alive: eels, bunker, shad, clams, porgies, sea worms, crabs; if stripers ate it, he used it. He would also occasionally use taboo baits. Although illegal, Jack would sometimes bait up with live fluke and immature blackfish. The bass loved them and no authorities ever boarded his boat to check. Jack never killed more than his limit of bass, and often released his catch; and he simply refused to be told what baits he could or couldn't use. If another boat came too close, he would just cut his line or toss the evidence overboard. His biggest bass of sixty-two pounds was caught on a live tautog. The bass was photographed and released. Jack would say of that fish: "Something that has lived long and hard to grow that big wouldn't be killed by me."

Jack knew that for this trip he would need nothing more than bunker chunks and chum to entice big bluefish to eat. He motored straight from Port Roosevelt Harbor and headed north toward

Connecticut. It was a crystal clear day, his bow pointed in the direction of the Stratford Shoal Lighthouse. That would be his first stop
but not where he expected to do best. He needed to give the tide
some time to run hard on outgoing water. That's when his secret spot
would yield the best results. If there were other boats out there, Jack
would lead them astray much like a hen mallard feigning a broken
wing leads predators away from her nest.

Jack loved the way the Sea Craft hull cut through the water. Once
on plane, it was like a sharp knife cutting through butter. The hull just
floated above the surface of the water, a ride that he often described
as being velvety smooth. Jack loved too the equally smooth, steady
sound the Mercury engine made as it trimmed out to peak running
efficiency. It was a comforting and hypnotic sound. A clear plastic
window enclosure wrapped around the T-top that framed the boat's
center console. The enclosure was useful when navigating rough
water and windy fall conditions. The plastic side windows prevented
cold spray from soaking Jack but, at this time of year, Jack kept the
windows unzipped—the salt spray was refreshing in the heat.

Within twenty minutes of leaving the harbor, Jack was anchored
up about six hundred yards off the lighthouse. He took down two
heavy bait rods from the rocket launcher rod holders attached to
T-top. Jack threaded tough eighty-pound test braided line through
the guides of both heavy-action graphite chunking rods. Each rod
was matched to an equally heavy-duty conventional reel with gearing
that allowed for high-speed line gathering. The outfit in its totality—
rod, reel, and line—could handle just about any fish that swam in the
Sound, including some of the small- to medium-sized brown sharks
that roamed deep recesses of the mid-Sound. Jack had even taken
some hefty tuna off Montauk with this rig. His game plan was to fish
one rod with an un-weighted chunk of menhaden affixed to a size
6/0 Gamakatsu circle hook, allowing the bait to remain in the upper-
to mid-level reaches of the water column. He preferred a circle hook
since its unique design allowed the barb to set in the corner of a

fish's mouth rather than deep in the gullet. It's easier on the fish, and there's lower mortality for those fish that are released.

Circle hooks were especially useful with big bluefish since it was a lot easier to remove the hook from the corner of the jaw and not run the risk of tangling with a mouth full of stiletto-sharp dentition. Jack rigged a length of strong piano wire as a leader that would be resistant to the biting force of even the largest bluefish. Bluefish can easily bite through fishing line so wire was used as the material that comes into contact with their teeth. The second rod and reel was rigged in the same fashion but with the addition of lead sinker weights that would keep the baited hook near the bottom. Between the two rigs, Jack would cover the most probable depths in the water column where bluefish would feed. If the fish herded bait to the surface, Jack would be ready with a stout casting rod and reel rigged with a popping plug, an artificial bait that chugs along on the surface when retrieved. The plug makes a popping commotion that bluefish find irresistible.

The next order of business was for Jack to prepare the chum block and get an alluring slick of blood and guts oozing into the water. He took the still-frozen chum blocks and placed them in a mesh bag specially designed for facilitating the flow of chum. Once the bag containing the smelly mixture was placed in the warm water of the Sound, it began to defrost, allowing the contents to flow with the current. Eventually, the elongated slick acted like a highway that big bluefish would travel back up-current to the source of the free meal, and hopefully, to Jack's baited hooks. As Jack placed the chum bag overboard, he secured it to a transom cleat with a length of rope. He shook the bag in the water to agitate and activate the chum mixtures: fish meal, ground bunker, fish oil, and a variety of fish parts, including tails, heads, and guts.

Bluefish, like most other predatory fish, have the ability to sense their world by acquiring critical bits of data from their watery environment. Jack knew that if he wanted to stimulate a bluefish to strike his bait, he must first appeal to its sensory receptors. Learn how fish react to the environment and you will learn how to better motivate them to accept your offerings. Through a unique sense of electro-reception, predatory fish like bluefish also have the ability to sense electrical impulses given off by distressed prey. Through years of evolution, bluefish have developed a keen sense of sight. The obvious connection between sight and prey is that what a fish can see will often get their attention and result in further investigation. Jack's quarry also have internal ears and a lateral line that aids in the process of hearing and feeling through vibrations produced in their environment. The lateral line is especially valuable in enabling a predatory fish to sense and feel the presence of other fish, prey in particular. Rows and clumps of receptor cells help bluefish to precisely locate food. It is able to detect disruptions in water like ripples made by struggling prey, and relay those to the brain through electrical impulses and unique nerve fibers. Fish also have the ability to smell via chemical reception. Through an arrangement of nostrils and an olfactory rosette, fish are able to detect and distinguish chemicals, often in minute quantities. Fish can actually taste through taste buds in their mouths and on their lips, tongues, and faces. That innate sense of smell was what Jack would use to his advantage to lure big bluefish to his baits.

As the chum bag emitted its arousing aromas, Jack placed his baits in the water. The reel was in free-spool as the first bait was allowed to descend toward bottom. He had marked some fish on his electronic fish finder at about seventy-two feet down and hugging the bottom. Jack let the bait hit bottom and then crank up three turns on the reel so the bait could hang seductively. Jack allowed the second bait to float enticingly on the currents without any hindrance from lead weights or any line resistance. With that part of his task done, Jack sat on a cushioned bench seat that backed up to the center console. The seat had a pivoting backrest that Jack positioned it in a way so that when sitting on the cushion, he was facing the transom of the boat. That way he could watch the slick develop behind the boat, and be sure to spot any surface activity. Jack was dead-sticking both bunker baits, leaving them each unattended in vertical rod holders mounted on the rear of the gunwales. He placed one rod on the port side of the boat and one on the starboard side. Jack kept a third rod at the ready rigged with a large top-water plug he could cast toward any fish breaking the surface as they traveled up the chum slick to its source.

Jack gave this spot about an hour an then moved a short distance to another location more suitable to the later phase of tide. He set up again and waited. To pass the time, Jack plugged in the earpieces to his iPod and sang along to some of his favorite Willie Nelson songs. Jack had idolized the singer since first listening to his music in Vietnam. It was the poetry of Willie's lyrics that captivated him, and he owned every song Willie ever wrote or sang, helping him during bouts of depression and posttraumatic stress syndrome after the war. Jack belted out the lyrics to *Good Hearted Woman* as the chum slick began to draw the first of its visitors.

CHAPTER 26

When Katie arrived at Fish and Game headquarters, Nick was pacing the floor in anticipation of her arrival. "What the hell took you so long? Gunther is having a shit fit. Seems someone leaked a rumor to News Long Island about giant snakeheads in the Sound attacking and killing people. It's all over the damn news tickers and airwaves."

"First, I needed to spend time with Karen to make sure we get the DNA results we want. Second, we hit construction traffic. What else is new on Long Island? And third, snakeheads? What moron broke that dumb ass story?" Katie said, amazed by the stupidity.

"Seems some hot shot New York City media mogul who has a house in Bridgehampton got wind of the incidents in the Sound and made waves with local police. He wanted to know if what was happening in the Sound presented a threat to the waters around the Hamptons. Guess he was afraid some of his summer guests might get their asses bitten off swimming in the surf. Well, the local gendarmes hadn't a clue what was going on so the mogul took matters into his own hands and went directly to the top rung on the political ladder."

"Okay, so he pulled some strings for answers, but where do the snakeheads fit in?" Katie said.

"The media guy assigned one of his investigative reporters to the case and she somehow concluded, after talking with local commercial fishermen, that the most probable culprits in these cases are some oversized snakeheads. Plus she saw a show on one of the cable channels about snakeheads and is convinced they've migrated up here to Long Island. She's also convinced they have an appetite for small dogs and small children. So she briefed her boss and he was all over it like flies at an outhouse."

"Snakeheads are an invasive freshwater species! There is no way they could survive the ecosystem of the Sound, let alone the higher salinity of the Atlantic Ocean. Those commercial fishermen were pulling her leg just for entertainment."

"I know that, Katie, but we'd better get in to see Ted before he puts out an APB on you or worse yet, a hit. The guy is pissed big time. Never seen him this much on edge."

Ted Gunther was beyond being pissed; he was on the verge of panic. Not only were his superiors on his back about the unsolved deaths and disappearances in the Sound, but now they were all over him about the snakehead stupidity and the resulting media frenzy it had generated. They expected him to diffuse the situation, put a lid on it, and then make it go away. One of the directors in Albany told him in no uncertain terms that . . . *if thing gets out of control you'll be feeding food pellets to trout at the Cold Spring hatchery for the rest of your career.* Ted Gunther was about to vent his pent up anger on the next two employees to walk into his office.

"Glad you could join us, Dr. DiNardo. I hope all is well with you? Would you be so kind as to tell me what is going on with your investigation? I mean, do we have a damn clue as to what sort of marine aberration is killing people? You do remember that body parts are showing up on beaches, dogs are disappearing, and the county is a little lighter by a few residents. Oh, and lest I forget, your buddy here told me more about your little encounter on the beach the other night. From what I hear your boyfriend, Rick, is lucky he's not now a castrato singing with the Vienna Boys Choir."

Katie gave Nick a piercing look. Had her eyes been lasers, Nick would have been fried.

"We have leads and we have new evidence, and thank you for putting in the call to the folks at the lab. My friend Karen is . . ."

"Yeah, yeah, yeah, I know all about that. I made the call as much to save my ass I did to save yours. Albany is swarming over this investigation. Even the governor is involved. He's planning a family vacation to Montauk and wants to know if it's safe for his kids to go in the water. His assistants are calling every hour on the hour to get updates. We have a press conference in two hours, my phone hasn't stopped ringing, and I have a killer headache. What are we going to say?"

"We can say we are close to understanding what is behind these unusual events and that we'll know better shortly what's going on."

"We are well beyond the understanding phase, Katie. We need to be recommending a course of action to the public now, especially with the holiday weekend coming up. Do you have any idea how much this county depends on tourism dollars? Last-minute cancellations could cost the local economy tens of millions. And on top of the lousy season the merchants have had this year because of the recession, this could be the straw that breaks the backs of many businesses and the county's tax revenue stream. This could all turn very ugly very fast."

Nick interjected. "Not to mention the risk of being eaten by some predatory marine creatures that are most likely fish. Preventing that seems to be priority one right now."

"*Brilliant*, Nick. *Wish* I had *thought* of *that.* Katie, the time clock is running out. Tell me what you got."

"Facts of the matter, Ted, are that other than the tooth DNA we are having analyzed at the lab, Nick and I are still uncertain what form of marine species perpetrated these attacks. Our evidence to date still strongly suggests some form of large fish-like animal but we have been unable to definitively prove that yet. From what I saw of the creature that attacked Rick, it definitely looked fish-like."

"Despite a lack of concrete evidence to finalize your conclusion, should we advise closing the beaches?" Gunther asked.

"When Karen finishes her DNA mapping, we should have our answers. But that is still two days from now. I can't go on record that some monster fish are the killers until then. But we need to say something. These things are a real risk to the public. The snakehead crap we can easily debunk."

"Yes, we need warnings, at minimum," Nick shot back.

Katie continued. "Let's look again at the facts we do know. Most of these incidents occurred late night or early morning. The dog attacks took place at dusk. The last attack we know of was the one involving Rick and that happened after midnight. The one common thread weaving through all events is that they occurred during the outgoing tide. If these fish are indeed some species mutation, they show a marked preference for dropping water and the accompanying currents and rips that form in the Sound during that tidal phase. The fast outgoing flow, especially around the full moon phases, moves bait around in a way that predators find favorable."

"So what are you saying here, Katie? Post a big tide chart on each of the beaches and warn bathers to run for their lives as the tide ebbs? I could just see that on Local 21 news."

"Something like that," Katie said. "Unless, of course we just close down the beaches"

"Where you going with this, Katie?" Nick said.

"Look. Since the newspapers broke the story, the entire Island is aware of the incidents. We could . . . "

"Correction, Katie. Make that the entire world," Ted said. This story is being followed now more closely than shark attacks. Why? Because so far this year, right here on Long Island, we have had more deaths and disappearances from whatever this creature is than all combined shark attacks in the entire United States. The spotlight is smack dab on us and it won't be long before every marine biologist on this planet is being quoted with an opinion. We need to manage the information flow before it becomes a multi-media three-ring circus with the three of us as sacrificial clowns."

Katie's retort was pointed. "This is much more than managing PR spin. I think we have but one choice here, Ted. We could shut down the beaches of the Sound completely until we have a handle on this. Even if Karen's DNA analysis doesn't prove my monster fish hypothesis, the immediate threat is still real. Those fish or whatever they are will still be swimming around, capable as ever of taking more lives. Remember, these are schooling creatures and there are most likely lots of them, not like singular and solitary rogue sharks. Knowing what perpetrated these crimes is just part one. The real issue is how do we eradicate the threat?"

"Katie, no one is going to close the beaches without hard evidence . . . especially this coming weekend. Even with the facts, it would be a battle. I need a Plan B. I need something softer to tell the press in about thirty minutes. After that, we can deal with Albany, the county executives, and local authorities about possible beach closures. That's not my call. That's not our call. We are being asked to provide facts. Even the police are looking our way. Their forensic teams came up short on this case."

"Look, Ted, after what I saw the other night on the beach, we have ourselves one big problem anyway we cut it. There are marine creatures out there capable of killing and feeding on humans. That's the bottom line."

"Softer. Give me something softer. I need to throw the press a bone."

"You just might be throwing them some bone from another victim." Katie was frustrated by the lack of hard facts and her partner sensed it.

"How about this?" Nick said. "We make a statement that there have been a number of tragic incidents in the Long Island Sound and that we are confident this is not the work of snakeheads. Right out of the gate, we lead with an encouraging statement. Diffuse that part of the situation and take the wind out of their sails from the get-go. We add that we have very strong leads that should result in conclusive findings within the next couple of days. In the interim, we suggest that bathers refrain from swimming in the Sound or at least stay out of the water during early morning, dusk, and nighttime hours."

"What about the tide issue?" Ted asked.

"We steer clear of that," Katie replied. "It will only confuse the matter for public consumption. In my opinion, tide relevance must converge with time of day. Time and tide appear mutually dependent with regards to the attacks. So at minimum, if we keep people out of the water during critical hours of the day, we eliminate one of two key variables. I believe this will lessen the chances of further attacks. I know you want a Plan B, Ted, but the only real choice we have is to close down the beaches entirely until we figure this out. We can't risk another injury or death."

"Once we go public with restricted beach access at certain times of the day we are doomed to evoke certain panic." Ted said. "We can write the headline now: *Killer Fish Prowl Long Island Sound Beaches, Eat Residents.*" Ted thought: just two more years until retirement and this shit has to happen to me. "And once the Hamptons crowd sinks their teeth further into this it will be the end-of-summer *cause célèbre*. They'll be making a movie before we even solve the case. But enough said. It's time to go face the music. I'll make the statement but you two be prepared to answer questions. And remember: be political. Don't commit to anything and try to be vague. We want to keep this short and sweet."

The press had gathered in the main meeting room in the Fish and Game building on the campus of the State University. It was a packed house. Local and regional press and TV crews were in attendance. As Katie, Nick, and Ted walked to the front of the room Katie spotted Detective Spinello standing along a sidewall. Their eyes met and he winked at her. It was a roguish wink and she instantly knew this press conference was not going to be fun.

CHAPTER 27

Jack continued to sing along with another Willie Nelson classic, "On the Road Again." He was in his own hypnotic musical trance when he glanced back over the transom. Jack came to immediate attention as he watched fish break the surface about three hundred yards off the back of the boat. He popped the iPod earpieces out and turned the device off. Now standing, he readied himself for the oncoming fish. He could tell they were bluefish by the way they behaved, slashing feverishly along the edges of the slick. His still-acute scout sniper eyesight focused intently on the chaotic feeding. Jack grabbed the rod rigged with the casting plug, known as a popper, and waited for the half-acre of bluefish to swim within range. He watched as they cut through the chum slick that had attracted all varieties of small baitfish. The feeding bluefish enjoyed an assorted buffet of floating chum and live prey.

The school appeared large, perhaps as many as several hundred individual fish, and they looked big. Confirmation of that came with the first hook-up. The fish moved rapidly up the chum slick and within minutes were within range. Jack made his first cast. The white and red popping plug landed in the middle of the melee. It took just one "pop" of the plug to elicit an explosive strike. The plug was thrown far into the air as a ravenous bluefish whacked it, but missed getting hooked. No sooner had the gyrating plug landed back on the water had another fish raced toward it and engulfed the lure, tough, sharp teeth penetrating into hard plastic. There was no way bluefish would let anything escape the killing field.

Feeling the fish's bulk, Jack set the hook and was pleased at the substantive weight attached to the end of his line. The bluefish fought hard for its freedom and made several desperate leaps from the water, attempting to rid itself of the fraudulent bait that was hooked to its jaws. It took a few minutes before Jack was able to place a Boga grip onto the jaws of the bluefish. The Boga grip is a device that enables an angler to safely extricate a fish from the water without actually touching the fish. With bluefish, that is a good thing since the gripping device kept fingers away from menacing and dangerous teeth. The tool is also equipped with a built-in weight scale. Hoisting the fish from the water Jack read the weight at fourteen and a half pounds. Not a bad start to the day but he needed to find bigger fish if he was to be competitive in the weekend tournament.

Jack made another cast and another bluefish of equal size pounced on the plug. As he fought the fish the free-floating line baited with a chunk of menhaden began to free spool off the reel, signaling that something had taken the bait. Jack reached over and engaged the anti-reverse lever on the reel, stopping the spool from spinning. As soon as the line tightened, the rod tip slammed downward as a big bluefish hooked itself. With two big fish on, Jack had his hands full. It got even more challenging as the third rod tip also slammed down on the gunwale. What interested Jack most was that there were fish at every level of the water column. He had checked the electronic fish finder mounted to the center console and it recorded a solid, dense mass of markings that covered the entire screen. Bait and bluefish were thick from the surface to the bottom.

Jack fought and luckily landed all three fish, one at a time. What could have turned into folly with three big bluefish on the hook at the same time ended well. As is common with binge-feeding blue-fish, each fish regurgitated stomach contents as their bodies would spasm violently in response to being removed from the water. By the time the third bluefish evacuated its last meal, the whole stern section of the boat was littered with a concoction of chum bits, partially digested sand eels and spearing, and half-bitten peanut bunker. Jack was usually diligent about quickly cleaning up this vomit mess but he was distracted by a number of other larger bluefish rocketing straight from the water out toward the outer edge of the slick. Those fish caught his attention because bluefish leaping in that fashion were not representative of typical behavior. It was if they were being chased. As quickly as the fish leapt from the water, the activity had ceased. Jack thought that very odd, but he was hopeful those larger fish would make their way back up the slick and onto his hooks.

Jack contemplated making a move to a second spot to search for bigger fish but, rather than pull up anchor and set up all over again, he decided to give this chum slick more time to develop. There were no other boats in sight. Jack felt no urgency to conceal his findings from other fishermen. There were good-size fish around and he knew from experience the predictable progression of events. If fish were here at this stage of the tide, he thought, they would move to the second spot just as he had expected, yet, they'd cycle through his location first. He'd been through the drill many times before and knew what was coming. Jack recalled an old axiom of fishing, *don't leave fish to find fish.*

Jack's predatory antennae were up and sensitized. Although he couldn't explain it, he often knew of things that would happen before they actually did. Ever since he was a kid, Jack had this prescient ability and it became much more acute as he got older. Sometimes it was fun to sense what would be but at other times it was downright frightening. Like the time he was drawn back home to his first wife. Jack was on his way to Montauk to fish the surf with friends when an overwhelming sense of trepidation overcame him. He feared that all wasn't right at home. He didn't know precisely what was wrong but that something was seriously amiss. Although he was far out on the eastern portion of the Island at Amagansett when the feeling came over him, he turned the old green Ford Bronco around and raced back to Port Roosevelt, He was stopped only once by the county's finest, but when he explained the situation, the understanding officer ran interference and escorted him the last dozen or so miles from Patchogue. As they both rushed into Jack's small colonial home, Jack's wife, Stella, was on the bed, lips blue from lack of oxygen, and just barely breathing. She was an asthmatic. The attending ER physician at St Dominick's Hospital told Jack his timing was not a moment too soon because his wife was on the verge of losing consciousness and would have surely died soon thereafter from the episode. From that time on, Jack always paid attention to his feelings, as bizarre as they might be. And at the moment, Jack was having one of those revelations: something very big was very near and he could feel its presence.

The early movement of the tide drew many small baitfish to the manmade feast. Small bluefish and bass keyed on the scent and scraps. It didn't take long for the hierarchy of nature to play out its timeless food chain scenario. Big fish eat little fish and big fish get eaten by even bigger ones. Jack was on high alert for he knew large predators were close by. He re-rigged two of the outfits with fresh bunker chunks. The strong, laser-sharpened circle hooks were large enough to hold anything he might expect to now catch. For insurance, he rigged the hooks with extra strong wire to prevent the big blues from biting through the leaders. Since most of the fish were in the mid to upper levels of the water column, Jack removed the lead weight from the rig that was fished deep on the bottom. He baited the hook so the bunker chunk floated naturally in the chum slick. Jack positioned one of the baits close to the boat and the other farther out. Each rod was placed back in a rod holder, recessed into the gunwale, one on the port side and one on the starboard side of the boat's aft section. He kept the plugging rod at the ready in the event another casting opportunity arose. As much as he enjoyed catching big bluefish on bait, he enjoyed catching them with surface plugs even more. With all bases covered, he waited.

It didn't take long for fish to respond, the way bluefish often feed. Jack watched as a pod of ravenous fish moved within casting distance. He once again lobbed the big plug into the mix and was instantaneously fast to a huge chopper bluefish. *Now this is more like it*, he thought. After decades of give and take with large bluefish, Jack could tell simply by feel that this fish would push sixteen pounds. When the bluefish jumped, he smiled. Jack knew he'd found the pot of gold. The fish was strong. Its time at sea fighting currents had built muscle mass like that of a well-conditioned athlete. And Lord knows, it ate well. Once bluefish attained this size, little else would threaten them save big sharks and tunas, some marine mammals . . . and man. The bluefish jumped again but this time a cavernous mouth followed it out of the water. In an instant, the line went slack. Jack watched as an enormous forked tail broke the surface. What remained was a huge black hole in the Sound. It was as if someone dropped a compact car into the water.

"What the hell was that?" Jack said out loud. "Holy shit, that was a fucking sea monster."

As if with synchronized movement, the tips of both baited fishing rods slammed downward simultaneously; line screamed off the reels. But the bluefish that had taken Jack's bait were not all that was on the end of the fishing lines. Jack was still in shock at what he had just seen, but ingrained habit and muscle memory caused him to reach for the portside rod and ensure the hook had set securely. His mind was still on the sight he had witnessed. Jack became distracted and did something he shouldn't have done. Fighting two big fish at the same time was fine when he had another fisherman on board, but to play the game solo was asking for trouble. At minimum, you'd lose one of the fish; worst case, you'd lose them both. Jack hadn't anticipated the third scenario.

While tightly grasping one rod in his left hand, Jack took hold of the other with his right hand and waited for the line to come tight and for the hook's barb to securely fasten into the jaw of the fish.

Once he felt weight, Jack swiftly swept the rod tip up to remain in contact with his hooked quarry. As his right arm came back to set the hook, the other rod surged sharply downward in the water. Jack reacted by again pulling back sharply on that rod. The energy generated by both Jack's rapid, awkward, and upward arm movements caused him to lose balance. Jack tried regaining equilibrium but he slipped on the fish vomit carelessly left on deck. He was pissed at himself for such an amateurish oversight. Jack's momentum caused him to tumble forward. He knew instantly he was in trouble as he lost all footing and fell completely over the transom and into the water. Instinctively, Jack tried bracing for the fall and dropped the fishing rods so that his arms and not his head would lead the way as he plunged in to the water.

Had Jack merely fallen overboard, all would have been well. He was a good swimmer and, putting the personal embarrassment aside, Jack would have been able to pull himself back over the corner of the transom and to the safety of his boat. But the situation deteriorated rapidly and things became much more complicated. Both fishing lines had entangled Jack's feet, wrapping tightly around crisscrossed ankles. His feet were bound together tightly as if he were shackled. Jack's first reaction was to cut the lines with the Leatherman, a multipurpose outdoor tool usually sheathed in holster on his belt. As Jack reached for the tool, he got a sickening feeling in the pit of his stomach. He had used the Leatherman when rigging the rods and had placed it on top of the center console. The sheath was empty. Jack was not one to panic. He'd come close to death many times during his tours in 'Nam. On several of his scouting sessions, his position was almost compromised and he came close to being captured by the Viet Cong. That would have met with a fate much worse than falling overboard and being stuck in some fishing lines. His brain raced to process the details of his current dilemma. He had to hurry but he knew he would figure out a solution. There had to be a solution. Jack's situation worsened rapidly. There was no time to think clearly because two very powerful fish pulled him across the surface of the water as they raced to the safety of their school. The super powerful fish stayed in the top portion of the water column, effortlessly pulling Jack along like a water skier, Jack bouncing across the small waves, his buttocks acting as a boogie board. Jack knew he was in trouble. He also knew what would come next.

Jack tried in vain to undo his feet from the braided lines. He even tried pulling on the lines to gain some slack and wiggle his feet free. But each time he did so, the fish pulled harder and the unforgiving braid line cut through his fingers and hands. Had the line been lighter weight monofilament, Jack might have been able to break it with a few tricks his father had taught him many years ago. Without his Leatherman, the combined strength of the two eighty-pound braid lines was more than Jack could handle with his bare hands.

The two fish headed out over deep water. It was what Jack had feared. The school was sounding and Jack's two captors would follow with him in tow. *Think, man, think. I can't have my life end with two fucking fish drowning me like this*. Jack had only one option. He had to pull back on the line as violently as the fish were pulling him forward. He would apply pure leg strength against the force of the fish. If he knew where the fishing rods were, he might use one or both to somehow twist the lines and break them. But Jack guessed that the rods were somewhere far behind him with the remaining line paying out from the reels. Jack was still being towed along the surface as he pulled both legs back up into his body in rapid and repeated motions as if performing some diabolical abdominal muscle exercise. His hope was that he might either pull the hooks free from the jaws of the fish or uncover some weakness in the lines that would cause them to break. Jack knew he was down to minutes if not seconds before the inevitable happened. He marshaled all the strength that remained in his tiring body and pulled his legs up aggressively in succession. The line did not part nor did the hooks pull free. Jack felt his legs involuntarily move from a horizontal position along the surface to an almost vertical downward facing angle. The fish were diving. Jack knew he was about to go under. He took several deep breaths, holding the last precious gulp of air as his head submerged. These demons would show no mercy. Jack stopped all leg movement to conserve oxygen. Without a means to disentangle from the death grip of the fishing lines, he would have no more than two minutes to live.

Both fish pulled in unison and dragged Jack into deeper water. Their collective strength overpowered him. He strained to look up but when he did he could faintly see daylight above the surface. *So this is how it ends*, he thought. He always kidded with his fishing buddies that when his time came, he wanted a big fish to be on the other end of the line. But this . . . Jack had to be thinking, *be careful what you wish*. This was not at all what he had in mind. Jack was down about twenty feet when the pulling stopped. For a moment, he felt free. *Could this be? Had the line finally broken?* He used his arms as a bird flaps its wings in flight. He thought he could propel himself upward toward the surface and toward a life-saving breath of air. He had only moved himself up a few feet when the slack lines once again became taught. The pulling had stopped but his adversaries were still there. Jack could feel their presence. He could feel their vibrations through the throbbing line. He also had a feeling these fish were now playing with him.

Jack had less than a minute to live. His lungs were burning as he started to surrender to the sea. That last minute would seem like an eternity as his mind processed many events of his life. Jack closed his eyes and saw Stella and his daughters. And he saw his grandmother holding out her hand welcoming him to the other side. *I love you, Grandma, but fuck the other side. I'm not ready for this*. Jack tried valiantly to fend off death but as he did his mind revealed others in the background. He could vaguely make out the faces of his father and grandfather smiling. Jack pointed at his father and shook his head as if saying, *I'm not ready to die, Dad*. But Jack's mind and body were surrendering. He was losing control. Oddly, he now felt at ease, a sense of liberation. Perhaps stored memories eased the pain of Jack's final moments. With but seconds of his life remaining, Jack sensed an abnormal presence and he opened his eyes. With fins erect and snapping monster-like jaws, they moved with deliberate and erratic motions. They swarmed around Jack and waited to strike.

There was still enough oxygen in Jack's brain to keep his mind functioning and aware. He closed his eyes and then reopened them to make certain his brain wasn't playing tricks. When his eyes opened a second time, much to his amazement, he saw not the horrifying assassins but the vision of a mermaid. *I must be dead,* Jack thought, *and she must be leading me to paradise.* Jack felt her gently caress him and he sensed his body floating upward toward the surface. *I'm on my way toward heaven.* Jack saw the light. It was an unmistakable bright white light, and he floated, closer toward the illuminated orb. The last thing Jack's mind processed before he lost all consciousness were words from his favorite Willie Nelson song, "Angel Flying Too Close to the Ground."

CHAPTER 28

Ted Gunther walked to the podium and called the press conference to order. He was surprised at the number of people who'd gathered in the main lecture hall of the Marine Sciences Building at the State University. Reporters from all local media were in attendance, from small community tabloids to the omnipresent *Long Island Newsweek* and the *New York Daily News*. The session had also gotten the attention of the *New York Times*. A reporter from the *Wall Street Journal* was also present; he occasionally would cover fishing and fisheries-related stories. But what troubled Ted even more were the TV cameras. He hadn't expected that much visibility. As his eyes scanned the room, he saw cameras with network logos from across the region: Local News 21, ABC, CBS, and Fox. And way in the back of the room he spotted a camera from SFN, the Sport Fishing Network. He had to chuckle at that one thinking, *Those guys will go anywhere for a fish story*. With all this TV coverage, Ted also thought that if he was to go down in flames over these incidents at least it would be in full color and high definition.

Ted's boss, William Charles III, was standing behind him, flanked by Katie DiNardo and Nick Tanner. Ted tapped his pen on the podium and tapped his toes on the carpet, sure signs he was ill at ease. He took a quick sip of water and began. "I'd like to thank you all for attending." The room instantly quieted. "I'll try to keep this short and then take your questions." Ted glanced over at Katie, put on his game face, and continued.

"Four days ago, a body washed up on a beach in Smith's Bay. The Division of Marine Sciences has been working with county police in an attempt to identify the victim and the cause of death. While there are no concrete leads to the case, there is considerable evidence to suggest that some form of marine life may have been involved in the incident, either as the direct cause of the death or as part of a post-mortem episode. Subsequent to that event, there have been several other local incidents of similar nature that have yet to be explained. We are not certain if all events are related in any way or if they are simply random and coincidental. The Division's two most experienced marine researchers, Dr. Katie DiNardo and Dr. Nick Tanner, have been assigned as lead investigators on the Smith's Bay case as well as to the other incidents. Their role is to assist local authorities in determining what contributed to the deaths and disappearances. In that role both, Dr. DiNardo and Dr. Tanner have thoroughly analyzed all available evidence. At this point in the investigation, we can unequivocally rule out the outlandish rumors that have been spread of alligators, crocodiles, komodo dragons, and monster snakeheads. None of those creatures have had anything to do with this case."

Ted Gunther noticed many heads in the audience nodding in apparent approval of his comments and he felt like he was on a roll. But just when he sensed that he had gained somewhat of an early advantage with this crowd, a voice rang out from the back of the room:

"Yeah, then what did? We don't want to know what's not involved in these incidents, we want to know what's killing people in the Long Island Sound."

Ted remained composed and responded firmly. "Please, we will respond to all your questions after our statement."

The voice shot back. "Why wait? Answer the question now. No need to rehash what we already know."

As best as Ted could tell, the heckler was barking his questions from behind one of the cameramen. Rather than challenge the questioner and risk more of an outcry from other media members, Ted choose to acknowledge the question. It was a good move on his part since other reporters were beginning to move toward the heckler.

"If you identify yourself, sir, I will answer your question."

After a brief moment of silence, a young man walked out into view from his position behind the News 21 camera. All eyes in the room turned toward him. "My name is Jake Dodd and I was a friend of who you referred to as the Smith's Bay victim. I think you may have grossly understated his condition when he was found. It was more like body pieces than a body."

Gunther interrupted. "No name has yet been officially released of any victim, Mr. Dodd."

"Yeah, I know. But his family and friends know it was him. He went fishing that night and never returned. The cops told his family that a print was recovered from a severed hand and they had a positive ID. Everything else is bullshit. In case you are not sure, his name was Jimmy McVee, one of the best surf fishermen on Long Island. Been fishing all his life and knew the local waters and its fish better than anyone. What got him had to have been something very strange. Jimmy was too good to make foolish mistakes on the water or to take unnecessary chances. I fished with him for years and I know."

Others in the room now stirred and a few shouted questions at Jake. Ted needed to regain control.

"Thank you, Mr. Dodd, for your input but since this an active crime investigation. I will leave the specific issues pertaining to the victim to the police."

"That's not good enough, Mr. Gunther. The people in this room and the residents of Long Island have a right to know what the hell's going on here. It's time to come clean about all this."

All TV cameras were trained directly on Jake Dodd. Ted heard the rumblings of others in the audience and he needed to diffuse the situation fast, but before he could again take charge of the meeting, the reporter from *Long Island Newsweek* stood up. Dorothy Whitman had been part of an investigative reporting team that broke a blockbuster story on corruption in a number of Long Island school districts.

It earned Ms. Whitman and her team a Pulitzer Prize. Her investigative reporting skills were as good as they come. She had an uncanny ability to quickly cut through the bull crap and get to the heart of a story.

"Mr. Gunther, I realize you want to get through your prepared remarks but if you don't mind, might I ask you a question?"

Ted sensed trouble but he didn't want to appear as if he was backing down.

"I've read your columns, Ms. Whitman. I enjoy your work. Please, ask your question."

"We've obtained some firsthand information that all the incidents taking place in the Sound recently are linked through forensic bite mark evidence, making the deaths all part of apparent serial killings. Furthermore, we have reason to believe that your folks have a pretty good idea what's behind these deaths. Are those two points accurate, Mr. Gunther?"

Ted did not like where this questioning was headed. Ms. Whitman certainly could cut to the chase. No wonder she won a Pulitzer. He knew if he answered in the affirmative, he would create a media feeding frenzy that would rival that of the feeding killers, but if he hedged his answer, Ms. Whitman would be on it in a heartbeat.

Just as Ted was about to answer, his boss leaned over to whisper in his ear. As William Charles III conveyed his message, Ted's eyes moved to lock onto Katie DiNardo.

Katie knew instantly where this was going. *Damn,* she thought. They are going to throw me into the breach.

"I'd like to ask Dr. DiNardo to respond to that question. She is our most senior marine biologist and has been intimately involved in the incidents in question."

Katie took a position in front of the microphone and did a once over of the crowd. All the cameras and reporters were focused on her. She was in the spotlight and she was uncertain what to say.

Impatient, Whitman broke the silence. "Okay, Dr. DiNardo, you are the expert, so what do you have to say about all this?"

Katie looked up again and spotted Rick standing in the far left-hand corner of the room. His presence gave her strength. "Yes, Ms. Whitman, we do have substantial bite evidence that is linked but as I have maintained throughout the entire course of this investigation, proving what actually caused the bites has not been an easy task, even for experts. And as I've said previously, we are not yet certain if the bites themselves were the actual cause of death or a by-product of postmortem assaults."

"That just doesn't cut it, Dr. DiNardo. Human beings are dead, similar and bizarre bite marks are in evidence in each of the incidents, and the gurus haven't a clue what's involved? I was born in the morning but not yesterday morning. What if I told you that a source told me that you actually have some strong evidence of what these creatures are? Say a tooth? Now how would you respond to that?"

Katie knew she couldn't dodge this one, but she still had to be careful. She glanced quickly at Rick and addressed the questions directly on, but just a bit cagey. "I'd say your source is pretty good, Ms. Whitman. At each of the incident sites, we have tried to gather as much organic evidence as was possible. For the most part, there has been little or any meaningful evidence. Bite marks have been our strongest leads. But the other morning at Plover Dunes where all those striped bass were found, we took samples of the flesh that had been bitten to see if perhaps there might be some DNA present that would give us a clue to the attackers. And at one of the other scenes, we discovered something that appeared to be a tooth. From what, we really have no idea." Katie hedged a bit with that answer but there was no way she was going to tell this crowd that her lover was almost eaten. "We are just following all possible evidence trails. But as you may know, organic material of that nature takes a long time to evaluate so no conclusions have been drawn yet. Without that DNA mapping, we cannot even begin to speculate as to what these unknown creatures are or aren't, or if they at all had anything to do with the killings."

Whitman contemplated that response and asked a follow-up. "Do the bite marks that you've seen suggest any known species of marine animal?"

"Simply put, Ms. Whitman, not that we know."

"Okay then, a simply yes or no from you. Do you believe that what caused those bite marks actually killed the people involved in the incidents?"

"I'm a scientist, Ms. Whitman, not one prone to wild guessing. While I do not yet know what did in fact cause those wounds, and the deaths in question, there is as much a chance that those bites were the cause of death as not being the cause of death."

Whitman ratcheted up the rhetoric. "This is no time for equivocation, Ms. DiNardo." The subtle change in how Whitman formally addressed Katie did not go unnoticed. The reporter was feeling a sense of superiority at having the scientist on the ropes. "People's lives may be at stake here in the coming days, especially with the big end of summer weekend upon us and water sports among the plans of many residents. As one concerned resident and a concerned parent, should I allow my children to go in the waters of the Sound this weekend or any waters around Long Island for that matter?"

Katie felt boxed and she was hoping for some help. She look at Nick and then at Ted Gunther. Katie was prepared to say, *No, you should not allow your children in the water under any circumstances and the beaches should be closed immediately,* when William Charles III, her boss's boss, finally spoke.

"Ms. Whitman, we are all concerned parents. Dr. DiNardo has responded as truthfully as possible given the facts at our disposal. While we do not have definitive answers at the moment, we hopefully will in a few days. My advice to you and everyone on Long Island is the same advice I will give to my own family. We have been confronted with some strange occurrences in the Long Island Sound that have had possible links to a number of unexplained deaths and I would encourage you all to exercise extreme caution when recreating in the waters of the Long Island Sound and be on alert for any unusual marine animal activity. Should additional information come to our attention that identifies a more severe threat or that warrants beach closures, rest assured we will act with all appropriate urgency. If there are no further questions, we will end this press conference."

Ms. Whitman again spoke, "I thank you for that sincere reply but lives are at stake here, perhaps many lives. After we learn what's doing this, how will we capture or kill it before it kills more of us?"

Those in the room became noticeably more restless as that question sunk in. Katie knew there was no answer. If her instincts were right, they would confirm the killer's identity within a day or two but determining how many of the things were out there was the great unknown. If it proved to be the deviant fish she feared, eliminating the threat was of a magnitude bordering on the impossible. She was relieved when William Charles III fielded this question."Ms. Whitman, until we know what enemy we are confronting, we will not know how to defeat it. Beyond that we can say no more. I thank you all for coming."

Ted Gunther realized this press conference would now lead to mass media exposure of the situation. That would lead to massive local and state-wide political pressure and worldwide coverage of the incidents. This was turning ugly fast and he was running out of options. All now hinged on Katie's DNA evidence. All he said to Katie before leaving the room was that she needed to push her friend even harder now to evaluate the tissue samples from the tooth and that he would call her. Ted and his boss exited the podium through a back door, talking strategy as they walked.

Katie and Nick walked to the exit at the back of the room where Rick was still standing. Just before reaching Rick, a man in his late thirties or early forties walked up and handed Katie a business card and said, "Call me soon, we need to talk." The name on the business card read Ned Mack Jr., PhD, Senior Scientist, Evolutionary Biology, Riverstone National Laboratory.

CHAPTER 29

Katie, Rick, and Nick stopped for a drink at Bailey's Pub in downtown Port Rosey. It was a small bar the biker crowd liked to frequent on weekends but it was now without any other patrons. It was a good place to decompress from the stress of the news conference.

"Three Blue Point Summer Ales," Rick said to the waitress as they were seated. He turned to Katie and said, "We got us a big problem here. The lid is about to blow off this thing major league. We may not have any time to play games with these fish on the weekend. That may be too late."

"Rick, I know that all too well. What scares the hell out of me is that we're not going to be able to stop this. I'm pretty certain this is an entire school of fish and there is no way we can catch them all, regardless of what they are. So whatever Karen tells me about the genetics of these monsters, great. What do we do next, throw depth charges at them?"

"Let's take this one step at a time," Nick said. "We really need to understand the adversary first. Perhaps when we know what it is and how it evolved, that might give us a clue to how we can destroy it."

"Nick, you didn't see those things on the beach the other night. Rick came within inches of being killed by creatures unlike anything I have ever seen or studied. Their eyes were penetrating like something from another world. When that fish came out from the water, all I could think was *sea monster.* I got the distinct feeling they could reason and plot and carry out an attack plan."

"Pure instincts, Katie, nothing more, nothing less."

"Here you go folks, three Blue Points. Can I get you anything else?"

"Not just yet. Thanks," Rick said.

Katie continued. "Perhaps, Nick, but in two days, our worst fears could be realized. Hundreds of boats will be on the water for the bluefish tournament, recreational boaters, kayakers, and swimmers will invade every port and beach along the Long Island shoreline of the Sound, not to mention an equally sized armada and mass of humanity across the Sound in Connecticut. And we have mutant fish of unknown origins killing people. Tell me that's not a formula for a master disaster?"

Rick wanted to be gentle but he couldn't hold back. "It's going to be a lot worse than that, Katie. After today's press conference, this story is sure to become sensationalized. Believe me when I tell you, there may be ten times the number of folks on the water this weekend than usual, drawn to the danger and the notoriety that will come from catching one of these things. That's going to be a worse frenzy than anything the fish might offer. And if some weekend warriors latch on to these beasts, it will be a mess."

"I know, I know, Rick. And here's where it gets even more complicated, if that's possible. If these things are in fact some genetic mutant, we don't know how they will react to all the activity on the Sound this weekend. Will they become reclusive and retreat to the depths of the Sound or will they respond to all the activity as stimuli and become even more aggressive? God, this is all making my head spin."

Katie's phone rang. "Oh, hello, Ted. What's up? I'm in Port Rosey. No, I haven't heard from Karen yet. My guess is that I won't until late tomorrow at the earliest. I'll let you know as soon as I hear something."

Katie listened intently do her boss and then spoke. "Who decided that? The Governor and Homeland Security. Wow! That escalated fast. Not sure how much that will help as a deterrent but it will surely keep the yahoos in check out on the water this weekend. Okay, I'll let Nick know and I'll be in touch."

"What was that all about?" Nick asked.

"Ted said that he and his boss had a conference call after the meeting with all agencies involved in the investigation and that included the Governor's Office and the Office of Homeland Security. It seems the way the press conference ended, they had the same reaction as Rick and they feel there will be a lot of news coverage and a lot more folks on the water this weekend . . . curiosity seekers. So the authorities have decided to divert additional marine police and extra Coast Guard vessels to this part of the Island for the weekend. They are also going to have police on quads and four-by-fours patrolling all the north shore beaches. That should be quite a scene but a good decision, nonetheless."

"That will be great for PR and for controlling the DUIs but not worth a darn for deterring any further attacks," Nick said.

"Nick, I have this nauseating feeling that no matter what we do, we won't be able prevent these fish from striking again. And given their numbers, how do we ever stop them from breeding? God, knowing what they are is just the tip of the iceberg."

"That may very well be true, Katie, but until we know what the devil we are dealing with, we won't have a clue to managing the problem. And for all we know, these things may be working their way out of the Sound."

"Oh that's great, Nick. Our problem then becomes someone else's nightmare. We can't let that happen."

Rick interjected. "How about we get a bite to eat and then we can take a run out into the Sound? I've got a full tank of gas and the outgoing tide starts to flow just before dusk. We might just bump into something. If for nothing else, the salt air might do us all a bit of good to clear our heads."

"Sounds good," Katie replied. "By the way, have you heard from Jack lately? I wonder if he's encountered anything else out there?"

"I'm sure if he had, he would have called but I'll ring him up in a bit and check in."

"Unfortunately folks, I will have to pass on dinner and the sunset cruise. I'll leave that to you two lovebirds. I have a prior commitment."

"What's his name?" Rick said, an impish glint in eyes.

"Rick, you stop that!" Katie shot back.

Nick just smiled and in retort said simply, "You should only know." He then winked at Rick and said he would talk to them later.

"Rick, I really wish you wouldn't kid around like that with Nick. He is a sensitive guy."

"Who was kidding?"

"Sometimes you are just beyond being a idiot. Let's get something light to eat and go on the Sound. And please, try to track down Jack. I want to ask him if he's encountered any other strange activities. I'm going to the ladies room. Order me a chicken salad sandwich. And another beer."

Rick dialed Jack's cell phone number. The call immediately went to voicemail: *Hello, you've reached Jack. If you are hearing this message, I'm mostly likely fishing and I don't want to be bothered. Leave a message at the beep and I'll return the call whenever. Thank you.*

That's my Jack, Rick thought. *Ever the diplomat*. Rick then dialed Jack's home phone number. Jack's wife answered.

"Hi Carole, it's Rick. How's your summer going? All set for the big weekend? Yep, barbeques and fishing, that's on the agenda for me too. Thanks, I'll try to stop by. Hey, I've been trying to track down Jack. His cell is on voice mail so I figured I would try the house."

Carole explained to Rick that Jack had gone out earlier that morning and said he might stay on the water overnight. She also said she was surprised that she had not heard from him yet. It was unlike Jack not to check in while out fishing.

"I'm sure he is okay, Carole. I've known Jack to throw out the anchor and enjoy a good sleep, especially after a hard day's fishing.

I'm heading out on the water with Katie after we get a bite to eat. I know most of his spots and will try to track him down."

"Okay Rick, thank you. By the way, it's nice to see you back with Katie. That girl is good for you. And if you see Jack out there please tell him to call home."

"Will do, Carole. Talk soon."

Katie had returned from the ladies room. "Who was that?"

"Jack's wife. He's still on the water. His cell phone is off. My bet is that he's sleeping somewhere out in the middle of the Sound."

CHAPTER 30

Jack Connors opened his eyes as his head poked through the surface of the water. To his astonishment, he seemed to still be alive and in one piece. How could that be? He remembered seeing the grotesque creatures encircle him, rigid bodies and jaws snapping, closing in for the kill. How could he forget the horrendous clicking and snapping sounds that brought unbearable pain to his inner ears. He remembered seeing the white light and the mermaid, an unexpected angel of mercy. *I must have been dead.* Then Jack realized he was still indeed among the living and had somehow been miraculously transported back to his boat. He touched the fiberglass. It was cool and very real. Unless they had room for Sea Craft boats in heaven, this one was still anchored in the Long Island Sound.

At the moment, Jack could not comprehend any of his circumstance but he needed to get out of the water. He was exhausted and while he had apparently survived a surreal encounter, the last thing he wanted to do was drown. Jack reached for the portside gunwale and tried pulling himself up and over but he was too weak from his ordeal. He shimmied his body along the side of the hull until he reached the motor. His hand grasped an open slot on the transom and he held tightly for a moment while catching his breath. Jack felt something bump his leg. Jolts of adrenaline shot through his body, a renewed strength took hold. With one Herculean surge of might, Jack pushed himself upward, catapulting his body from the water, over the motor, and onto the deck where he collapsed on his back.

God. Don't tell me those things are back. Jack righted himself and, on all fours, moved to have a look over the transom. What he saw made him laugh.

There beneath him in the water, swaying in the current, was his chum bucket still attached to the rope he had secured to one of the aft cleats. Jack was so relieved, he vomited in the water.

While Jack was coming to grips with the reality that he was still alive, Rick eased *Maya* out from her slip and into the southern end of Port Roosevelt Harbor. The ferry to Connecticut was just pulling out from the dock, filled with walk-on passengers and cars. Rick gave the big boat berth. She could cause quite a stir with her thruster engines while maneuvering to turn bow out and head north out into the Sound. Rick was in no rush. He had two miles of a no wake zone to navigate before he too made it to the outside. Since the ferry was a vessel of commerce, it did not need to heed the channel speed restriction and it barreled its way along, passengers on the top deck waving to all who would acknowledge them. Rick always felt that since he too was a commercial enterprise, a professional captain, and an active waterman, he should also be exempt from the speed limitation. But the bay constable thought otherwise and Rick paid his fair share of speeding fines into the town coffers. He would joke that one of these days they'd be able to add a new wing onto town hall from all the tickets he'd paid for his eagerness to reach the fishing grounds. But there was no need to race around this evening. Katie was with him and he would savor the time. He really didn't expect to see much out there and, if he found Jack, that would make for a fine outing.

As Rick guided the twenty-seven foot sea foam–colored Contender into the channel, Katie remembered the business card. She pulled it from her notepad folder and reread the name, Ned Mack Jr. He had an impressive title: Senior Scientist, PhD, Evolutionary Biology, Riverstone National Laboratory. Katie wondered if he knew Karen. Those biologist types at the Riverstone Lab were a tight-knit group. Katie also thought it odd this fellow would make contact at a time when one of his colleagues was working on a hush-hush project for her. Katie wondered if Dr. Mack had some part in the DNA analysis or if he had some of his own information to share. She decided to wait until Karen called before contacting him. Katie did not want to risk divulging any more information to anyone at this time than was needed; the situation had gotten too tense, and more than anything else she needed the results of the DNA mapping.

"Hey, Rick, look at all those fish breaking the surface. They look like little tunny?"

"Nope. Atlantic bonito. They've pushed spearing up on that long sandbar and are enjoying a mighty fine evening feast. They come in here sometimes in late summer if conditions are right."

"Wow, they are efficient and deliberate in their movements, not at all like the pandemonium that accompanies a bluefish frenzy."

"Yes they are, just like little tuna. Perfect marine predators."

"Rick, I can't imagine any predator more perfect that those bastards that tried to kill you the other night."

Rick looked at Katie and just shrugged, and then he mashed forward on the throttle as he cleared the no-wake zone. The two 250 horsepower Yamaha engines jumped to life. Within seconds, the boat was up on plane and heading toward Sandhill Point. The evening was warm and the Sound calm, a light breeze blew from the southwest. Within minutes, Rick's boat cruised past Old Colonial Light and the promontory upon which it sat. The boulder field in front of the light was just becoming visible as the slowly dropping tide flowed eastward. Small bluefish and bass were feeding on the surface and flat seas prevailed as far as the eye could see. On this evening, the Long Island Sound looked more like a big inland lake than the huge saltwater estuary that it was. Rick pointed across the Sound to the visible power stacks off Bridgeport, Connecticut, almost fourteen miles away. The evening was exceptionally clear with no limitations to visibility. Katie nodded. She was familiar with that portion of the Connecticut shoreline since her youngest sister had attended Fairfield University and she made the ferry trip across the Sound often to visit. It beat having to deal with all the traffic getting off the Island and onto the New England Thruway.

Rick motioned for Katie to move closer to him. He put his lips to her ear and, over the roar of the engines, said, "Let's run into Smith's Bay and over to the mouth of the Squeteague River. We might see something there as the tide runs out of the river and dumps into the Sound."

Rick pulled back but Katie held his face with both hands and kissed him, first on the cheek and then squarely on the lips. Rick backed off the throttle and the Contender settled back like a horse responding to the command *whoa*. The boat sat about three hundred yards off White's Pond, a tidal pond outlet popular with local fish erman. Rick and Katie made quick but passionate love. A pod of the killer fish swam beneath the boat and sensed every vibration made by the two lovers.

"Holy smokes there. That was as intense as it gets. Best dessert a guy could get. Mind if I jump in the water to cool myself down?"

"Don't start that again. Do you have to ruin the moment?"

"One quick dip. Down and up."

"That's what you said on the beach, *in and out,* and look at what it almost got you—killed!"

The alpha male was fast becoming agitated. He sensed the presence of food; the vibrations transmitted through the boat's hull communicated with his lateral line and he locked in on the signals. The alpha male knew there were living things above him . . . living things he could eat. His frustration fueled the ferociousness of the entire pack as his body produced and released aggression pheromones. The pack followed his lead; they too sensed another meal. The pod of killer fish had been moving east from Eagle's Neck, where they began the evening hunt. Having broken away from the larger school, this band of about a dozen fish moved in a defined pattern, covering grids of territory until they found food. Unlike their normal and smaller relatives, these mutants had evolved with a higher degree of intellect. Their hunting methods were in part instinctive and in part learned behaviors.

Holding onto the starboard gunwale as one would hold on to the edge of a swimming pool, Rick lowered himself into the water. Despite being at peak seasonal temperature, the water was refreshingly cool. Rick's body was still in overdrive, the effects of the quickie still lingering within. His body wanted sleep after the intense lovemaking, yet he knew Katie would have none of that.

The alpha male now had a visual sighting of its prey. It looked strangely familiar, as if it had seen this one before. It had eaten that type of prey recently but it needed to be sure before it would attack. The big fish didn't want to risk an encounter that might cause him harm. The pack circled directly beneath Rick, no more than thirty feet down. Each time Rick moved his legs or kicked his feet, the pack became more aroused and more focused. Their bodies tensed, their fins became rigid, their jaws snapped and clicked . . . and their eyes glowed a ghastly and piercing yellow.

"Rick, please put your clothes back on and let's get going. Don't let me regret my affectionate overture. Keep this up and you will ruin the evening. We have work to do. Let's get going."

"There's still plenty of light left and the tide is just beginning to run strong. And my boat is fast. Give me a minute and we'll be on our way."

The killer fish swimming below had reached the height of agitation and were ready to strike. The pack had been stimulated to a frenzied state by the continual discharge of bodily hormonal chemicals that triggered violent behavior. Pheromones released by these altered fish were especially potent as a result of the genetic mutations they had undergone. Each fish reacted to the scents and body language of the others. They waited for the cue from the pack leader. The one-hundred-pound alpha male was in a crazed state, his glowing eyes locked on to Rick's feet. The fish knew from previous attacks that when he bit off the feet, his prey would be incapable of mobility. Once unable to move, his subordinates would advance for the lethal assault. The pack was ready, wound like a coiled spring. They would circle beneath the *Maya* one final time before ascending the water column to strike.

Rick's VHF cracked to life. "Captain Rick, vessel *Maya*, do you read me? Come in Rick. Any chance you are out here this evening?" It was Jack.

"Katie, please answer that," Rick said, as he quickly and forcefully pulled himself up and over a shallow part of the gunnel and onto the deck. He owed Jack a big debt of gratitude.

The alpha male was as pissed off as an animal could get at missing another opportunity to kill Rick. The fish was so filled with rage that he lashed out at one of his lesser pack mates and severed its tail. The rest of the pack fed as their fallen kin bled out and descended toward the bottom.

CHAPTER 31

"Captain Jack, come back, Jack. This is Katie. Over"

"Ah, a name that is music to my ears. Where are you, Katie? Over."

"With Rick, on the *Maya*. We're slightly to the east of Sandhill Point. Where are you? We've been worried. Carole too. Over."

"I'm about half a mile off the southwest edge of Stratford Shoal. Got myself into a bit of a mess. Long story. I'm sorta okay but could use some company." Jack was still too dazed and physically exhausted to say much more.

Rick took the microphone from Katie and spoke, "Jack, it's Rick. Hang on, buddy. We'll be there shortly."

"Ten-four, good buddy. Tell Carole I'm okay. Thanks. Over and out."

Rick turned the ignition key and the two Yamaha engines roared to life.

"I don't like the sound of Jack," Rick said. He aimed *Maya*'s bow north toward Connecticut. With more than an hour of daylight left and unimpeded visibility, Rick was able to discern the shape of the Stratford Shoal Lighthouse, his visual point of reference. Although Rick had all the latest radar technology aboard *Maya*, he would need only rely on that one visual structure to reach Jack, whose boat would be but a short distance south and west of the lighthouse. It would take about fifteen minutes to reach the light. The location of Jack's boat would be apparent from there. If Rick had any problems locating Jack's position, he would hail him on the VHF and get exact

GPS coordinates. Rick didn't anticipate having to do that. There weren't many other boats on the water and he'd immediately recognize the profile of Jack's boat.

Rick manned the helm and thought it a bit ironic that he was aiming for a sea marker that for years others had tried to avoid. The shoal was a dangerous piece of real estate that got its name by being positioned equidistant between Old Field Point on Long Island and Stratford Point, Connecticut. Even though it was closer to Old Field Point by half a mile, the lighthouse was tagged a with name representative of the Connecticut point of land. Some say that came about as a result of the lighthouse being positioned approximately one thousand feet onto the Connecticut side of the Sound. The Stratford lighthouse had functioned as a beacon of warning for sailors since its activation in December 1877. Its primary purpose was to mark the perilous Middle Ground Shoal, a three-quarters of a mile long piece of very shallow water and rocks. When the area was first charted in the early 1600s, what is now the shoal were then two small islands in the middle of the Sound. Time, tide, and effects of severe weather worked in concert to erode the islands and leave behind treacherous shallow rocks and boulders. It was those shallow rocks and the surrounding deep water that attracted all varieties of baitfish and game fish to this area. At times, it could be one of the most productive fishing area in the Sound. At other times, it could be the most dangerous. As one of Jack's favorite places to fish, especially for big bass and bluefish, Rick was not at all surprised to find him there.

Katie had grabbed the binoculars and scanned the water for Jack's boat. Rick's Contender was fast and it ate up those nautical miles in short order. The lighthouse was now just a quarter of a mile away.

Rick backed down on the throttle and trimmed up the engines slightly as the boat approached close to the lighthouse. He didn't want to take any chance of hitting an unseen rock.

"Why so close, Rick? Jack is off to the southwest somewhere."

"Let me have the glasses, Katie. I need to do something first."

Oddly, Rick put the glasses to his eyes and focused not on where Jack's boat might be but rather on the windows of the lighthouse and then the light tower.

"What are you doing?" Katie said.

"Looking for a sign of the long-departed keeper. I do it all the time I'm out here in the evening or at night."

"What are you talking about?"

"A ghost, Katie. The ghost of a lighthouse keeper gone mad. The isolation got to him and he killed himself. His restless spirit is believed to still reside in the building."

"Rick, we are out here to find Jack and you are looking for apparitions. Sometimes I really wonder about you and your priorities in life."

"One night I was out here fishing for bass and I saw a shadow in the tower. It was a man-like silhouette that lingered as the Fresnel lens broadcast its alternating signal. I would have sworn at that time that it looked straight at me and pointed a finger."

"Intriguing, Rick, but I'm more concerned about Jack right now than some dead lighthouse keeper giving you the finger."

"Okay, let's go. No one's home."

The sun was low in the sky and shone brilliant red, orange, and yellow hues. It looked like a giant hybrid orange and grapefruit, collared by the intensity of it its corona. Katie snatched the binoculars from Rick and searched an arc of an area due south of their location. She slowly moved the glasses west and along the horizon. The boat moved slowly off the shoal on a heading due southwest.

"Damn!" Katie had moved the binoculars too far above the horizon and caught the full force of the sun's brilliance. She was momentarily blinded by the light; blinking and floating spots appeared before her eyes. "That was pretty stupid," she said. "I could have fried my retinas."

"Nah, you're way hotter than the sun and your patented stare is like a laser beam." Rick was ever in a playful mood, regardless of the circumstances."We'll give this a few more minutes and then I will call up Jack to get coordinates."

Katie's vision slowly returned to normal and the spots had totally vanished. She refocused her sight on the horizon but this time without the aid of binoculars. Katie formed a visor-shaped arch with her hands that filtered out the direct rays of the sun. Visualizing quadrants on the water, she resumed scanning, up and down, back and forth, thoroughly covering each mental square of water. Her eyes moved on a horizontal plane until they made contact with the bottom edge of the corona. That is when Katie saw the reflection.

"Rick, give me the glasses. I think I see something." With the aid of the binoculars, Katie confirmed the shape of a boat.

She handed the glasses back to Rick. "Take a look. What do you think? It's in line with the North Harbor power stacks."

Rick took one quick look and knew immediately from the hull's silhouette that it was Jack's boat.

"It's him," Rick said. He brought *Maya* up on plane.

Jack was sitting on the bench seat behind the center console. He was slouched over, head in his hands, looking like the weight of the world was on his shoulders. He looked up at the sound of the oncoming boat and instantly recognized Rick's boat. He always liked the sea foam green hull. It was his favorite color. Jack waved. Both Katie and Rick acknowledged.

Jack braced himself on the backrest of the bench seat and tried standing up. He was fatigued, weak, and had trouble steadying himself. Jack's ankles bore deep cuts from the line that had entangled him; they had bled but the blood had clotted. Although the bleeding had stopped, the pain was intense. Jack was unable to place much weight upon his feet. His hands too were badly cut from when he tried to break the strong braided line. He had pulled so hard that the line cut right down to the bone on both index fingers. Somehow Jack had also dislocated his right shoulder. He was torn up pretty good.

Rick placed rubber bumpers on each of three starboard side cleats so he could tie up directly to port side of Jack's boats without risk of any damage to either hull. As Rick tied off both boats, Katie jumped from the *Maya* and into the Sea Craft. She was visibly shaken at the sight of Jack's condition.

"Jack, what happened to you? How did this happen?"

Jack still had a distant stare in his eyes but he smiled at Katie and then shocked her.

"It was them, Katie, the killer fish. They did this, almost killed me. But the bastards lost the fight. The mermaid saved me."

"Okay there, old buddy," Rick said. "And what mermaid might that be?"

Katie thought Jack might be hallucinating. She also saw the blood and Jack's wounds and knew he might be in shock. Jack needed immediate medical attention.

"There really was a mermaid. Those fuckers had me surrounded and were about to make the kill, and when I opened my eyes, there she was . . . a mermaid. I thought it was an angel but I'm not dead. I'm here, still alive."

Rick had never seen his friend in such a state of ill being. He turned on his VHF and tuned it to Channel 16, the emergency channel. He gave the county marine police their exact coordinates and told them of the medical emergency. The Coast Guard at Eagle's Neck also responded but Rick told them he felt local authorities could handle the situation. They'd have an ambulance back at the launch ramp that would rush Jack up the hill to Saint Dominick's Hospital. He'd be in good hands within minutes.

Katie found a windbreaker that Jack has stowed on board and slipped it over his arms. He winced in pain as his right shoulder flexed.

Katie knew Jack was traumatized and she did not feel at ease asking him questions, but she had to know. "Did you seem them, Jack? Did you see the killer fish?"

Jack's response was labored and measured but he replied. "Yes I did, Katie. They were huge. Grotesque. Vicious."

"Jack, did they look to you like any fish we know of? Did you recognize them, Jack?"

Rick broke in to the conversation. "Katie, I can see the rescue boat making way. They should be here in a few minutes. We need to get Jack ready for the transfer."

Jack responded to Katie's question. "They were monsters, Katie, like no fish I've ever seen. And there were lots of them, but the mermaid saved me."

The rescue boat arrived and tied off on the starboard side of the Sea Craft.

An EMT jumped aboard and took control of Jack. She introduced herself as Rosemary and asked Jack how he was doing. Jack nodded okay, a strained smile formed on his face.

"Let's get you cleaned up here. You are going to be fine," she said. Rosemary worked to clean Jack's wounds and got an IV started. She motioned for one of the police officers to assist her and hold the IV bag. Then she immobilized Jack's shoulder.

Rick knew one of the two police officers that remained on the rescue boat. He and some friends had chartered him in the past. He asked Rick what had happened. Rick's reply was that they had only arrived on scene a short while ago and were trying to figure out the same thing, and that Jack was a friend.

When the EMT had Jack stabilized, she covered him with a high-tech blanket and helped him onto the rescue boat. Jack went willingly but he turned back to Rick.

"Let Carole know that I'm was okay and please take care of my boat."

"Will do, Jack, don't worry."

The officers untied their boat. Within minutes, they were cruising at a moderate speed back to Port Roosevelt. The sun had begun to set and the Sound remained flat, calm. They couldn't run the boat at full throttle since the bouncing would surely have caused Jack more discomfort and pain. The unhurried pace would have to suffice.

Rick jumped aboard Jack's boat and tidied her up. He put all Jack's gear back in its place and scrubbed down the deck. He had fished on this boat in the past and knew two of Jack's favorite rod and reel combinations were missing. He thought that odd. Rick also knew Jack to be a neat freak when it came to the Sea Craft so he couldn't understand the mess strewn about the aft deck. It appeared as if chum bags had exploded with fish guts and body parts blown all over the place. That was not at all typical of how Jack fished. Rick would have to wait to get answers when Jack was in shape to talk about what had happened.

"Rick, I'm going to call Carole and tell her about Jack."

"That's fine. We need to get this boat back to port."

Rick fired up the Sea Craft. Katie would pilot the Contender back to Port Rosey. She was a very capable boat handler. Rick motioned for Katie to follow him in. It was a nice evening for a cruise but this was now just all business. The wind was slight out of the southwest and the Sound remained calm as a small pond. Katie thought about what Jack had said about his encounter with the fish and she wondered about the possibilities. What she could not get her mind around was Jacks' reference to a mermaid. He had to be hallucinating.

With favorable sea conditions, both boats entered the mouth of the harbor and were back at the docks by 9:10 p.m. Rick tied up *Maya* in his slip and then walked over to the public launch ramp where Jack had put in. Luckily Jack had a spare key to his truck on the boat key ring. Rick watched Katie maneuver the boat alongside the dock. She expertly reversed the engines and allowed *Maya* to come up gently against the cushioned dock rails. He had taught her that maneuver and was proud to see her execute the technique with precision.

"Nice going. Let me get Jack's trailer and we'll get the boat loaded."

Rick was excellent at maneuvering boats efficiently onto trailers, not like some of the neophytes who put on a show each day at the ramp. Within minutes, Jack's boat was sitting on the rollers of the trailer and securely strapped down.

Rick told Katie he would leave the boat inside the Caris boatyard for safe keeping overnight. He had a key to the gate since he fished at night and would often avail himself of the ice machine after shop hours so that he could preserve his catch. He'd deal with getting the boat back to Jack's house the next day.

While Katie waited for Rick to finish up with Jack's boat, her cell phone rang.

"Katie, it's Karen. Are you sitting down?"

"No, I'm standing by Rick's truck in Port Rosey. Just got off the water. Bit of an incident with his friend, Jack, that may be tied to these fish. He's in the hospital and we're about to go see him."

"Hospital? What happened?"

"Not quite sure but what do you have for me?"

"This gets pretty heavy, my friend. Perhaps we should have a face-to-face. There's too much to discuss over the phone. I'm still at the lab. Just got the final results of the analysis. I could meet you at the Boulder Point Diner in about an hour. Are you good?"

"Yeah, but just tell me, are they some kind of local fish?"

"Yes and no. It's not that simple. I'll explain it all when we meet. See you in an hour."

Rick had Jack's boat safely in the boatyard and walked back to where he had parked his truck. "Let's head up to the hospital and check on how Jack's doing, and then we'll go get a bite to eat. I'm famished."

The hospital was a short drive up the hill from the ramp. Official visiting hours were over, but Rick and Katie fibbed a bit to get their visitor's badges. They told the receptionist they were Jack's son and daughter. But once on the floor, they met with the head nurse who told them Jack was sedated and asleep. Jack's wife was in the room with him.

"How's he doing?" Rick inquired.

"He'll be fine and you'll be able to visit tomorrow," the nurse replied. "He lost a fair amount of blood and his system was in shock from the injuries. But all his vitals are back close to normal. He must have been through some ordeal and just needs his rest."

"Would you like me to tell your mother you are here?"

"No thanks. We'll let them be for now. Just tell her that Rick and Katie were here and that we'll see her in the morning?"

"Will do. Have a good night."

Katie wasted no time with the next priority. "Rick, we need go to the Boulder Point Diner to meet with Karen. She has her findings from the DNA analysis and I cannot wait any longer to know the results."

"Let me just hit the men's room and clean up a bit. I smell like bluefish chum and fish vomit."

"Fine, I'll wait by the stairs and give Nick a call. I'm sure he wants to hear Karen's finding firsthand."

Katie paced the floor. Soon she would have answers and then there would be even more issues and challenges to deal with. Knowing the enemy would just be the beginning of a new battle. She dialed Nick's cell phone but it instantly went to voice mail. She left a message to meet her at the diner and to come alone.

CHAPTER 32

Karen Hammond took a booth in the back of the Boulder Point Diner where there would be privacy. Karen brought a notepad but all of what she would tell Katie DiNardo would be recalled from her photographic memory. The pad was for doodling while she deliberated her findings over and over again just to make certain she had not missed one relevant detail in her analysis. Karen was a no-nonsense woman, her life governed by the scientific process. She dealt only in facts, details, and validated conclusions. Hyperbole, idle speculation, gossip and rumors were not at all part of her persona. She was the antithesis of the drama queen. If it wasn't based on hard facts, Karen Hammond wanted nothing to do with it. She had painstakingly evaluated the tooth tissue sample and ran repeat tests to confirm her findings. She brought one of her colleagues into the process to help expedite the DNA mapping and validate the results. The conclusions were rock solid.

"Hey there, good buddy." Katie's voice broke Karen's contemplation.

Katie and Rick sat directly opposite Karen on the window side of the booth. They could talk directly without being overheard.

"Katie, when you dropped off the tooth, I gave you the rundown on the methodology I would use to analyze the tissue. I have access to the latest and best DNA mapping technology, but I want to run through some basic genetic stuff with you first to set the groundwork before I give you the drumroll and my conclusions. Are you okay with that?"

Katie knew Karen all too well and that she would have no choice in the matter. "Yeah, okay, I'm fine with it but make it short and sweet. You do remember I too am a scientist?"

"Well, I'd benefit from the primer," Rick added. "Remember, I'm just a fishing guide."

"I need to begin with the genome. As you know, a genome contains all the genetic material and biological data that is necessary to form any and all life organisms. Every organism on the planet has a genome. It is the basis of an organism's heredity or genetics. The biological information imbedded in a genome is encoded in its DNA."

Katie groaned.

"Indulge me, Katie, and you shall have your answers. There is a purpose here. As you also know, DNA separates into distinct genes that carry information for proteins needed by an organism to function. These proteins determine many aspects of an organism's existence, including appearance, size, shape, overall health, and can affect temperament, personality, and behavior. This is true of all creatures in the animal kingdom, including fish."

"Got it, Karen, right there with you . . . straight from freshman bio. Continue."

"In addition to chromosomes in the nuclei of cells that determine genetic information, there are tiny bits of matter in the cytoplasm of cells that also carry DNA information: the mitochondria. They play a crucial role in heredity. They are also responsible for the production of energy for the body, destruction of cells, and, most important, mutations and aging. Those are very significant and relevant distinctions for this analysis. The mini-lecture is now done. On to the findings."

"Thank God!"

Before Karen could continue, another voice interrupted.

"I got here as quickly as I could. I was otherwise preoccupied." It was Nick Tanner. He slid into the booth next to Karen.

"Hot date?" Rick poked. "Was he nice?"

"Perhaps. But it's none of your business. What did I miss?"

"Just a quick overview, Nick," Katie answered. "Karen was just getting to the good stuff."

"Okay. Let me continue. We used all the latest and greatest technology available and ran multiple tests. The major finding is that the tooth came from a male fish with genetic markers most closely aligned with that of one of our local species of fish, with a few major and notable exceptions."

"Damn! I knew it," Nick said. "We were spot on all along. What species?"

"*Pomatomus saltatrix.*"

Katie's jaw dropped. "Bluefish!"

"These aren't just ordinary bluefish, Katie. There have been some major cellular and genetic alterations. *Significantly mutated creatures* would best describe these fish."

"How about mega-monsters?" Katie said "I've seen them and they have been transformed into fish that look nothing like ordinary bluefish, or any other fish we know of."

"No shit! One almost got my leg," Rick added.

"That's because you're an idiot, Rick. Karen, please continue."

"And that is why I spent a few minutes on the overview. Although the straight forward DNA mapping proves these things are genetic variations of bluefish, an analysis of the mitochondrial DNA revealed genetic changes that could have had a profound impact on how your creatures evolved, grow, behave, and, more important to your investigation, what their vulnerabilities might be."

"Now we're getting somewhere. Keep it going."

"Okay. You know that mitochondrial DNA is maternally inherited and as such can be used by geneticists to trace maternal evolutionary lineage back ages. One example is that *mtDNA* has been used by scientists to trace back the lineage of modern dogs to wolves. And some enterprising labs have even offered services where clients—for a hefty fee—swab their cheeks for DNA and then have it mapped to see where their ancient roots reside. Africa, Asia, Europe, another universe . . . mitochondrial DNA tells the story. The whole ground zero concept of *Mitochondrial Eve* is founded on the same principle of mapping back mtDNA in time to discover the origins of the human race—the mother of all humanity."

"So are you absolutely certain about the fish being some aberrant form of bluefish?" Katie asked.

"Katie, I am 99.99 percent certain. I wouldn't have told you otherwise. I know what the stakes are and I'm as sure as science allows me to be. My colleague validated the findings and we ran additional tests."

"His name wouldn't happen to be Ned Mack?"

"Yes it would. I had to bring him into the fold for his expertise in cellular and evolutionary biology. How do you know his name and why do you ask?"

"We'll talk about that some other time. Did you answer the questions I initially posed regarding any anomalies in the genetic makeup of the tissue? Has anything caused changes or mutations to chromosomes, genes, or DNA?"

"I used *FISH* to help me profile the DNA and answer those questions. If you've forgotten, it's the acronym for fluorescence in situ hybridization. That process enabled me to map the genetic material from the tooth DNA, including specific genes and segments of genes. That is what allowed me to analyze chromosomal abnormalities and other genetic mutations. It's how I was able to tell you the fish tooth came from a genetic mutant. We also learned from the mitochondrial DNA that the ancestry of your killer fish does not extend back all that far in time. Maybe a few decades. That is where we see a fork in the road so to speak with the DNA. My suspicion is that it was most likely some chemical or environmental event that caused permanent cellular mutations that have been passed on to subsequent generations of fish. This carry-thorough of genetic mutation in some ways defied known science."

"Can these fish breed? Did you see any evidence of hybridiza-tion?" Nick said.

"Yes and no. We saw no evidence to suggest the chromosomal changes that had taken place would affect fertility, and there was no evidence of any hybridization. These are definitely descendants of bluefish stock and they can breed, most likely just among themselves."

Katie pushed. "Tell me about vulnerabilities."

"Let me put that answer in the context of all the primary find-ings. First, we were able to determine that whatever the cause, the myostatin gene in this sample showed evidence of being deactiv-ated . . . turned off. What that means is that this fish would have had an abnormal ability to grow muscle mass at a very rapid rate."

"So is that it?" Katie asked. "Big, bad bluefish that have had their myostatin gene turned off?"

"No. It gets much more complicated. The size of the tooth itself indicates a very large animal. From what you've told me about the dimensions of these fish, I suspected there must have been other sig-nificant chemical and cellar changes as well. My associate was able to find enough remnant blood contained within the sample to run some chemical analysis. The toxicology findings were surprising and aston-ishing. Without getting too technical, Dr. Mack discovered traces of unusually high levels of testosterone and abnormally elevated levels of somatostatin."

Nick interjected. "Somatostatin is known to regulate aggressive behavior in fish. I read a scientific paper a while back about levels of somatostatin in extremely aggressive Cichlids. Between the *statin* and the pumped up testosterone, it's no wonder our fish behave as aggressively as they do."

"Hey Rick, maybe you should get yourself tested," Karen chided before continuing with her findings. "You are absolutely correct, Nick. But we also found high concentrations of somatotropin, a growth hormone."

Rick couldn't contain himself any longer. "So what we have here is a perfect genetic storm of sorts that has created some super fish?"

"Yes we do, Rick. Simply put, the combination of an overabundance of growth hormones, a deactivated gene that inhibits growth, off-the-chart testosterone, and a neuropeptide that increases aggressive behavior in fish have all contributed to the size, temperament, and behaviors of these killer fish."

"So what we really have here is one big, mean, son of a bitch killing machine."

"Like you didn't know that already, Rick, from your skinny dipping episode," Katie said.

"I guess you are never going to let me live that one down. But remember, were it not for my swimming escapade, we may not have had a tooth for your buddy Karen to analyze."

Katie shot Rick one of her piercing signature stares.

"So far what you've told us is all bad news. These aberrations make the magnitude of this problem far greater than what I thought originally. How are these creatures vulnerable? Can you tell me something I can use to eradicate them?"

"This is where it gets really interesting. We also discovered that the ends of various chromosomes from the sample tissue had begun to erode, a result of a deficiency of the protein telomerase."

"This is beginning to make my hair hurt" Rick said. "Where does all this altered state mumbo jumbo end? What the hell kind of fish are these?"

"*End* is a fitting choice of words, Rick. Telomerase works to create natural end caps called telomeres that are on terminal tips of chromosomes. Telomeres function to prevent shortening of the chromosomes and deterioration of genes. They also are essential for the effective transfer of genetic coding from parent to progeny. This is true of mice, men, and fish."

"Fine, Karen. But where's the vulnerability in all that? Let's get to some usable findings so I can stop these things."

"Here's the connection, Katie. Chromosomal erosion is part of the aging process in all organisms. Based on the information we've analyzed, we believe that aging was accelerated in the fish from which the tooth was obtained. If this is true of all your killer fish, they may not live as long as normal bluefish."

"Can you tell how long their lifespan may be?" Nick said. "That could be a critical element in this entire puzzle."

"No I can't, Nick. While there is a link between the fraying of chromosomal endings and aging there is no linear correlation that a certain degree of fraying translates into a specific rate of premature aging. A group of Nobel scientists found that telomeres in humans could almost function as a biological clock but not as a predictor of how long someone might live. Those same scientists also found that shortened telomeres in older humans lead to certain illnesses and to an inability to effectively handle stress. If those findings are transferable to other organisms—including your bluefish—they may represent a meaningful piece to your puzzle."

Katie listened intently, but she needed to synthesize all this information into a logical sequence of findings that could be acted upon to help stop the killings. Her mind wandered back to her graduate school days and her intense study of bluefish. Katie could rattle off every known scientific fact and figure about bluefish, their life cycles, and their behavior.

"Katie. Are you still with us?" Karen said.

"Yeah, yeah . . . just thinking. "There seems to be a big disconnect here, Karen. If aging is accelerated and shortened telomeres prevent the effective transfer of genetic coding from parent to offspring, then these fish must mature sexually at a young age. Otherwise, these aberrant traits would not be inherited from one generation to the next. Add to that your belief that the mutations do not extend back all that far, and there is a big void in the logic. It is not possible for the fish we are dealing with now to be the ones that originally mutated."

"Katie, the aging scenario is but a hypothesis. We can only prove what has emerged from the DNA mapping and the blood tests. Aging is a wild card in all this. If the fish age very prematurely to a point where they could not successfully spawn, then that casts an entirely different light on this. The killer fish would have to be ones initially affected by whatever transpired more than three decades ago."

"I'm not so sure," Nick added. "Bluefish live to a max of about twelve years and are sexually mature at two years. Factoring in your possible aging scenario, even if they aged more rapidly than normal bluefish, they would most likely live beyond two years and, therefore, would breed at least once, perhaps more. So, my bet is that the killers in the Sound right now were spawned from the initial mutations. They are at least several generations of offspring removed from that first affected population of fish."

"I tend to agree with Nick. These bastards may be aging faster than normal but they may be capable of breeding, which means if they have been doing so for decades, there are a shit load of them in the Sound and perhaps elsewhere."

"Your problem just got a whole lot bigger," Rick suggested. "Unless these things start dying of old age there is no way we can catch them all, even if we got the commercial guys to trawl the entire Sound. I guess depth charges are totally out of the question?" he added sarcastically.

"I suspect these fish are also smarter than your average bluefish which adds to the complexity of the situation," Nick said. "And lest we forget, the concoction of genetically altered chemistry mixing in their blood has created a bit of an unstable marine monster with capabilities we don't understand."

"What possibly could have caused so many cellular and chemical alterations in one species?" Katie asked, trying to make sense of Karen's enormous data dump. "I've never encountered a scenario like this before with any marine creature. Not even close."

"There could be many triggering events. Look at all the speculation about what caused the massive die-off of juvenile lobsters in the Sound. Reasons have run the gamut from hypoxia to pesticides."

"But this is a little different, don't you think?" Rick replied. "This is not a die-off but the creation of some Frankenfish."

"Rick's right," Katie said. "We are breaking new ground with all this. If we're not careful we could lose all control of this situation, and in a hurry too. I'm beginning to feel like we may be on the losing end of this battle."

"I've never known you to give up on anything in your life, Katie," Karen said.

"It's just that to win in a battle, you need to understand your opponent better than you understand yourself. And we are not there yet with this. Nick, we have to let Ted know these findings." Katie heard all she needed to hear.

"I agree I gotta run. Let's huddle up in the morning."

"Hope he's a nice guy?" Rick jabbed.

Nick gave Rick the middle finger salute, and as he walked out from the diner, he dialed a phone number on his cell.

"Hello?"

"It's me, Nick, I'll be back in a bit. Just finished up the meeting at the diner. Okay, sweetie, I'll expect you to have dessert waiting for me."

Nick looked back into the diner and gave the peace sign as Katie and her companions had gotten out from the booth and prepared to leave. The next few days would be like nothing any of them could ever have imagined. Katie dialed her boss's cell phone number but the call immediately went to voice mail.

Once in the diner parking lot, Katie and Karen hugged and each kissed the other on a cheek.

"Thank you, Karen. My problem is so much bigger now. Your efforts have put this into perspective."

"Not to worry kiddo. Keep me in the loop and if you need any other assistance just give me a shout. Take care, Rick."

Katie and Rick watched as Karen walked to her car. Once safely on her way, Katie asked Rick to take her home.

"My place?" Rick inquired hopefully.

"No. Not tonight, Rick. My place. This is all so overwhelming. I just need to be alone and I need to get some rest. Tomorrow is going to be a long, tough day." It was already past midnight and Katie knew she'd have trouble sleeping with all Karen's information crashing around in her head.

"All the more reason for me to stay with you. I promise, I'll be good."

"Rick, if you want to maintain harmony in this relationship, just drive me home and let's call it a night."

"Okay, you win." Rick hated concessions. "But don't forget, we need to check on Jack in the hospital tomorrow. Make sure he is okay and hear his story. He might have something to add to all this."

"Fine. We can do that but first I need to contact Ted and arrange the meeting. That's my priority right now. Why don't you go visit Jack first thing in the morning, and if there is anything I need to know, you can all me. Tell him I'll stop by to see him after my meeting. If there's anything left of me, that is."

"You'll do fine, as always."

Katie just nodded in the affirmative and then closed her eyes. She slept the rest of the way home.

Once in her condo, and although mentally and physically exhausted, Katie DiNardo could not stop thinking about the killer fish and Karen's findings. This was the biggest challenge of her career and she was frightened like never before over what could transpire during the next few days. Her job could be on the line, but more than that, she feared these mutant bastards might kill again. That was the last thing she wanted on her conscience. Katie paced the first floor of her abode as much in the hope of tiring herself out as to clear her head. Neither objective was attained. As a last resort, she mixed up batch of her grandmother's favorite sleep remedy: warm milk and honey with a bit of dried chamomile. As she waited for the milk to warm, Katie removed her slacks and, as she did so, she felt something in one of the pockets. She pulled out Ned Mack Jr.'s business card. She would call him in the morning. Katie changed into pajama shorts and a tank top, drank her concoction, and tried Ted Gunther's cell phone again. Still no answer. Now she waited for sleep, which that would take time in coming.

CHAPTER 33

Later that morning . . .

Jonathan Bennett had graduated in June from Saint Luke's High School. The seventeen-year-old was one of the top scholar athletes on Long Island and in all of New York State. His accomplishments in the swimming pool earned him an all-expenses-paid four years to Penn State University. This future Nittany Lion broke every high school and Long Island record in the men's freestyle, backstroke, and breaststroke events. He also maintained a straight-A average. Jonathan was driven by two goals: he wanted to make the US Olympics swimming team and he wanted to become a veterinarian. Both those objectives demanded hard work and personal dedication. Not many could achieve either of those two goals, but this kid was up to the challenge.

Jonathan also loved his two fiercely loyal dogs—a big-boned black Labrador retriever named Scoter and a Japanese Akita called Yuuki. He was saddened by the realization that this was the first time since the dogs were puppies that he'd be leaving them for such an extended period. He wished he could take his dogs to school the following week, but only fish and some other innocuous pets were allowed in the dorms. Jonathan wanted to spend as much time as possible with Scoter and Yuuki before his freshman college semester began. The trio would often swim together in the back northeast corner of Treasure Cove, an appendage off the main portion of Port Roosevelt Harbor.

The manmade cove was dredged by the Salt Marsh Dredging Company in the early 1900s. Initially called Dead Man's Pit, the town's first chamber of commerce quickly changed the name to Treasure Cove in an effort to add some mystery and panache to an area that was beginning to establish a tourism trade. To the best of any local historian's knowledge, not an ounce of treasure was ever buried there nor had a single pirate ever stepped foot on the sandy shores of Treasure Cove. The closest the area came to hosting a renegade buccaneer was the time a somewhat on-the-fringe clammer hid among the beach roses and poison ivy to spring out and flash unsuspecting women joggers. He was finally caught by the harbormaster after exposing himself to a packed ferry on its way out of the inlet. Following a brief psychological evaluation at one of the local hospitals and some prednisone treatments for the poison ivy that had invaded his groin area, the clammer was back on his skiff raking in bivalves.

A number of large sand dunes, remnants of the dredging activity, rimmed the cove. When crested, the dunes offered a stunning view of the Long Island Sound and, on clear days, the Connecticut shoreline. The cove is a very popular mooring location, especially on the weekends after Memorial Day. It sometimes appeared there were more partying boats anchored up in the cove than there were boats on the entire Long Island Sound. The small cove at times would resemble a parking lot with not only moored boats, but also various craft tied together forming big party flotillas, littered with booze, bikinis, and boom boxes. Large boats easily made way into the area since the moorings were in deep water, capable of accommodating long-keeled sailboats and substantial motorboats. From rafts and kayaks to forty-footers, the cove attracted them all.

Jonathan typically avoided weekend or holiday swims with his dogs. With this being the last big vacation week of summer, he decided to take Scoter and Yuuki for an early morning swim before most folks would engage in water activities. Six a.m. was way too early for the party crowd to arrive at the cove, or for those already moored to wake up from the previous night's festivities. Jonathan was aware of the weekend bluefish tournament but any fishermen who would be inclined to do some pre-tournament scouting would leave the harbor and motor directly out into the Sound, not bothering to make a pit stop in the cove. To Jonathan's surprise, there weren't many boats in the cove and the few that were moored there were at the extreme opposite end from where he and the dogs would swim.

Jonathan had a ritual he performed before actually swimming with the dogs. He would first toss out one stick as far as he could throw it. Scoter, the Lab, had a marked advantage at this game. Retrieving was in his genes. Jonathan would then throw two sticks in slightly different directions. Yuuki liked that, since he now had a fair chance to get in on a retrieve. Once both dogs were into the game, Jonathan would chuck a tennis ball beyond the last mooring. The tide was at flood stage and the cove was full of water that extended well into the sod banks. The extra water made for a longer swim to the mooring.

The dogs sat at attention on the sand, watching the flight of the tennis ball and awaiting Jonathan's command to *fetch*. When he did, the dogs leapt forward in full swimming stride. Jonathan then dove in and joined them. It was off to the races with Jonathan setting the pace. While either dog could run much faster than their master on land, the dog paddle in water was no match for Jonathan's superstrong freestyle stroke. Each dog kept an eye on the other and an eye on the tennis ball and stayed close to Jonathan. The real fun began as the trio approached the mooring ball that acted as a turn-around, the halfway point. Jonathan slowed his pace and let the dogs compete for the coveted tennis ball. As always, Scoter reached the ball first and gently snatched it. Retrievers have been bred with soft mouths since duck hunters are not too fond of mangled waterfowl. It is a signature trait of the breed. Once the tennis ball was secured in Scoter's mouth, he swam around the mooring and headed down the homestretch.

His objective was to get the ball back to the beach. That's what he had been taught to do.

Jonathan made the turn next and swam behind the Lab while Yuuki brought up the rear, foiled again by a waterdog. As Jonathan eased around the mooring ball to begin his power stroke, he felt the water beneath him bulge oddly upward, and he felt something brush against his right leg.

"Yuuki, back off," Jonathan commanded, thinking the dog had gotten too close and wanted to play. He felt the water up-swell again and looked back. To Jonathan's surprise, Yuuki was a full five yards behind him. Again he felt something surge past. The water was about thirty feet deep and one thought raced through Jonathan's mind: *Shark.* Jonathan's swimming pace accelerated as he called out to Yuuki to hurry up. But as Jonathan turned back around facing forward, he saw the most frightening vision of his young life: a gushing of water erupted ahead of him, like a geyser at Yellowstone, and in an instant, Scoter was catapulted fifteen feet into the air. It was surreal and appeared to Jonathan to be taking place in slow motion. He could see the big black bundle of fur twist and turn in the air as if it were some disoriented and uncoordinated acrobat. As the dog crashed back onto the water, it amazingly still had the tennis ball in its mouth.

"Swim, Scoter! Swim!" Jonathan yelled with alarm, knowing intuitively that his pet's life was in peril. Scoter must have understood Jonathan's command and the urgency of the situation for his webbed paws paddled as fast as his retriever legs could move. Jonathan saw the huge forked tail break the surface just behind his beloved Labrador. He panicked and slapped the water with his arms in an attempt to distract whatever it was that was on his dog's tail. Scoter was but twenty yards from the safety of the sand when another bulge of water pushed him upward a second time, tossing him about like a rag doll. It was almost as if the thing beneath the water was maliciously playing with the dog. Yuuki also sensed danger and he began to snarl and growl; the matted hairs on his back stood straight up.

His bark must have resonated with some sensory mechanism in the killer fish because it and its pack mates stopped chasing Scoter and turned their attention toward Yuuki, swimming straight past Jonathan to circle around the Akita. By now, Scoter was within a few yards of safety so Jonathan's attention was riveted on Yuuki. With the pack of killer fish closing in on the dog, the boy reacted from his heart not his brain. Adrenaline pumping hard, he swam back toward Yuuki and toward the creatures beneath him. He needed to save his dog.

An alpha male lead the attack from below. He was sizing up his floating adversary, knowing from past encounters that the dog's legs would be his first bite target. He would sever all four legs. From there the kill would be easy and then his pack mates could dispatch the human. The alpha male toyed with his victim, finning on the surface of the water and nudging first Jonathan and then Yuuki. Jonathan was paralyzed by the sight of the creature but he yelled for help. The boats in the cove were too far away to hear him, or their occupants too deep in sleep to respond. While the lead fish played cat-and-mouse with his prey, the others encircled Jonathan and Yuuki, swimming in sinister procession. In all, there were ten fish in the pack, including the alpha male.

The lead fish bumped Yuuki hard. The dog growled, a primal, guttural snarl. The fish continued to torment the dog, completely ignoring Jonathan, and moved beneath Yuuki. With a short flick of the its head, the fish hurled Yuuki from the water, all the while its mates engaged in a death procession waiting for their chance to feed.

Yuuki landed back in the water, ready for the fight of his life. Akitas are fearless, built for battle. Strong and muscular, this centuries-old breed was used to hunt boar and bear. But the dog was out of its element. This life-and-death struggle would only end favorably for the dog if it could outwit its demonic foe.

The alpha male finally had had enough of the game. It was done playing with the dog. It surfaced and moved to within a few feet of Yuuki. The fish swam around him once, twice, and then a third time.

The dog watched, measuring every move the fish made . . . studying his would-be assailant. At one point, Yuuki locked eyes with the fish. He showed his own dominance by holding fast to his stare and not flinching. By now Jonathan realized there was no way he could help his dog and, fearing for his own life, he slowly backed away from the confrontation. But Yuuki's look and demeanor communicated to Jonathan his dog was not afraid, and that something remarkable was about to happen; and then it did.

The fish assumed an aggressive posture like others of its kind when ready to attack. Its fins became erect, its movements erratic. It made one final pass around the dog and then rushed in to inflict the first lethal wave of pain. Yuuki's instincts were sharp, his senses acute, and before the fish could deliver the mortal bite, Yuuki gathered all the strength from within his powerfully built body and went on the offensive. As the fish opened it huge maw and turned its head to the side, Yuuki lunged forward, ears back flat, teeth exposed, and clamped his massive canine jaws down hard on the most vulnerable part of the creature's head. The strike was perfect. One upper fang penetrated the fish's orbital eye socket, tearing into the eye as the other upper fang penetrated near to the fish's olfactory nerve, a critical sensory mechanism used by the fish to smell its surroundings. Yuuki shook his head violently, ripping flesh and bone, his long top fangs digging deeper into the creature's head. Yuuki's lower canines dug in as well and acted as supporting anchors strengthening the dog's grip. The fish felt fear like never before and sensed it was in peril.

Without a complete sense of sight and an olfactory network, the killer fish would be vulnerable, especially to younger males wanting to assume the alpha leadership role. The pack's patriarch wouldn't allow that. In an attempt to rid itself of the dog, the fish went airborne like a surface-to-air missile. Jonathan watched in horror as Yuuki ascended from the water, teeth deep into the beast's head, looking somewhat like a cowboy being flung about by a bucking Brahma bull. The dog's tenacious death grip bore down on the fish with all his will and spirit. It was as if the dog had reverted back to the primitive wolf. Yuuki knew instinctively that for the moment the advantage was his. He would die before he would let go.

The creature also knew instinctively it was in deep trouble if it didn't extricate itself quickly from this situation. The alpha male was equally tenacious, jumping from the water twice more. But the dog miraculously hung on. The fish almost hoped that his pod mates would come to his rescue. But they wanted nothing of the confrontation and just kept circling. They took their cues from their leader who was now not in any position to lead. His body automatically shifted into survival mode. His teeth clicked involuntarily, sending out a danger signal to other fish in the pack, and his body released endorphins into his system to ease the pain. Now fear pheromones and aggression chemicals released into the water. The other pack fish sensed fear in the alpha male and fled, leaving their leader to fend for himself.

The mutant fish had only one choice. He whipped his tail upward and sounded straight to the bottom of the cove. The fish tried to scrape the dog off by running its back along the hard bottom much like migrating salmon trying to remove sea lice. But amazingly, the dog held fast to the fish's head. As valiantly as Yuuki had fought, he could only hold his breath for a short period of time. The dog released its grip on the fish and swam quickly toward the surface, thirty feet away. As filtered light silhouetted Yuuki's body, the killer fish looked up, glad to be rid of the dog. The killer fish saw all four of the dog's legs paddling feverishly, appearing as easy targets. The fish was tempted to strike but extreme pain in the creature's eye and head triggered a reflex flight response. The alpha male swam off to find its pack, glad to be rid of the unyielding canine.

Yuuki bobbed up through the surface of the water and howled in victory. In response, Jonathan and Scooter swam out to meet their pal and savior.

CHAPTER 34

Katie managed to get a few hours sleep thanks to her grandmother's potion. The clock alarm blared with its usual musical fanfare at six a.m. Katie was still exhausted and, despite the urgency of the day, she slapped the snooze button four times before finally dragging herself out of bed. Katie put up a pot of coffee and hopped in the shower.

As the warm water sharpened her senses, Katie played through in her mind what she was to tell Ted. He wasn't going to like what she had to say, but this was now crunch time and some tough decisions needed to me made; decisions that were well above her pay grade. No matter how Katie cut Karen's findings, there was no escaping the fact that the killers were genetically altered bluefish and there could be hundreds or even thousands of them swimming in Long Island Sound. Without public notification and beach closures, these monsters could easily kill again. And the worst was that Katie had no clue how to stop the carnage. Ted Gunther was going to have a shit fit when he heard Karen Hammond's findings.

Katie dialed her cell phone. "Morning Nick, it's Katie. Are you ready for this?"

"As ready as I'll ever be. Been giving this whole thing a lot of thought. Our options are pretty limited. Katie, this is a mess."

"I know, Nick. It all makes me just want to throw up. The reality of it all is hard to comprehend. I'll see you in a bit. Okay?"

As Katie dressed, she noticed Ned Mack Jr.'s business card lying by her car keys. She would call him on the way to the office. He might just have something to add to the equation. With some luck, he'd be at his desk. But first she called Rick to find out if he'd heard anything about Jack.

"Hey there," she said.

"Did you sleep well?"

"Hardly."

"You would have slept better with me."

"Excuse me while I barf. Have you heard anything yet about Jack?"

"Not yet. I was just getting ready to call Carole. Why? What's up?"

"Just on my way into the office to meet with Ted. I have one other call to make before I get there so I can't really talk much now. Keep me posted on Jack and I'll give you another call after my meeting."

"Good deal. If you are up for it, I'm buying drinks later."

"We'll see about that, Rick. I have to get through this meeting before I can think about my social calendar. Bye."

While pumping gas at the Sunoco station, Katie re-examined Ned Mack's business card: *Senior Research Scientist, Evolutionary Biology*. She thought the coincidence odd given the findings on the killer fish. Katie dialed his number.

The phone rang several times with no answer. She started the car and pulled out of the station, letting the phone ring. Ten, eleven, twelve rings. She was about to end the call up when she heard a voice on the other end, "Good morning, Ned Mack here."

"Good morning. This is Katie DiNardo at Fish and Game."

"I know who you are, Dr. DiNardo. I've been waiting for your call. Any closer to solving your problem? I worked with Karen Hammond to analyze your tooth DNA. Interesting findings if I may say so."

"Interesting, yeah. Thanks for your assistance. Is there other information about the findings you care to share?"

"Not so much about the findings. Are you sitting down, Katie?"

"Are you serious, Ned? I'm driving and on my way to a very important meeting."

"You may want to pull over. You are going to want to pay attention to what I have I say, Dr. DiNardo. It may shed a whole new light on your problems."

Katie was in downtown Port Roosevelt and pulled into the town parking lot. She drove to the back of the lot, where the party boats were moored, and turned off the engine.

"Okay . . ."

Ned Mack Jr. told Katie the story of the East Coast nuclear power plant accident. While Ned wasn't aware of all the details of the accident, he did know bits and pieces from conversations he overheard his father having with coworkers.

"The leak was covered up and I think my father's death was not an accident."

"That story is beyond belief, Ned. Why disclose it now?"

"I believe the mutated fish that are doing the killing are a direct result of that specific radiation leak. My dad was also a fisherman and he told a friend that, at the time of the accident, there was a very large school of bluefish in the bay. He expected to see a massive die off of that school, but it never happened."

"That doesn't mean those fish weren't contaminated and then died elsewhere," Katie said.

"That may very well be true but when I connect the findings Karen and I made to the incident at the power plant the specific mutations we are seeing in those fish make a lot more sense."

"It does make more sense, but . . . I need time to absorb all this."

"Let me leave you with this, Katie. You have evidence of bite marks associated with the killings and attacks, patterns that you now know closely match to the dentition of bluefish. Karen and I have irrefutable scientific evidence of cellular and chemical transmutations . . . and DNA that alters the killer bluefish. The only open question is how those mutations occurred. Aside from that radiation leak, very little else could have caused the magnitude of those genetic changes in the fish."

"Ned, thank you for all this. Perhaps we can talk again."

The only thought that went through Katie's mind as she ended the call was: *Holy fuck! Jesus Christ! We are totally screwed!* Katie realized all too well the implications of what she had just been told and now she had to figure out fast how to tell Ted Gunther this bombshell news. Her problem was on the verge of whirling completely out of control.

CHAPTER 35

"You're late."

"You should only know why, Nick."

"Another amorous Ricky encounter?"

"No bullshit, okay? We gotta talk before we meet with Ted."

"He's in his office, Katie, doing his nervous dance. He got your messages and he's eager to hear what we have to say. So make it fast."

"I just got off the phone with one of Karen's colleagues, Ned Mack Jr., and what he had to tell me will blow your socks off. I'm still trying to digest it all."

"Is he the guy who helped analyze the tooth?"

"Yes, but he disclosed something to me that has been buried for thirty years and that has a direct link to the killings we've been experiencing."

"That sounds almost clandestine."

"There was a leak, Nick. A fucking radioactive leak . . . years ago . . . along the East Coast. Mack believes there is a connection between that leak and the killing fish that now swim in the Sound. He has some compelling reasons and evidence."

"Are we now talking fish that glow in the dark?"

"Nick, these bluefish or their descendants came into direct contact with contaminated discharge from a leak in a spent fuel rod cooling pool. It was radiation that mutated the cellular structure and chemistry of these fish. Ned Mack's father ran the operation back then. We are dealing with firsthand intelligence."

"It's somewhat plausible, Katie. But this is one of life's Jesus Christ moments. You'd better be right and you'd better bring an oxygen tank into the meeting with Ted for when he passes out."

"Sounds to me like we are up shit's creek on this one, Katie."

Of all Katie's expectations about the killings, this was about as bad as it could get.

Ted looked over at Nick, hopeful he might get a more supportive response, but Nick just shrugged his shoulders and poured salt into the wound. "It's pretty bad, boss. There could be hundreds, maybe thousands of these things in the Sound, and eradication, if that is at all possible, is going to take time. And time is something we don't have much of."

"Okay. Okay. I get the picture. Any suggestions about what we should do before I take this upstairs?"

"I think the first thing we need to do is warn the public," Katie said.

"You mean close the beaches?"

"I don't believe we have to go that far but we need to prohibit swimming all along the central north shore of Long Island."

"What about the west end and the north fork? And how about informing Connecticut and Rhode Island?"

Nick responded. "The attacks have all been centralized in the Sound. Nothing has yet happened west of Smith's Bay or east of Boulder Point. The central Sound seems to be where these fish prefer to hunt. I suggest we recommend prohibiting swimming in that zone and advise town officials on either side to use discretion."

"We can't mandate the closure of any beaches," Ted Gunther said. "All we can do is recommend. Each town board will take counsel from our department and the police, and they will each have to make their own independent decisions. If threats to public safety are not addressed adequately then the counties and the state can intervene, but we aren't closing anything."

"Ted, we really have no choice here and we really don't have much time," Katie said, stressing that there was no other option. "We need to recommend public warnings and prohibit swimming. If these fish attack again, based on what we now know, we will have no reasonable defense in a wrongful death suit for our lack of action."

Ted knew his back was against the wall on this one and that he needed to mobilize support among the top levels of leadership at Fish and Game, even the EPA. "You're right, Katie. We don't have much time. Nick and you have to ride shotgun with me. Let's run this up the flagpole."

Ted Gunther, Katie, and Nick spent the next four hours on conference calls with top state officials, county executives, and police chiefs. They even patched in the governor's office. Much to Katie's dismay, and despite her presentation of Karen's findings, the entire group of officials found it all too hard to believe and declined to issue warnings or close beaches without first engaging independent science consultants to review the circumstances of the case, even dismissing Ned Mack's disclosures as nothing more than unsubstantiated rumors. Bureaucracy at its finest.

The local town officials were the most vocal. While they bitched and moaned during the early stages of the investigation about not having enough information on the killings, now they turned their backs.

As one official put it: "This is the last big weekend of the holiday season. Residents who live here and tourists who come here to visit do so because of the surf and sand. We are an island, surrounded by water, and you expect us to just close down access to that water because of some science fiction mumbo jumbo? If you are wrong, our economy will lose millions at a time we can ill afford to do so, and we will have created unnecessary panic."

Katie viewed their concerns as a lack of fortitude, and all she could think of was: *Not a pair of cojones among them.* She knew she was right, yet she also knew how hard it was for others to believe the story. Katie feared that the panic created by going public with this would pale in comparison to the panic that would ensue if the killer fish went on an eating binge over the coming weekend. It would be like a coastal buffet with humans as the main course.

Katie was proud of Ted for supporting her as aggressively as he did but, in the end, he caved in to the pressure. He was too close to retirement to try and shake up the system and put his pension at risk. In his mind, he elevated the problem and took the burden off his own shoulders. To some extent, his conscience was clear but he cared deeply about the welfare of those he felt obligated to protect. He just hoped it wouldn't again turn tragic.

CHAPTER 36

Katie was physically and emotionally drained. Most of all, she was scared, not for her own well-being but for the unsuspecting public that could further fall victim to the killer fish. She was frustrated at her herself for not being able to do more to halt the deaths. Katie feared it would take a miracle to get through the coming weekend without another tragic incident, especially with all the beach goers that would be in the water and the fishermen in their boats. She was distraught over the inaction by those leaders entrusted to protect the public interest. How they could rationalize away the crisis and turn a blind eye toward potential mayhem was beyond Katie's comprehension. And then there was the not-so-minor issue of the bluefish tournament. Her intuition kept telling her that something very bad was going to happen and neither she nor anyone else would be able to stop it. Katie just wanted to go home and crash in her bed, but this was one of those times she really needed to be with Rick.

When Rick answered his cell phone, the voice at the other end said longingly, "If you're still buying, I'm ready for those drinks."

"Guess it didn't go too well?"

"Rick, you have no idea. Those bastards put their heads in the sand and refused to do anything but wait this out. They even refused authorizing another press conference."

"Where are you?"

"Just leaving the office parking lot. How's Jack?

"He's doing much better and seems almost back to normal. But he's still talking about the mermaid. And the more he talks about it, the more whacky the whole situation sounds."

"I still wonder what that's all about? Odd that he would continue to recall that part of his ordeal. Maybe it was just one of those near-death visual experiences."

"How about we grab a few drinks and dinner? We can talk about it then."

"I'd like to go home first to take a shower and freshen up a bit. To say I was sweating today would be a *gross* understatement."

"It's five-thirty now. I still have to call the captains about tomorrow's plan for trying to lock in on your monster fish. I'll pick you up at seven. We'll go to Casa Mariachi."

"Sounds good. I do love their shrimp fajita. And a couple of margaritas would do me well right about now. Make your calls and I'll be ready when you get here."

"Good deal. See you later. Love you."

"Love you too."

Katie's head was spinning and she was troubled by yet another gnawing question: *What the hell's up with Jack's mermaid?* Had Jack actually seen something or was he experiencing hallucinations from some form of post-traumatic stress? In all the years Katie had known Jack, he was nothing less than rational and always in control. While he rarely talked with her about his sniper days in Viet nam, Rick did pass along some of Jack's stories. Jack had come close to meeting his maker a few times in southeast Asian jungles, and he apparently came close to the end again, this time a lot closer to home. Katie couldn't help but wonder if his vision of a mythological aquatic creature had something to do with the killer fish, or more importantly, why he was still alive.

Rick called each of his captain friends one by one to review the plans for the weekend scouting mission and to reaffirm their specific role in the plan. All captains would be on the water for both days of the bluefish tournament.

Captain Sandy Bassonet had two orthopedic surgeons expecting to be put on the winning bluefish. The prize money paled in comparison to what they each netted from their joint practice. They just wanted bragging rights, and Captain Bassonet would work his butt off to accommodate that goal, but he wanted bragging rights too.

Captain Valerie Russo had canceled her charters and would host Nick Tanner on board. Rick thought that a bit surprising but was glad those two had hooked up. She knew the Sound as well as any other captain and Nick knew fish better than anyone who'd be on the water those two days. He probably knew more about bluefish too than anyone, except Katie. They'd make a good team.

Captain Al Robinetti would forego any charters for the weekend, opting to fish with his son and daughter. As a skilled captain and one trained in the scientific process, his powers of observation would be invaluable.

Captain John Sullivan's two party boats would be packed to the rails and, as usual, he'd be fishing deep water out toward the middle of the Sound. Sully would be in constant contact with his brother, the skipper of his second boat. Given Jack's experience, Rick suspected these fish might be around the Middle Grounds and the adjacent shoal during daytime hours. With the two party boats chumming the waters all day, and with all the bait that would be in on more than 130 tempting hooks, the stage was set for possible encounters.

Captain Joey Marrone had charters for Saturday and Sunday but would not be fishing for bluefish. Rather, he and his clients would be in search of little tunny, a highly-coveted pelagic game fish that visit the Long Island Sound during late summer and early fall. Since these fish are constantly on the move, Captain Marrone would travel far and wide along inshore areas of the Sound in hot pursuit. His range would provide a good assessment of what was taking place throughout a large area from the western Sound out toward Plover Dunes.

Although the captains would be shoving off from different ports and harbors along the Sound, they'd all be connected via VHF radios and cell phones. If they encountered anything unusual, they would use the cell phones since other boats often monitor VHF channels for fish reports. What Rick wanted to avoid at all costs was a potentially dangerous situation if the killer fish were spotted. The entire fleet would want in on big fish no matter what they were. The captains would all check in with Rick again once they were on the water in the morning. Rick expected to burn a ton of gas as he and Katie patrolled the entire area of coverage, from Smith's Bay east to Mount Misery Harbor. He was pleased with his plan and more confident than ever that his team of captains was the best for the task at hand.

Katie had showered and walked through a fine mist of Acqua Di Gio, her favorite fragrance. Rick liked that too. For added measure Katie applied a bit of perfume to her pulse points: the crook of each the elbows, the back of the knees, the nape of the neck, the wrists, and her cleavage. She dressed in jeans and a tee shirt that proclaimed *life is good*. Moccasins and a baseball cap would round out Katie's outfit. She liked the scent, and she felt comfortable. It should be a delightful evening. All she had to do was wipe the killer fish from her mind.

Rick was right on time. Katie was sitting in an old wooden rocker on her small front porch, the soft light of dusk framing her petite and attractive body. She radiated with an aura that caused Rick to momentarily forget about dinner. She rose from the chair and walked toward the car as Rick exited his vehicle to the passenger-side door. He was mesmerized. The entire killer fish episode had brought Katie back closer to him than she had been in a very long time. Rick had no intentions of squandering this opportunity to win back Katie's affections once and for all. Rick noticed the small overnight bag clutched in Katie's right hand, and as she approached the truck, her perfume began to weave its magic. The spell was cast.

"Wow! You look great and you smell even better."

"Well . . . you always did like Gio's water. And you don't look so bad yourself. Is that a new tee shirt?" Katie said with a playful smile.

"Only the best for you. And it's clean. It even has a picture of a bluefish on the back."

"You really know how to spoil the perfect moment, don't you?" But Katie was very happy to see Rick and, just before getting into the truck, she got on her tip toes and kissed him gently on the lips. It was one of those kisses that said, *Thank you, I love you, and there'll be more later.*

The drive to Casa Mariachi took only about ten minutes. With one hand on the steering wheel, Rick held Katie's hand with the other; their fingers interlocked. They listened to music but didn't say much. Katie was a big fan of Jimmy Buffett and Rick loaded up the CD player with a few of his albums. Katie was tapping away to the beat of the music and singing along with words that evoked visions of cheeseburgers, tropical paradise, and forty-year-old pirates past their prime.

Katie was really getting into the songs when the fish demons popped back into in her mind. Suddenly she removed her hand from Rick's. Katie's brief respite from the day's ordeal was overshadowed by the omnipresent horror of the killings.

Rick immediately sensed the change. "We'll get through this, Katie. There has to be a solution. Trust me. We'll figure this out."

Just as Jimmy B belted out the lyrics, *it's five o'clock somewhere,* Rick pulled into the restaurant parking lot. Mama Lydia owned Casa Mariachi and greeted Katie and Rick with hugs and kisses as if they were family. Carlos, the head waiter, acknowledged the couple as Señor Rick and Señorita Katie, and said, "Your table is ready." They had the nice corner booth in the back of the restaurant so that Katie and Rick would have privacy, that is, until the mariachi band showed up to play Rick's favorite Mexican tunes. Carlos knew the drill and immediately arrived at the table with the house special Mariachi

Margarita for Katie and a cold bottle of Negra Modello for Rick, a big bowl of chips and salsa between them.

The mariachis belted out "*Maria en la Playa*" and Rick sang along. When the song ended, the band segued right into Katie's favorite tune, "*Caballitos,*" and upon reaching the part where the little horses neigh, Katie whinnied along with the band. She was finally starting to relax from the day's ordeal. Katie and Rick drank and talked and held hands. It was just like old times. Their conversation was mostly of the way things were and the way they could be. They both deftly avoided any mention of their current challenges, personal and professional. There was no mention at all of *the fish.* This was the mental escape Katie needed. It was also one of the best evenings they had had together in a very long time. Carlos brought them their favorite shared dessert, a bunuelo, filled with vanilla ice cream and topped with whipped cream, honey, and cinnamon. They devoured it and laughed at their excess consumption. Rick pushed the last bit of the dessert onto Katie's side of the plate and as he did so, their eyes locked in intense magnetic attraction. They both leaned toward the middle of the table and kissed. The real dessert was soon to come once they arrived back at Rick's place.

As the couple made love, the fish killed again.

CHAPTER 37

Rick leaned over the bed and kissed Katie gently on the forehead. "Wake up. It's time to get going."

Katie squinted with one eye and peeked at the alarm clock. "Jesus Christmas, it's only four o'clock, Rick. Come back to bed."

"I'd love to, sweet pea, but the tournament begins at sunrise and we need to be on the water by six."

Rick nudged Katie and pulled the sheets back from the bed. Katie had slept naked and, for an instant, the invitation to rejoin her in bed pulled at him like a moon tide pulls and pushes water in and out of the surf. Rick hesitated for a moment. He would have liked nothing better than some early morning delight, but he knew what had to be done. This was going to be one hell of a day.

"Let's go, up and at it. Want breakfast? I'll make my not-so-famous eggs McCord."

Grudgingly, Katie moved to the edge of the bed and sat up. It didn't take long for the killer fish to take over her thoughts. She cupped her head in her hands. "I dread this day, Rick. I wish it was already over."

"Go take a shower and I'll have coffee and eggs ready when you get out."

While Katie showered and Rick prepared breakfast, the mutant fish cruised the near-shore waters of the Long Island Sound in search of their morning victims. Dozens of pods of the savage killers had located a massive school of Atlantic menhaden swimming lazily beneath the surface. The fish tore through hap-less mossbunker like buzz saws. It was another blood and guts massacre. The most violent attacks came from school's lead alpha male. The fish was still pissed off at the dog. The canine had made a bull's-eye bite that ripped open the fish's right orbital eye socket, an injury that had robbed the alpha male of its right-side peri-pheral vision; a serious disadvantage for a predator, a potentially fatal flaw for the leader of the pack. Although the alpha male was weakened by this disability, he prevailed. While challenged for the leadership position of the entire school by a number of would-be successors, after killing two of his challengers, the rest of the ambi-tious and younger males had backed off. They would yet again defy their leader at the right moment, but for now they would be con-tent to follow his lead. With the school of menhaden decimated, the voracious killers retreated to the offshore depths of the Sound until their next foray inshore.

Katie emerged from the shower. A long towel wrapped around her breasts covered all but her legs. Rick had his back to her as she moved behind him. Katie embraced Rick from the rear with a bear-sized hug. Her head was turned sideways and rested in the middle of Rick's back.

"Those eggs smell yummy." Katie was indeed hungry, but break-fast was the last thing on her mind. As Rick moved within Katie's grasp, she eased up on the hug allowing him to turn fully toward her. Once Rick shifted completely around, the two were standing face to face. He knew that fighting against this moment would prove fruit-less. The towel opened partially as Katie pushed herself closer to Rick, her genitals rubbing against his. Her nipples stood at attention. She could feel the moisture move between swollen lips. Rick felt himself getting hard and knew the eggs would have to wait. The intensity of the moment did not call for long lovemaking. It was over almost as quickly as it had begun.

"I love quickies," Katie quipped, "and I love your *Huevos McCord*."

Rick smiled but he sensed Katie was trying to divert attention away from the day's primary task. Rick was now all business. He had a bad feeling about the tournament.

"Katie, put the dishes in the washer, and I'll go get my gear. We need to get a move on. We have a lot to do this morning."

Rick's forceful tone brought Katie back to the reality of the moment.

The ride to the marina was short and quick. There weren't many other cars on the road at five-thirty on a Saturday morning. Those that were out and about were driven either by fishermen or night owls returning home from Friday night partying. Rick's boat sat snugly tied in the slip. Fishermen were launching other boats at the ramp while a few early bird vessels sat out in the back end of the harbor awaiting the tournament director's flare, signaling the start of the contest. Rick loaded his gear into the boat and then he and Katie walked toward the launch ramp. Katie detoured to The Fisherman's Deli to get some sandwiches for lunch while Rich picked up a few buckets of chum at the bait shack.

As Rick waited for Katie to exit the deli, he watched a thirty-two-foot long Yellowfin offshore center console back into the water. Rick did not recognize the guy driving the truck but he did recognize the voice on the dock that belted out a greeting. The voice turned his stomach.

"Hey, sport. Been in a long time. Want to pick up where we left off?"

All Rick could think of was: *What the fuck is this guy doing here?*

"Lenny Kramer. Never expected seeing you here."

"Decided to splash my new ride in this tournament. I hear tell that there are some *really* big fish around. Like the boat? It cost a bundle."

Lenny's tone suggested to Rick that the blowhard might know something about the killer fish. The guy was connected to many social circles and the killings had become a hot topic of cocktail hour conversation. Or perhaps he was bullshitting.

Rick wanted to just walk away. This guy was trouble and he didn't want Katie crossing paths with the asshole.

"Nice boat you got there, Lenny. It's rigged out to the nines."

"Best of everything; three-hundred-grand worth of boat, motors, tackle, and toys. Even flew Captain Henry Reichert up from Key West for this. He's the best. Know him?"

The dig at Rick didn't go unnoticed. *Once a prick always a prick.*

Rick spotted Katie walking out of the deli and wanted to put an end to this chitchat with Lenny Kramer. If it continued much longer, nothing good would come of it.

"Can't say I know him. But that is a sweet rig you got there. Good luck in the tournament."

Lenny was never one to let up. "With this boat and captain, no luck needed. All skill."

Arrogant fucker, Rick thought. *I hope Captain Marvelous forgot to put in the drain plug.*

"I'm sure you will do well," Rick responded.

Katie was now standing beside Rick. Lenny couldn't resist that moment either.

"Who's the pretty chippy there, Captain Rick?"

Rick ignored the question and motioned to Katie to head back to his boat. With a halfhearted wave, he bid Lenny Kramer farewell. He hoped never to see that bastard again.

"See you at the weigh-in, Ricky boy. I'm going to win this thing, and then buy dinner for that sexy girlfriend of yours."

"Who *is* that guy?" Katie finally asked.

"He's the reason I'm not still guiding in Alaska."

Once back aboard *Maya*, Rick started up the engines and turned on the VHF to check in with the other captains. Each harbor along the north shore of Long Island hosted the tournament and Rick's friends launched from several different locations. Captain Bassonet was the only one whose clients were registered in the tournament, so his day would be devoted totally to bluefish. The rest would go about their normal charters and, if bluefish presented an opportunity, they would seize the moment.

Katie had fished with Rick enough to know the morning drill. The engines had warmed sufficiently and she detached the bow and mid-ship ropes from the cleats. Rick smiled. He loved having Katie on his boat. The tournament would officially begin at sunrise and most of the participating boats were sitting in the lower harbor. Just west of the ferry dock, Lenny's boat sat at the head of the pack. With nine-hundred horsepower motors sitting on the transom, it wasn't like he needed the extra advantage. It was sort of like bringing an Abrams Battle Tank to a bumper car ride. But that was Lenny: the guy had to control every situation. Rick counted thirty-seven boats awaiting the start flare. He added that number to all the ramps from the Throgs Neck Bridge in the Bronx out to Orient Point and said to Katie, "I bet there are at least a few hundred boats out there for this tournament, not counting the folks from the Connecticut side."

"It could get chaotic and dangerous out there," Katie replied, "especially if our fish decide to play."

At the precise moment of sunrise, the starter's flare cracked and illuminated the dawn sky. It sounded somewhat like a NASCAR race as boats flew out of the harbor along the outside edges of the channel. Lenny Kramer's was the only boat in the restricted five-mile-an-hour zone running wide open at full throttle. Rick's thought at seeing that was, *what a dick head*. Rick also thought there was no need to rush. He'd take his time getting out of the harbor and give some of the other captains a chance to get set up. Rick put his arm around Katie's shoulder.

Rick pushed the throttle forward and pointed *Maya*'s bow toward the harbor inlet. The events that would shape this tournament would haunt their thoughts for the rest of their lives.

CHAPTER 38

As Lenny Kramer's boat, *Semper Victoris*, roared toward open water, Lenny tapped Captain Reichert on the shoulder and pointed to the middle of the Sound. While neither Lenny nor Reichert were familiar with the water of the central Long Island Sound, Lenny paid handsomely for current local knowledge. He had contacted a number of captains, paying them each a full day's charter fare for the GPS coordinates of the largest bluefish. Having assembled quite a list of hot spots, Lenny had his sights set on a specific area west of the Middle Grounds, some of the deepest water in the Sound where the biggest bluefish had been caught recently. *Semper Victoris*'s nine-hundred-horsepower would have them out to their first fishing spot in less than ten minutes.

Captain Reichert backed down on the throttle, they approached the waypoint numbers. Lenny patted the captain on the back. "Let's get this done." He then reached for one of the three bunker chum buckets. Lenny was eager to begin fishing. Working together, he and Captain Reichert placed the frozen menhaden in a chum bag, attached it to a gunwale cleat on the down current side of the boat, and tossed it overboard. The goal was to establish an inviting slick of defrosted bunker parts that would draw big bluefish up toward the boat to feed, and hopefully to eat one of the baited hooks. While they waited, Reichert rigged the fishing rods, setting three off the stern of the boat, two baited with chunks of bunker and one with mackerel, varying depths.

Lenny was not a man of much patience. The computer-traded market in which he operated happened at speeds measured in micro and nanoseconds. Sitting and waiting for a fish to bite was not high on Lenny's list of prime-time activities; he liked his fishing fast. Establishing a productive chum slick takes time. Bits and pieces of bunker and scent needed to permeate the water before fish could be attracted and stimulated to feed. It had only been about half an hour into the drift when Lenny got antsy.

"Henry, cut up those mackerel and start tossing them overboard. And put some of that bunker oil overboard too," Lenny barked.

"Maybe we should give it some time Lenny. We don't want to over-feed whatever may be beneath the slick."

"Bluefish never stop attacking and marauding. Just like me. Throw more shit overboard."

Reichert was not one to challenge his boss. He was being paid a ton of money for this tournament and he didn't want to piss the guy off. Lenny had a short fuse.

"Okay Lenny, you got it."

With that, Reichert cut several mackerel into small chunks and tossed them into the slick at a moderate pace. He also picked up a large squeeze bottle of bunker oil and sprayed a liberal amount in the water.

"Spray more," Lenny ordered. "Remember, when I win this thing, you get half the fifty Gs."

Reichert was indeed motivated by money to spray more oil in the water, regardless of contempt he may have held for his boss. But this time, Lenny may have been right. After only ten minute of tossing out the mackerel chunks, Reichert pointed to a commotion at the far end of the slick and said simply, "Bluefish."

They both watched as the fish moved up the slick and closer to the boat. As best as they could tell, these looked to be big fish. At once, the middle rod and the portside stern rod bounced to life. Lenny grabbed the rod closest to him and Reichert took hold of the portside rod. "Good one," Lenny said. Reichert's fish, although a respectable bluefish, was smaller, so he left it in the water and moved to net Lenny's fish. The plan was to net fish rather than gaff them so as to avoid bleeding that would rob any fish of needed ounces at weigh-in.

It was indeed a good fish that registered fifteen pounds, two ounces on the certified boat scale. "Solid fish," Reichert said, but Lenny knew a winning bluefish would have to be bigger. The previous year's first place weight was sixteen pound, seven ounces. Nonetheless, Lenny motioned to Reichert to put the fish in the fish box. "If we have to, we'll use it as bait later on in the day. These fucking things are cannibals and love to eat their own kind."

As Lenny and Reichert discussed the fate of the first bluefish, they failed to notice that the other rod with a fish on took a violent bounce and shot back up with a limp line.

"Pull in that other fish, Reichert. We'll use that one too."

Reichert turned to reel in his bluefish but instantly realized something was amiss.

"Looks like it got off." Reeling in all the line, Reichert was even more astonished. "It bit through the hundred-pound wire leader."

"Not possible. You must have tied a shitty knot."

"No, Lenny. The knot didn't slip. The fish bit right through the wire. But it wasn't that big . . ."

"Forget it," Lenny said as he reached to grab the middle rod that was now doubled over. The bluefish was a carbon copy of the first and it too endured the same fate: tossed into the fish box. Over the next hour, Lenny and Reichert caught a half dozen more bluefish but none larger than the first. Lenny once again grew impatient and abusive.

"Move this fucking boat, Henry. We need to find bigger fish, I'm paying you to find big fish; now get on with finding them."

Reichert wasn't so convinced they needed to change locations. While he was fishing unfamiliar waters, he was a good captain with much fishing experience. In his opinion, they had done well so far.

They caught good-sized fish and had a strong slick working in their favor. He would risk going against Lenny's wishes.

"You are also paying me for my advice and I think we should give this drift some more time. I'm feeling like we can draw some bigger fish up as the tide gets stronger."

"'I paid for the advice of others too and I think we should move back over there by the lighthouse." Reichert was prepared to dig in his heels on this."I'm saying we stay. We move, it is a big mistake. You want to win this thing or not?"

Lenny hated giving in but he grudgingly conceded to Reichert's position.

"Keep drifting. This better work, Henry."

"I'll put out a new chum bucket and get some more mackerel chunks in the water. I feel good about this."

Semper Victoris had drifted a mile and a half since the day's fishing began. The boat moved over deep water as the electronic fish finder marked big fish down near the bottom of the water column. Captain Reichert took notice.

"Lenny, we have some large marks on the finder showing fish beneath the boat, down about one hundred feet. Let's see if we can get those fish to come up." Reichert re-baited each hook with fresh pieces of bunker and mackerel. He cut up some additional bunker and mackerel to seed the water with new scent. Lenny was invigorated by the mention of big fish. He stood at the ready to take hold of the first rod that showed signs of life. The wait wasn't long; the rod with the bait set deepest went off first. Lenny was all over it and made sure the fish was on tight by setting the hook a second and a third time.

"Good one! Good one!"Lenny proclaimed. The stout rod strained under the weight of the heavy fish. "This could be the winner, Reichert." Lenny held tight as the big fish pulled line off the reel. It seemed intent on heading back to the bottom. Lenny muscled the fish, turning it and getting it to swim toward the surface. Suddenly, the rod shot down toward the water and then its stored energy caused it to spring back up in one instantaneous motion. The line had been severed.

"Son of a bitch. What the fuck is going on here, Reichert? You gotta check those knots."

"Let me see the line, Lenny." The captain inspected the area of the break and it became immediately apparent that the fish had bitten through the steel wire.

"These must be some bluefish, Lenny. The wire is severed again. It isn't a knot failure."

"Then put some stronger fucking wire on here, Captain. Let's get with the program. That fish could have been first place and fifty large."

Reichert remembered that he had some stronger wire in his gear bag. It was what he had used on his most recent shark fishing charter in Florida.

"If this doesn't do it, nothing will," Reichert announced as he tied and twisted the wire to Lenny's line. "Two hundred pounds of wire shark leader. Nothing in this water can bite through it."

"I hope so, Henry," Lenny replied, feeling somewhat relieved and vindicated by the extra strength leader.

With all fishing rods re-rigged with shark wire leaders and baited with fresh chunks of bunker and mackerel, the two anglers waited yet again for the next fish to bite.

CHAPTER 39

Long Island's "Biggest and Baddest Bluefish Tournament" was well underway. Based on reports Rick and Katie listened to on the VHF, many bluefish had already been caught. A fish of about seventeen pounds was atop the leader board. Fortunately, no strange incidents had yet to be reported. Unfortunately, Katie needed answers. Rick had decided to set up his chum slick in deep water, between Mount Misery Ledge and Mount Misery Inlet, the general location of one of the unexplained attacks. The chum bits had attracted large rafts of small baitfish, and only small, cocktail-sized bluefish had come in to feed on the bait. Both Rick and Katie knew full well the fish they were after could show up anywhere at any minute. Rick would give the slick more time to attract their intended targets, but he also wanted to make the rounds of the entire area so Katie could observe conditions on the water that might offer clues to their behaviors.

The VHF crackled to life, "Captain Rick, Captain Rick, come in *Maya*. Come in Rick."

"Hi Valerie, Rick here. How goes it?"

"Going great," Captain Russo replied. "We are a drifting between Eagles Neck and Sandill Point. I have a good slick going and Nick has a bunch of electronic devices hooked up: some transmitting, some receiving signals."

Rick turned toward Katie and silently mouthed "Nick," and then he winked. Katie shrugged her shoulders and just smiled.

"Great. Any worthwhile activity to report?"

"That's a negative, Rick. Other than a ton of boats out here today, it has been quiet so far. If I did have action I would have called you on the cell."

Katie grabbed the microphone. "Val, it's Katie. Please tell Nick to call me on my cell. Thanks."

"You got it, Katie. Will keep you guys posted. Talk later. Over and out."

"Captain Russo and Nick. Pretty interesting pairing," Rick said. "Maybe I had the guy figured all wrong?"

"Enough with his sexual preferences, Rick. Who gives a crap?"

Katie's cell phone rang. "Hi, Nick. Did you bring any water sampling equipment with you?

"Sure did, Katie."

"If our killers show up in your slick, take some samples. I want to check for any traces of pheromones. Never know what we might find. And be careful."

"You got it, Katie. I have a feeling these things may be more unpredictable or smarter than we think. Plus, all these boats and water activity may have affected their normal patterns. But then again, it may not. Stay tuned."

"I'm right there with you. Talk later."

Although all was quiet inshore where Katie and Rick drifted, it was a different story out where Lenny Kramer and Captain Reichert fished. They were enjoying nonstop action with big bluefish. Reichert's decision not to move was paying dividends.

"Got to hand it to you, Henry. Your call was right on the mark." Lenny was happy. It had been fish after fish for the past hour. He had a second big bluefish in the box and was fast to another. "We need a twenty-pounder to seal the deal. This one could be it, Henry." When Lenny was in a good mood, it was Henry; if he was in a pissed off mood it was Captain Reichert; and if Lenny was in a really foul mood, then it was simply Reichert.

The bluefish on Lenny's line fought harder than any of the previous fish. It was indeed the biggest of the day. It was the *Fifty Gs* trophy he had wanted. The fish never jumped like big bluefish do. It stayed deep and fought like a heavyweight. But Lenny knew this fish would be his. He sensed fatigue. The runs were shorter, there was less head shaking to try to throw the hook, and Lenny was gaining line back onto the reel. As the fish was brought up through the water column, Lenny and Henry got a first look at the huge shining body; light reflected off the bluefish flanks. The fish had a long, thick body and a broad head, well-hooked in a corner of the jaw. Yet the big bluefish refused to relinquish.

The alpha male and his pack sensed the struggling fish. The first signals to reach him were the vibrations being broadcast by the fish fighting for its survival. Those sensations bombarded the alpha male's super-sensitive lateral line and directed him to prey like radar. The stressed bluefish emitted pheromones the alpha male recognized as indicators of fear. The pack of killer fish were now wired and excited. Once the alpha male homed in on the distressed fish and actually saw it, its own state of being transformed and it become wildly frenzied.

"Just look at that son of a bitch, Henry. I bet it is all of twenty pounds."

"That's a real trophy bluefish, Lenny. With a little luck, it may do the trick."

Lenny was ecstatic. Not only was this the biggest bluefish he had ever hooked, but it could be his ticket to top-dog bragging rights for a year. He couldn't wait to see the expression on Captain Rick McCord's face when he put this fish on the scale. *Up yours, hot shit fishing guide*, he thought.

The big bluefish had begun swimming in a death circle and was on its flank, a sure sign of exhaustion. With each pull of the rod, the fish offered less resistance and came easily to the surface.

"Let me get the net ready," Reichert said.

"No!" Lenny shot back. "I'm going to grab this bastard myself."

"I wouldn't do that if I were you, Lenny. That's a big fish. Why risk losing it or worse yet, getting bit?

"It's totally beat, hooked solid, and I completely dominated it. Now I'll add the exclamation point. I'll snatch it right behind the back of the head and he's mine—macho man style."

Although Lenny certainly had the hand strength to accomplish landing the big fish in that manner, this was yet again a moment of a too large ego winning out over compelling logic. He had his mind set on this and that was it. Reichert knew better than to challenge him.

"Okay, Lenny, but let me take hold of your rod when you grab the leader."

"That's fine, Henry."

The bluefish was just about eight feet under the surface of the water. A few more cranks of the reel handle and Lenny was able to grab hold of the leader. Reichert positioned himself to Kramer's left, the side where Lenny held the rod. With the leader now in hand, Lenny gave the rod to Reichert and pulled on the line the last few feet to get the fish to the surface. Lenny's prize was completely spent. It fought to the point of total collapse and its captor was poised to deftly grasp the big blue on the top part of the head and just behind the gills.

Lenny bent over the portside gunwale. The alpha male watched from below. He and his pod circled thirty feet beneath the boat. The commotion generated by the tussle between Lenny and the bluefish had the killer fish agitated, aggressive, and hungry. They waited but they were growing impatient. The alpha male was locked in on the big bluefish. He would not let this opportunity pass as happened with the dog. This was an easy meal and one he would not let slip away. The other fish would follow is lead.

Lenny pulled the leader tight with his left hand so the bluefish's head rested alongside the boat. With his strong right hand, the big man grasped his quarry's large head. It was as large a bluefish as

Lenny had ever seen. He held the fish with outstretched arm and shook it above his head as a gesture of conquest. Lowering his arm, he turned to the captain, "Henry, we did . . . " Before Lenny could compete the sentence, the alpha male rocketed from the depths. Reichert saw the monster first. His eyes froze on the creature. He wanted to scream a warning to Lenny but he couldn't. Fear had taken hold. By the time Lenny turned around to face the fiendish creature, it was too late. With powerful sweeps of its tail, the alpha male launched its body from the water. The killer's cavernous mouth was wide open, stiletto teeth ready to rip and shred. Momentum carried the killer upward as it engulfed the bluefish that Lenny had held moments before in triumphant jubilation. Lenny was face to face with the devil. Another strong push of the tail forced the alpha male farther out of the water and along a line that took it beyond the bluefish. The alpha male was eye to eye with Lenny as it bit down with immense force to sever Lenny's arm just beneath the shoulder muscle.

Lenny screamed as the alpha male dropped back into the water with his trophy and his arm. Blood spurted from Lenny's shoulder with each beat of his heart. Muscle, sinew, blood vessels, and bone were all clearly visible. Reichert finally gasped in horror.

"Do something, you pussy!" Lenny screamed with one of the last proclamations of his life. "What am I paying you for, Reichert?" Lenny was Lenny right until the end.

As the big man bled out from the fatal bite, his body began to spasm violently. Lenny involuntarily lurched forward into Reichert with such force that the two fell overboard. Lenny's blood was like icing on the cake for the riled-up pod of killer fish. They savagely attacked and fed on the bodies of both men.

CHAPTER 40

Katie and Rick were disappointed. They spent much of the morning and early afternoon drifting in the Long Island Sound from Mount Misery Ledge west to Smith's Bay, without a trace of the marine life they were hoping to see. Rick had checked in continuously with the other captains. They were all enjoying some good fishing but none had seen anything out of the ordinary. There were plenty of bluefish around but nothing that could qualify as the suspected mutant killers. Katie had suggested Rick make the run back to the east toward Plover Dunes and then move offshore to the middle of the Sound. Rick started *Maya*'s engines and steered a course east past Sandill Point. Captain Marrone gave him a high five, followed by a wave and a blown kiss from Captain Russo, whose boat was anchored among the rocks off the Old Colonial Lighthouse. As *Maya* approached the entrance to Port Roosevelt Harbor, an orange Coast Guard response boat blasted from the inlet on a course that zeroed in on Middle Grounds.

"Someone must be in trouble," Katie said.

"Someone definitely is in trouble." Rick watched as both the county marine patrol boat and the Port Roosevelt Fire and Rescue vessel also exited the harbor and trailed the Coast Guard boat in hot pursuit.

"Wonder what happened?" Katie said.

Rick didn't have a VHF marine scanner on his boat but he knew who did. "I'll give Sully a call. He's got one on the big boat. . . ." "Sully, it's Rick. What's with all the police and rescue traffic?"

"Seems there was an incident offshore near Stratford Shoal."

"What kind of incident, Sully?"

"A passing fisherman reported seeing a boat adrift with no one on board and lots of blood on deck."

"Any ID on the boat?"

"Yeah, Rick. A thirty-two-foot Yellowfin. *Semper Victoris*."

Rick glanced toward Katie, with that *oh shit* look in his eyes. "I know one of the guys who was on that boat, Sully. Any word on the incident?"

"'Negative on that that, Rick. If I hear more, I'll let you know."

"Ten-four Sully. Later."

"It's them, Rick," Katie said emphatically. "I have no doubts. That guy Lenny got into them and it was all she wrote."

"It must have been quite the scene with Lenny Kramer hooked up to one of those creatures. I'm surprised they didn't spit the bastard out. But I kinda feel bad for his captain."

"No time for sarcasm, Rick. Looks like the games have only just begun."

"Maybe the Coast Guard will find them swimming around somewhere?"

"Not a chance in hell, Rick. If the fish were in a frenzied feeding state, it would be curtains the minute those two hit the water."

"Want to head out there and take a look?"

"No. That pod of fish has fed and will be on the move. Let's head farther east and then work our way back. Something has to break open soon," Katie said.

"Okay. We'll stay about a quarter mile off the beach heading east, angle out to the middle, and then work our way back inshore. That will give us a wide triangular grid area to search."

The killer fish had indeed fed but for them, full stomachs only meant temporary satisfaction. Had Katie known what was taking place beneath the surface, she would have been beyond terrorized. Pods of killer fish ravaged prey throughout much of the central

Long Island Sound. In total, there were several hundred monstrous mutants feeding indiscriminately on bunker, bass, small bluefish, and anything else that crossed their paths. When tearing through prey, they created an oily slick that floated to the surface, emitting a scent oddly reminiscent of watermelon. With all the blood, guts, and body parts that remained suspended lower in the water column, it was peculiar that such a pleasant aroma filled the air, like a perfume masking the stench of death.

The individual pods of fish continued with their macabre predation. They moved about the Sound and steadily joined an ever-building school of others of their kind. Their numbers grew as they amassed like an army and collectively fed. The oily slick also grew. A wide swath of the slimy emulsion did not go unnoticed. Captain Sully was at the helm of his party boat, the *Port Rosey Princess*, when he first spotted the growing slick. The melon-like scent wafted in the breeze and he knew something big was happening. Although his boat was packed with fares who were eagerly catching solid numbers of bluefish and striped bass, Sully knew a move was in order. He blew the boat's horn signaling *lines up* and announced over the loudspeaker that he'd be making a short run and to get ready for some faster and even more furious bluefish action.

The *Princess* had traveled only about a quarter mile when Captain Sully pulled back on the throttle and coasted to a stop. All his electronic fishing finding equipment was lit up like a Christmas tree in Rockefeller Center. Bait and game fish filled the screens. Many of the marks identified exceptionally large fish. Captain Sully once again blew the boat's horn, but this time the blast signified *lines down*. In an excited tone, the captain blurted out instructions: "Get the diamond jigs to the bottom. Reel up ten to twelve fast turns of the handle and drop the jig back down; reel up again. Come on, come on. Tons of fish. You should be hooked up by now."

"Fish on!" came first from the boat's stern, repeated on midships and then in the bow. Within seconds, all anglers on board were fast to bluefish. The mates had their hands, full running from one passenger to the next to gaff their prizes. The scene was utter mayhem as Captain Sully hailed his other party boat to join the festivities.

Fares celebrated their good fortune, hooting and hollering in blissful glee as fish after fish came over the rails and onto a deck that now looked like a crime scene. The mates dutifully unhooked each fish and tossed them unceremoniously into coolers and buckets. They had to continually hose down the deck to rid it of regurgitated matter that poured from the mouths of bluefish writhing in final attempts to get back onto the water. A woman in the bow proclaimed she had a big one on and needed a mate's assistance. Her fishing rod strained under the pressure of a large bluefish struggling on the surface of the water. She pulled back on the rod as hard as she could just as the killer fish surfaced and grabbed her bluefish. The line severed and the rod shot back, releasing all its stored energy. *Smack!* The rod struck her in the face and broke her nose. As blood streamed down her cheeks, two anglers positioned on either side of the startled woman stood flabbergasted. It was soon their turn to encounter the demons. Both their rods smashed down onto the rails and shattered as huge horrific heads emerged and cavernous mouths gobbled down the bluefish they had hooked. They gasped at the sight and backed away from the rail as two huge forked tails disappeared under the boat with their fish and their fishing rods.

The scene on the *Princess* was now pandemonium. Rods broke, people screamed, huge unknown fish surfaced all around the boat terrorizing passengers and crew alike. Captain Sully had never seen anything like it. He stayed calm despite the brewing bedlam and instructed all anglers to bring in their lines immediately. Sully had gotten a good look at the creatures and he now knew they were what Katie was after. He hastily dialed Rick's cell.

"Rick, it's Sully. All hell just broke loose. We saw Katie's killers."

"Where are you now, Sully?"

"About a mile north of the lobster pots, off Sandhill Point."

"What did you see?"

"Fish like I have never seen before, Rick. Big, ugly, and vicious. Tore through everything like buzz saws. We sustained a few minor injuries to passengers who had those things hooked."

"Is it still happening, Sully?"

"There's an enormous slick but the fish seem to have moved off toward shore. A few of my fares videoed the whole event so there may be some useful visual evidence."

"That's great, Sully. I'm sure Katie can use that."

"Let's just hope they don't sell it to News 21 after you get back to port."

The killers had indeed moved south and east. Many hunting pods had met and merged, forming the most lethal school of fish ever to swim the waters of the Long Island Sound. The mutant fish headed straight in the direction of crowded private and public beaches along the central north shore.

Katie's cell phone rang. It was Nick.

"Katie, dearest, they're back!"

"Nick, you saw them?"

"Yes, they came up around the boat several times and then sounded. We're anchored up in the rocks off the Old Colonial Lighthouse. And I got water samples. Running a few quick tests now."

"Nick, were they aggressive?"

"They surfaced, circled the boat few times, one charged the engine and bit the propeller, and then the entire bunch sounded. Guess we weren't appetizing enough."

"Did you get a good look at them?"

"I did. The one that hit the motor gave me a good profile. Katie, the fish had deformed features: a body like a huge bluefish, the maw of an African tigerfish, replete with massive teeth, and large armor-like scales of a tarpon. Pretty impressive package that looked to be about one hundred pounds. These are certainly formidable adversaries."

"Any idea which way they headed?"

"Beats me, Katie. They were up, around, and down and we haven't seen a trace since."

"Okay, Nick, but be careful. There is one big freakin' school of those things swimming around now, and a couple of guys in the tournament just went missing and are presumed dead. Sully had them in huge numbers. Created havoc with his party boat fares. There may be more of them headed your way. If you see them again, let me know ASAP."

"Roger that, Katie. Will do."

Katie and Rick compared notes. It was obvious their killers had begun to turn up the heat and were on a roll. Based on the reports, Katie was confident this recent feeding behavior would continue throughout the day. But she lacked confidence that any eradication plan would be effective. She had no clue how to rid the Sound or all of Long Island of these creatures.

"Rick, I think we should just zigzag our way back west. With all this activity, we have a good chance at bumping into these fish somewhere along the way."

Rick nodded his approval and steered *Maya* in a serpentine pattern toward the beach and then veered offshore about a half mile. As Rick rounded navigation buoy 9 offshore of Plover Dunes, his cell phone rang again. To his surprise, it was Jack Connors.

"Hey, Rick. They released me from the hospital. I'm at the fueling dock in front of Charlie's Bait and Tackle. Come pick me up."

"Jack, are you sure you are up for this?"

"Just come get me. I'm fine."

"Okay, Jack. See you in a few."

CHAPTER 41

Two thirteen-year-old twin brothers and their younger sister man-euvered standup paddleboards through Mount Misery Inlet and out into the open Sound. The trio paddled east parallel to the shoreline about two hundred yards off the beach. The eight-year old girl trailed her big brothers and kept yelling at them to wait up, but as older siblings often do, they ignored her. The brothers figured since she had on a life vest, they didn't need to babysit her. Every once in a while, they would turn around to make sure their sister was still there. She was a strong little kid, an up-and-coming soccer and field hockey player, but the boys constantly competed against one another in every sport they played. It was no different with paddleboarding. They paddled feverishly to see who was faster and who could reach an ever-expanding finish line. They just never stopped with their competitive games. The young girl paddled slow and steady and was somewhat like the turtle that expected to beat the hare. While far behind her brothers, she implored them to slow down. They never did and the distance between them grew.

"Look at those kids on the paddleboards." Katie said as the boat approached Mount Misery Inlet. "Do you think we should head over and warn them?" Katie didn't see the little girl.

The boys had reached a point off Pavilion Dunes, a concession stand and food court set back from Pine Beach. This popular stretch of municipal sand and water had attracted a throng of beachgoers on this picture perfect, late summer day. The boys needed a cold drink and were lured onto the beach by some similarly-aged girls frolicking in the surf. One of the brothers turned back to his sister off in the distance and whistled. He pointed to the beach and gestured for her to follow them in. She was too far away to clearly see him.

Jack waited on the dock. He was still feeling the effects of his ordeal but hospitals don't like keeping folks in bed longer than need be. The insurance companies frown upon that and Lord knows, insurance companies do control health care in this country. Once Jack's vitals were back to normal, he was shown the door, and there was no better way for Jack to begin his recuperation than to get back on the water.

"Ahoy, Jack," Katie shouted.

"About time. Been waiting here all of five minutes." Jack smiled.

"Grab a line, Jack, and tie her off. Gotta top off this tank. Been doing a lot of running around today."

Katie jumped onto the deck and hugged Jack. "I'm so glad you're okay. You had us scared. How are you feeling?"

"I'm good, Katie. Been through a lot worse. Thanks for the concern."

"Well then, I guess I will go pee. Rick, need anything from the shop?"

"Yeah, a second mortgage on my house to pay for this fuel bill. But a few more orange Gatorades will do."

Rick moved to Jack and gave him a firm hug.

"Glad you are okay, Jack. We were all worried. Now, what the hell were you talking about with those mermaids?"

"Rick, I wish I knew. I fell overboard. I saw those horrible fish creatures. Closed my eyes and when I opened them, I saw the mermaid. That's all there is to it. Probably delirious at the time too. Don't know if it was real or imagined, but whether in the water or in my mind, she was real to me at the time."

"Those creature are out there now, Jack. Sully, Valerie, and Nick all saw them today. When we head back out, we will continue to search for them."

Rick's cell phone rang. It was Captain Sandy Bassonet.

"Rick, Sandy here. I'm in Port Rosey Harbor. I think we just eyed your monster fish. One of my fares landed an eighteen-and-three-quarter-pound bluefish off the sand flat and something came up behind the fish as we netted it. Tried to eat it. That fish was one badass. Big as a tarpon and a mouth full of teeth."

"Were there others?"

"Saw just the one. But we did watch some nervous and turbulent water move out the harbor and though the inlet. Could have been a bunch of these things on the prowl."

"That's very possible, Sandy. At least you got your big bluefish. That one could end up in the tournament money. Thanks for the heads up. If you see more, give me another call. And stay safe."

"Who are you talking to now?" Katie had returned from the bait shop.

"Sandy. He had an encounter with the fish in Port Roosevelt Harbor."

"That's right next door, Rick. These fish are definitely on the prowl today."

"Jack, untie us and let's get a move on."

Maya inched away from the dock and toward the inlet. The pod of killer fish that had been in Port Roosevelt Harbor moved out from that inlet and in the direction of Mount Misery Ledge. The fish headed toward a fleet of recreational fishing boats gathered along a deep drop-off on the northeast corner of the ledge. Other fish of their kind also moved toward that location. The stage had been set for a congregation of demons. The fish were attracted to a large collection of bait and to the vibrations emitted by all the fishing activity, their lateral lines bombarded by the sensory signals of vulnerable and struggling prey.

The alpha male with the mangled eye played the leadership role in organizing the assemblage of killers. Despite his disabled vision, he was still the strongest pack leader; his other senses had sharpened to offset the damage to his eye. Other males deferred to his cues and followed his direction. It seemed as if the encounter with the dog made him more resolute in his killing ambitions. The fish never forgot the dark silhouette of the canine framed against a bright sky. And it never forgot the missed opportunity to kill and feed. Now it needed to even the score for the damage to its eye.

No one yet realized the aquatic apocalypse that was building. Rafts upon rafts of bait moved onto Mount Misery Ledge as gulls and terns dived among the smorgasbord of small fish. The actions of the birds were a signal for all anglers in the area to move their boats to the vicinity of the ledge. No one wanted to miss a rare opportunity to cash in on this special bounty of predatory game fish that zeroed in on the area to feed. Their numbers grew to hundreds as all pods joined into one massive community of assassins, plotting their next major assault.

On the way out from the harbor, Rick spotted Captain Joey Marrone. He had moved outside the inlet following a school of little tunny, locally known as albies. His husband and wife charter wanted to catch tunny fish on fly rods, rounding out their "slam" of bass, blue-fish, and albies. Joey was one of the best at this game and his reputation had his boat booked on days when most other light-tackle guides stayed tied to the docks and drank beer. Both fares were fast to fish. Rick idled up alongside his boat. "I see it's going well today, Joey?"

"Yeah, Rick. Been a good one. A ton of fish around. But neither hide nor hair of the things you are after."

"They have been spotted, Joey, so be careful."

"Be careful of what?" the husband angler on board asked. "Can I catch it on a fly rod?"

Jack turned and replied, "Buddy, you don't want to know, and no, not if you value your life."

Katie's phone rang. It was Nick again. Katie, "I ran those water samples. Not good."

"What do you mean?"

"Highest levels of concentrated aggression pheromones I have ever recorded in samples. For me to get these kinds of readings, the stuff must be pouring out of them. These fish are stoked for a big fight. The only other thing I can compare these results to is what I have read of bull elephants in *musth*, whose hormones and testosterone get so elevated they start attacking and killing everything in sight."

"Nick, call Ted and tell him to contact authorities to close the beaches. Tell him it is imperative to prevent further injury and loss of life. I have a feeling all hell is about to break loose. And tell him we have video from the party boats."

"Ten four, Katie, will do. We'll head your way."

The enormous oily slick now extended for miles from Smith's Bay east to Mount Misery Inlet. Frenzied feeding and fishing activity on and around the offshore ledge kept the killer fish feeding deep in the water column. The edge of an adjoining shoal dropped to a depth of about one hundred feet. That's where the dominant alpha male and his pod prowled and fed. That is, until the beast sensed the little tunny farther east from the ledge. Tunas of all sizes were a preferred food source of the mutant killers. Other than sharks, they were the only other fish in the ocean fast enough to catch them. As minute traces of molecular tuna scent aroused the alpha male, his body language signaled the others to follow. It headed toward Mount Misery Inlet. Although the killers began to move from the ledge, the inviting slick had attracted another marine predator whose presence had surprisingly gone unnoticed.

The school of little tunas had dispersed into several dozen groupings that corralled small baitfish on the surface and slashed through them with speed and accuracy. Their surface feeding actions were plainly visible to the trained human eye and captain Joey Marrone moved his boat to where he thought the fish might surface next, giving his husband and wife team a better shot at hooking up. Rick had also noticed the feeding activity and moved *Maya* over for a better look. He shut down the engines and he and Katie and Jack just watched the fracas.

"Rick, do you smell that?"

"Yep. There must be quite the slaughter going on under the water."

Jack also replied, "That's the smell of fear and carnage. Those little tunas are very effective hunters."

The trio watched as water boiled all around the boat and little tunny tore through peanut bunker and anchovies.

"This never ceases to amaze me," Rick said.

"Look," Katie answered, "Joey's two clients are both hooked up to albies."

The husband and wife were indeed hooked solid to two little tunny. The fish moved off with blazing speed, trying to regain contact with their school. The couple's fly rods were bent in parabolic splendor as line poured from the reels. The fish were determined to escape, but the skill and patience of the anglers overcame the tunnys' fight for freedom.

The short but intense fight was now in the end game. Both fish swam beneath the boat in ever-tightening circles, a sure sign of submission. The anglers had no intention of killing their catch. The fish would be released, but Captain Joey would have to act fast. All tunas, regardless of size, battle so aggressively they can actually fight themselves to exhaustion, then death.

The husband was first to get his fish to the boat. Joey grabbed the leader and the fish's tale slapped water in repetitive syncopation. With timing honed from many such landings, Joey thrust his hand at the fish, grabbed it by the tail and deftly hoisted it into the boat. After a quick photo for the scrapbook, the fish was tossed back into the water head first to give it a jolt of rejuvenating oxygen through its gills.

The wife now had her fish close to the boat. The drill was repeated once again. The hooked fish made tight circling motions close to the boat as Joey grabbed hold of the leader. The young captain kneeled down and readied himself for the grab. His hand was inches from the fish's tail when the woman screamed. Instinctively, Joey recoiled and released the leader. And then he saw the reason for the angler's scream. The ghastly monster had swallowed her prize fish whole and just laid suspended alongside the boat, its freakish yellow eyes locked onto hers. Killing her would have been easy; the shallow draft vessel had low gunwales and the creature could have jumped into the boat deck and seized the woman. Fortunately, the fish was distracted by more of its kind ravaging other fish. The creature turned and disappeared.

Katie heard the scream, but before Rick could call Joey Marrone, the water thirty yards east of his boat erupted with flying tunny swimming for their lives. Killer fish were everywhere, catapulting form the water with whole or half-bitten fish in their mouths. There were hundreds of them The water began to ran an eerie red from the blood of their victims. The entire scene was made even more chilling by the blast of a warning siren coming from the beach.

"I guess Nick got through to Ted and he listened," Katie said.

"And not a moment too soon," Jack added.

All eyes focused on the chaos building along the beach: lifeguards ushered bathers from the water; parents collected their kids; police vehicles cruised up and down the beach. The National Guard also showed up and two rescue helicopters flew east to west along the beaches. Katie was beyond relieved that the officials finally heeded her advice. She now knew there was no way to stop these fish from killing.

CHAPTER 42

Rick's eyes were glued to the binoculars. He searched the surf line for any sign the killers had moved close to the beach. He scanned the area immediately in front of the concession stand and noticed the two young male paddleboarders jumping up and down, waving their arms wildly and pointing out into the Sound. And then he remembered the girl.

Killer fish boiled on the surface in every direction. The water had turned a turbulent and frothy white with patches of pink and red where the mutants had fed. Their violent attacks transformed an otherwise tranquil Sound into a tumultuous maelstrom, sucking down anything that crossed the path of the killing machine. Nothing in the water could possibly survive the onslaught. It was as if all the aberrant creatures in the Sound had turned on at the same time to feed in the most frenzied and violent way.

"Jack, Katie, we have to find the girl on the paddleboard. I can't see her. The two boys are on the beach but she's not with them. She's got to be out here somewhere."

"Oh my God, Rick, she wouldn't stand a chance against these things."

"Katie, take the binoculars while I steer. Jack, there's another set of glasses in the port side, forward gear compartment. We need all eyes on the water."

By now, several of the other captains had motored into the area. Sandy Bassonet, Al Robinetti, and Joey Marrone had moved east following the fish. Rick called each one and told them to do a grid search of the area for the girl. Katie spotted Nick and Valerie out by the shoal marker. She called Nick and told him to move closer inshore. Five boats searched for the small paddle boarder.

The situation instantly went from bad to dire; Rick spotted the girl's two brothers paddling out from the beach. They too seemed intent on joining the urgent search for their sister. The boys paddled north and east. Rick focused his attention in the direction of their paddling but his concentration was broken by killer fish crashing into the boat as they pursued little tunny. One maddened fish was so attracted to the electrical impulses of the motors, it latched on to a propeller. Rick gunned the engine and teeth flew in all directions.

"That's one way to deal with the bastards," Jack said.

"Yeah, Jack, until my props blow up or they chew off the lower units."

Several of the mutant fish vaulted completely out from the water not more than ten feet from *Maya*'s bow. The trio on board got the best view yet of these fish since they first began their quest to find the killers.

"Holy Mary, Mother of God, those the fuckers that tried to drown me!" Jack exclaimed.

"And those ugly freaks tried to eat me," Rick said.

Katie remained vigilant in her search for the little girl. Out of the corner of her eye, she saw the brothers paddling excitedly toward a clump of exposed boulders that were a about four hundred yards from shore and a half mile due east. Katie trained the glasses on the boulder field and, much to her amazement, there was the little girl lying belly down on her paddleboard with her arms and feet dangling in the water. She looked to be playing hide and seek with her brothers, perhaps payback for them abandoning her for their girlfriends.

"Rick, quick, head for the rocks off Heron's Point. The girl is there."

Rick throttled up the motors, but he had to proceed slowly with all the big killer fish leaping unexpectedly from the water. The last thing he needed was one or more of those mutants thrashing about wildly on deck or worse, knocking him, Katie, or Jack overboard. Katie kept diligent track of the girl's whereabouts. She was aware that the entire biomass of bait, fish, and killers was moving steadily east and in the direction of the girl. Katie also saw the two brothers closing in fast on their sister's position. She feared the worst if the killers were distracted from their feeding frenzy.

The other captains realized what was happening and each also slowly made way toward the boulders. Rick and Valerie were the closest, only about two hundred yards from the girl, when the alpha male noticed the vaguely familiar object floating on the surface. The paddleboard silhouette resembled a body with four extremities, and it looked like something the alpha male had killed before. It also looked like that damn canine, the only creature to ever cause the alpha male pain. This was a big and easy meal. With most of the other creatures preoccupied feeding on other fish, the alpha male moved in the direction of the girl. His band of aquatic thugs followed. They circled the boulders deep, careful not to reveal their presence. The leader of the pack was wary of the object on the surface and, until he could better determine what it was, he didn't want to risk another dog-like encounter, or worse, further injury to his eye. The alpha male and his tightly wound pack slowly made their way up the water column, inching closer to the girl. Readying to make a final pass before striking, the male's attention was diverted in the direction of the two boys. He sensed movement of the boards as the duo paddled toward their sister. The brothers called her name but she remained silent, hidden by the boulders and by her low profile. Oblivious to what was going on beneath her and the feeding frenzy further offshore, the girl was determined to surprise her brothers. But first she wanted them to worry just a bit.

The vibrations sent out by the boys' paddles had grabbed the full attention of the alpha male. The resonating sound was both irritating and inviting. For the moment, the creature left the girl and focused all his senses on the two moving objects. The fish was agitated and hyper-aggressive. It angled its good eye toward the surface of the water and recognized the creatures standing on the floating objects as food. The big male made one wide circle beneath the surface to gain speed and momentum for the attack. He would hit the closer of the two paddleboarders. The subservient male of the pack followed. His prize would be the trailing paddler. Once the prey was incapacitated, the rest of the pack would move in to feed while the victims were still alive and dying.

The alpha male's charge was swift and powerful. He impacted the first paddleboard with a force that not only knocked the boy ten feet into the air, but catapulted its own body an equal distance above the surface. The second fish followed the dominant male's lead and he struck the brother's board with equal strength. For an instant, the two fish and both brothers suspended in air in what seemed like surreal slow motion. Jaws snapped and muscular bodies contorted as the fish watched through wicked glowing eyes for anything within reach to bite. The boys tumbled about, but looked in horror at their attackers and knew for the first time in their young lives the meaning of primal fear.

Both male fish crashed down with a force that displaced a mountain of water. Surprisingly, the initial focus of the attack was the inanimate objects. The fish bit and shredded the paddleboards to pulp, and only then turned their attention to the boys who now swam in panic toward shore. It was as if they knew that once the boards were destroyed, the boys had no means of protection or escape. The beasts toyed with the brothers, circling them and brushing against them with their bodies. They seemed to take joy in the torment. The boys stopped swimming and huddled together. They could no longer swim to safety.

To be certain the twins presented no further risk, and the younger male fish lunged at the boy . . . but did not bite. He was testing his prey. With a flick of its powerful head, he thrust the boy into the air.

The alpha male readied himself to bite off the boy's legs as soon as he landed back on the water. The alpha male's body became rigid and his fins erect. A horrendous clicking sound once again emanated from rapidly snapping jaws, a signal to the underwater world that he was about to kill again.

As the boy landed back on the water, the fish moved in for the kill but were halted by yet another infuriating sound. The boy's sister screamed and pounded her paddle on the surface. Rick's boat was very close to the girl and Katie yelled to her, "Stop! Stop!" Her plea went unheeded. The girl moved her board out from the boulders and paddled toward her brothers in distress. That was a big mistake. The entire pod of fish readied for the attack. They would not allow their meal to escape.

The evil clicking built to a crescendo as each member of the pod joined in the alpha male's death song. The intense sounds attracted the attention of many other mutant killers that began to converge upon the male and his pack. They too snapped jaws in harmonious and sinister symphony. The clicking also attracted other marine creatures, animals no one expected to see at a time like this.

The alpha male was intently focused on his two prizes. He would not be distracted this time as he had been with the dogs. He remembered; he had made an almost fatal mistake. But not now. He was ready to kill. The fish move deep beneath the boys and circled them. He would attack from behind and sever the legs just above the knees. It mattered not which boy he hit first, for the second male would strike as soon as it scented blood. With femoral arteries cut, the boys would bleed out within a minute. And then the remainder of the pack would kill the girl. They always deferred to their leader.

The alpha male was as physiologically frenzied as an animal could get. Adrenaline, testosterone, aggression pheromones, and a mutated mixture of organic chemistry fueled its rage. Its eyes radiated a ghoulish phosphorescent yellow. The maddened fish circled one last time and charged the boys, its sights set on four dangling legs. The creature, with it jaws spread wide and its chain-saw teeth clacking, was within several feet of the brothers when it felt a powerful and painful blow to its midsection. The impact pushed the alpha male to the surface, inches from its would-be prey. The upheaval had Katie thinking the fish had attacked the brothers. She screamed, "Oh my God! It's got the boy!"

Katie, Rick, Jack, and all the other captains were so preoccupied trying to prevent the inevitable attack they were unaware of hundreds of other creatures that approached from the west. It was an aquatic cavalry to the rescue: pod upon pod of bottlenose dolphins.

The alpha male was completely disoriented and in excruciating pain as it was struck broadside yet again. This time its internal organs ruptured. The mutant fish was strong and fought to regain equilibrium. The dolphin would deny that opportunity. The mammal broke the surface of the water to refill its lungs and then submerged. The dolphin rammed the alpha male one more time, totally disabling it. As the creature listed to one side, the dolphin grabbed the killer behind its head and inverted it in the water so that it was oriented belly up. The killer fish was deprived of an opportunity to swim and, therefore, to move oxygen through its gills. As the dolphin held the alpha male upside down, the killer fish entered a state of helplessness known as tonic immobility. The monster fish was rendered harmless as a little puppy. The dolphin swam slowly and kept the alpha male oriented this way for several minutes, during which time the killer fish suffocated to death. The second and subservient male also succumbed to the same fate, as did hundreds of other killer fish. One by one, the dolphins targeted the mutants and delivered their own brand of Darwinian justice. The water was a tumult of mayhem. Killer fish in great numbers were attacked, immobilized, and suffocated to death. Dolphins leapt triumphantly from the water, cart-wheeling in gestures of victory.

Those aboard the *Maya* watched in amazement as the dolphin swam past the boat still clinging to the dead alpha male. It released its hold and the fish sank to the bottom. In the end, this apex mutant monster would end up as crab food. The mammal looked up and its eyes met Jack's, who immediately experienced a flashback to his own encounter with the killers. Now Jack remembered the images in the water as he had struggled to save his own life. It finally became clear. He spoke aloud. "Mermaid. That was the mermaid. A dolphin saved me. Pushed me to the surface."

Katie just looked at Jack and smiled.

Rick was able to extricate the two brothers from the water as Amanda and Nick did the same with the girl. The kids were all frightened beyond their wildest nightmares, but they were safe.

As both boats floated side-by-side, Nick had realized first what had taking place.

"Katie, this is amazing. These dolphins are behaving just like orcas killing great white sharks."

Nick referred to the phenomenon of a culture among certain populations of orcas that had learned how to incapacitate and kill great whites. The most notable of those confrontations occurred off the Farallon Islands near San Francisco when a female orca attacked and drowned a large white shark. The entire incident was captured on video by stunned whale watchers. This population of dolphins had apparently acquired a similar behavior, perhaps from their experiences ramming sharks with their snouts. However they had come by this skill, Katie was the most grateful.

"I have never in all my life been so happy to see dolphins. Do you think they got them all, Nick?"

"Tough to say, Katie. My bet is that there were hundreds of those things around. By the looks of this mayhem, I think the dolphins got the job done."

Oddly, what was just moments before a maelstrom of fiendish activity in the Sound had been almost instantly transformed into a sea of tranquility. The only disturbance to the now calm waters of the Long Island Sound was the frolicking of dolphins. Once the demonic fish were destroyed, the mammals appeared to celebrate their victory.

They put on a display of aerial acrobatics that brought tears to Katie's eyes. She knew that without their miraculous intervention, the killings would not have stopped. In Katie's mind, it seemed only fitting that in the end it was nature way's that solved a problem created by man. She hugged Rick tightly and then gave Jack a kiss on the cheek.

Rick piloted *Maya* back into Mount Misery Harbor where they docked and called the kids' parents. "Wait till mom and dad hear about this," the little girl said. "You two are in big trouble." Everyone laughed. Jack called his wife to tell her he was okay and that they would be going out to dinner. She asked what the occasion was, and Jack said simply, "Life."

Nick Tanner and Valerie Russo were still out on the Sound. Nick had gathered up all his scientific gear and sat on the front seat of Valerie's boat. He stared out at the water and contemplated the astonishing drama that had unfolded before his eyes. It was the most amazing experience of his professional career. Valerie nudged her way onto the seat with Nick and put her arm around his shoulder. She kissed him in a way Nick had never before been kissed. Nick liked it.

Much of the world was now watching what had taken place. Folks on the beach had videoed the entire event that was now airing on all TV networks and going viral on all social media. The party boat video also hit the airwaves. Reporters were playing up the angle of good triumphs over evil. It wouldn't be long before Katie and Nick would be answering more questions than they cared to. At least this time, they would be viewed in a more favorable light. Some even called them heroes.

As the final phase of the tide ebbed to the east, the scent of death flowed strong beneath the water. Hundreds of mutant fish bodies carpeted the seabed of the Long Island Sound. It would be the final resting place for all but a pair of the killer fish. Two young males escaped the onslaught of dolphins. A superior flight response was triggered when fear pheromones flooded their sensory mechanisms as their pod mates faced certain doom. The remaining two fish swam east without ever stopping and exited the Long Island Sound. They headed toward Montauk and the open Atlantic Ocean.

When the time was right, one of the males would undergo a change to his physiology. What had gone undetected in all the lab tests of the mutated DNA was that the killer fish were also genetically protandrous hermaphrodites. To ensure preservation of the species that male would transform into a female.

AUTHOR'S NOTE

Writing a novel is indeed an adventure and a journey of self-discovery. Having written mostly nonfiction, I wasn't sure what to expect when I embarked upon the project that culminated in the publication of this book. I had an idea for a plot, a few characters, a laptop, and a notion that I could string enough words together to tell an interesting story. As the process unfolded, I expanded my knowledge of fish, fisheries management, marine biology, and the demanding art of writing science fiction. Along the way, I was also blessed to have met some interesting and supportive folks. The process of writing a book, especially a book of fiction, is much like running a marathon: when you hit the dreaded wall of potential physical and emotional defeat, you aren't quite sure if you can make it to the end. But somehow you rise up and get over the hurdles, the obstacles, and other challenges that seem to all conspire against you. Eventually the writer prevails and ideas somehow become words; words become sentences, paragraphs, and then chapters.

After much toil, frustration, staring at the ceiling, and long walks on the beach with my dog, a book somehow materialized. Words seemed to find me more than I found them and for that I feel blessed. There is this mysterious place within where words are born. At times, I knew not where the ideas or words came from but they did, in a manner and way that told me this book needed to be finished. In the end, a story had been told and a book had been written. For that, I am most grateful and humbled by the sources of any and all inspirations that motivated me to continue writing.

As is often the case with any accomplishment in life, there were many family members, friends, and colleagues who me cheered me on to the finish line and through the good, bad, and ugly times that accompany the writing process. I thank them all for their encouragement and support. First and foremost my family: Gabrielle, Jacqueline, and Victoria, who endured the three years of research, writing, and nonstop chatter about the plot and the characters. To my high school English teacher, Mr. Philip Heary, I say thank you. You were the first person in my life to encourage my writing and whose words of support have stayed with me all my life: "You have something there. Keep writing." Wherever you are, Mr. Heary, you helped light a candle that still burns brightly.

My sincerest gratitude is also extended to late Jack Samson, venerable editor and author, who totally amazed and motivated a young writer by buying his very first article for publication in *Field & Stream*. That article was written in 1974 and represented the beginning of my writing journey. And to angler and editor extraordinaire, Fred Golofaro, of the *Fisherman Magazine*, thank you for your friendship and for supporting my fishing stories for almost four decades. To the memory of Charles H. Ross Jr., a mentor at Merrill Lynch. He helped me grow and gave me many opportunities to see what I was capable of accomplishing in business and in life. At times, he believed in me more than I did in myself. I will forever be indebted. Thank you to the late Herbert M. Allison, a brilliant Merrill Lynch executive and leader who instilled in me a belief that the solutions to all problems in life and in business lie in fully understanding and managing the details. Thank you to Bob Banfelder and Donna Derasmo, whose advice and encouragement helped me push on through some of the down times that accompany the process of writing fiction. A singular thanks to the Lorian Hemingway Short Story Competition that first inspired me to try my hand at fiction. And thanks to "Jannie" and "Rabbit" for being friends when one was needed most.

To Dr. Mark Di Benedetto, with whom I have had many conversations about fish, fishing, and fisheries during my wellness office visits. You help keep me going. To Dr. Jennifer Iannacone, a remarkable veterinarian who, over the years, has shed light on canine behavior that helped me write one of my favorite chapters in this book, and who shared in my sorrow when I said goodbye to Jenny. To Jay Cassell and Tony Lyons at Skyhorse Publishing, whose confidence in my work has been unwavering and fully supportive, and to Steve Price for his insightful and constructive advice. And a very special thanks to Jay McCullough, for helping me refine and shape the final version of this book.

A very heartfelt thanks goes out Frank and Tony Amato, Kermit Hummel, Steve Piatt, John Shewey, Ted Venker, Kevin Blinkoff, Jimmy Fee, and Troy Letherman: publishers and editors who've supported my writings about fish and fishing and who've motivated me to keep plugging away. I'd also like to thank some fishing buddies with whom I have shared great times on the water. You all know who you are but special thanks goes out to Captain Adrian Mason, Captain Rick Gulia, Pete Palmieri, Chuck Moore, and Tim McCloskey. Thank you Gemini, Santee, Jessie, Jenny, Grizzly, Bear, Grizzly Too, Catherine, and Leo . . . you all helped me to better understand our natural world and the bond that exists between animals and humans.

Lastly, I thank my Labrador retriever, Bailey, who sat with me every step of the way while writing and editing this story. She and I took many walks along the beach as I worked through the elements of this story. Her unwavering friendship, loyalty, and often humorous beach antics helped immensely to clear my head; Chapter 33 is for you.